PRAISE FOR THE JONATHAN QUINN SERIES

"Brilliant and heart pounding"—**Jeffery Deaver**, *New York Times* bestselling author

"Addictive."—**James Rollins**, *New York Times* bestselling author

"Unputdownable."—**Tess Gerritsen**, *New York Times* bestselling author

"The best elements of Lee Child, John le Carré, and Robert Ludlum."—**Sheldon Siegel**, *New York Times* bestselling author

"Quinn is one part James Bond, one part Jason Bourne."—**Nashville Book Worm**

"Welcome addition to the political thriller game."—***Publishers Weekly***

ALSO BY BRETT BATTLES

THE JONATHAN QUINN THRILLERS

THE CLEANER
THE DECEIVED
SHADOW OF BETRAYAL (U.S.)/THE UNWANTED (U.K.)
THE SILENCED
BECOMING QUINN

THE LOGAN HARPER THRILLERS

LITTLE GIRL GONE
EVERY PRECIOUS THING

THE PROJECT EDEN THRILLERS

SICK
EXIT NINE
PALE HORSE

STANDALONES

THE PULL OF GRAVITY
NO RETURN

For Younger Readers

THE TROUBLE FAMILY CHRONICLES

HERE COMES MR. TROUBLE

THE
DESTROYED

Brett Battles

A Jonathan Quinn Novel

For more information about the author, please visit
www.brettbattles.com.

This one's for charter Team Quinn members
Bill Cameron and Robert Browne

CHAPTER
ONE

DAR ES SALAAM, TANZANIA

I SHOULDN'T HAVE come, Lawrence Rosen thought as he stared out the window of the cab. *I should have stayed home and pretended I'd never received it.*

But he had received the email. And opened it.

And read it.

Mr. Rosen—

April 12th, 2006. A flight to Portugal. You were one of the prisoner's escorts. I'm sure you haven't forgotten about the trip. I'm willing to make sure your name isn't included when the story is leaked, but only if you speak with me first.

One chance. Saturday. 8:30 p.m. Kilimanjaro Restaurant in the Majestic Hotel, Dar es Salaam.

There was no signature, and when he tried to send a reply, he received a message telling him the address didn't exist.

THE DESTROYED

For twenty-four hours he had done nothing, hoping he could just forget about the whole thing. But the sender had been right. He did remember the flight, and he certainly remembered the prisoner. It was a taint he could never wash off.

When Saturday came, he boarded an early morning flight headed southwest from his current home in Dubai to Tanzania.

"How much longer?" he asked his taxi driver.

"Soon, soon. Fifteen minutes, no more."

Rosen looked at his watch. It was after eight already. Fifteen minutes would probably be more like twenty or thirty, meaning he'd barely arrive on time.

This is a mistake. I should've ignored the email.

Easy to say, but how could he have done that, really? If his name came out in association with what had happened, he had no doubt he'd be the one receiving a prisoner escort.

"WELCOME TO THE Majestic," the doorman said as Rosen approached the hotel entrance at exactly 8:28 p.m.

"Kilimanjaro's?" Rosen asked.

"Twenty-third floor, sir. The elevator is past the reception desk."

As hotel lobbies went, the Majestic's was impressive— white marble floors adorned here and there with purple rugs, ultra-modern furniture upholstered in fabrics of green and pink and beige, and columns that rose to the ceiling two floors above, covered with purple and gold tiles. The reception desk was halfway back along the left wall, a black granite countertop manned by half a dozen smiling women.

Rosen walked quickly to the four elevator doors along the back wall. Only a few seconds passed before the one on the far right opened. He entered and pushed the button for the twenty-third floor. Just as the door started to close, a man and a woman rushed in.

"Ah, twenty-three. Perfect," the man said.

Rosen smiled weakly as he moved into the back corner to give the others some space.

14

"Honey, do you mind if we stop at the room first?" the woman asked.

The man shrugged, and hit the button for the nineteenth floor. "Okay by me."

Up they went, the new elevator barely making a sound as it shot past floor after floor. The car slowed on eighteen then stopped on the nineteenth floor. The doors slid open, and the woman stepped off. Rosen was too lost in thought to notice that the man with her did not leave also.

"Clear," the woman said from the nineteenth-floor lobby.

The unexpected word jolted Rosen back into reality, but by then it was too late. The "husband" was already pointing a gun at Rosen, his other hand pressing the button that kept the elevator doors open.

He motioned with the gun out the door. "This is where you get off, Mr. Rosen."

MILA VOSS KNEW it would be dangerous before she even sent the email to Lawrence Rosen. She knew very little about his life now, how connected he might still be, how he might react to her not-so-subtle threat. As it was, finding an active email address for him had been pushing things. She had to be very careful to minimize her exposure in his world, a world that had at one time been hers, too.

But it was a chance she had to take, because he could either confirm or dispel what she already believed.

After that?

Get through this first, she told herself. *Figure out the after later.*

Her first concern had been whether he would come at all. But twenty-two hours earlier, a flight had been booked from where he currently lived in Dubai to Tanzania, using an alias he'd traveled under previously. When she checked that morning, the airline listed a "Mark Walker" as having boarded.

Still, she wanted to be positive, so she took another big risk by hacking into the Dubai International Airport video security system. She located the footage of the gate servicing the flight to Tanzania, and scanned through the faces as passengers handed over their tickets until she spotted the one she was looking for.

Lawrence Rosen was definitely on his way to her.

Her next concern was that he wouldn't come to the hotel alone. To ensure her own safety, she had taken a room on the fifth floor two days earlier, then planted micro cameras outside the hotel, in the lobby, and outside the Kilimanjaro Restaurant. Her plan was to wait in her room until Rosen was seated in the restaurant. If everything seemed fine, she'd go up and join him. If not, she'd take the emergency stairwell down to the ground floor and get the hell out of there.

She began monitoring the feeds in earnest four hours before the appointed meeting time. If he'd arranged for anyone to act as backup, she was confident they would arrive sometime in that window.

At just after six p.m., she spotted two men and a woman in the main lobby who concerned her. They seemed a little too interested in their surroundings, too aware of what was going on. She labeled them as potential threats and continued looking for others.

As eight thirty drew closer, she became more and more anxious. Though Rosen's plane had landed several hours earlier, there was still no sign of him. Had he decided at the last minute *not* to come? If that were the case, she'd have to write him off, and employ more aggressive tactics to find out whether she was right or not.

Just before eight thirty, a cab pulled up out front, and Rosen stepped out. Mila felt an odd mixture of relief and renewed tension. He was here. She was going to talk to him.

She watched as he walked across the lobby to the elevators, and stepped into one. She was just thinking that things would go as planned, when the three people who had concerned her earlier entered the frame. One of the men stopped and gave his companions a quick nod as they stepped into Rosen's car just before the doors closed. The man who stayed in the lobby turned away from the elevators, and began casually scanning the room—looking for her, no doubt.

Dammit! Rosen isn't *alone.*

She nearly shut her laptop and sprinted out of the room right then. The only thing that stopped her was a sense of unease. There had been something odd about Rosen's reaction to the others' arrival. The view from the camera had shown him move to the back corner when they joined him, like he didn't know them. Faking it? Possibly, but she *had* worked in the secrets business for many years, and during that time had developed a strong ability to read others.

She replayed the last few moments before the doors closed.

No, she decided. *He doesn't know them. But if that's true, who the hell are they?*

She switched to the camera covering the Kilimanjaro waiting area outside the elevators on the twenty-third floor. Half a dozen people were hovering in front of a podium where two hostesses were standing. After a moment, a group of three diners was led inside, while the others continued to wait.

Mila focused on the elevators. Minus the fifteen seconds that had already passed, the car Rosen was riding in—the one she'd labeled number four—could reach the twenty-third floor as quickly as fifty-five seconds. If the other passengers got out on a lower floor, it could take as long as two minutes, maybe more.

Fifty-five seconds passed, sixty, then the door to car number one opened and a party of six exited.

Twenty more seconds and another *ding*, followed by the door to number two parting.

When the clock reached two minutes, she frowned. Number four still hadn't arrived. That didn't make sense. It should have—

Ding.

She tensed as the light next to number four lit up.

There was a pause, then the doors slid apart.

THE NINETEENTH FLOOR was only half finished. One wing of rooms looked ready to go, but the hallway leading through

17

the other half was still in the process of being painted, and had yet to have the signature purple carpet laid down.

The man with the gun walked behind Rosen while the woman led the way down the unfinished corridor.

"Look," Rosen said. "I don't know what you want or who you might think I am, but you've made a mistake. I'm just here for a business meeting. You let me go, I won't say a word."

"No mistake," the man said.

"Of course it's a mistake!" Rosen argued, looking back over his shoulder.

If the man had been close enough, Rosen would have gone for the gun, but the guy was several feet back, out of range.

"Turn around," the man said.

Son of a bitch. This was a trap from the beginning, Rosen thought.

As they neared the end of the hall, the woman opened a door and walked inside.

"Keep moving," the gunman ordered Rosen.

This was his chance, Rosen realized. As he stepped across the threshold, he reached out, grabbed the handle, then jerked the door closed behind him and engaged the lock.

The only direction Rosen could go in the small area beyond was left. He raced down the short hallway, and entered a room lit only by the light of the city flowing in through the windows. He tensed to take on the woman.

She was there, all right, but she wasn't alone. Another man stood beside her, a gun in his hand.

Rosen felt the blood drain from his face.

Behind him, the door opened, and the gunman from the hallway joined them.

"Whatever it is you want, I'll get it. Money? Is that it? Tell me how much you want."

"Larry, don't embarrass yourself," the new man said.

Rosen stared at him for a moment, then his eyes widened. "Scott?" As soon as he said the other man's name, the full reality of what was going on hit him. "No. No. I haven't *said* anything. I kept my mouth shut. I…I've never—"

"Then what are you doing here?" his former colleague asked.

"Just a business meeting," he said. But his words closed the trap completely, and he knew it. "You know about the email."

"Of course we know about the email."

Rosen began shaking his head. "I wasn't going to say anything. I wanted to see who sent it, that's all. I wanted to be able to tell you who it was."

"You should have said something *before* you got on that plane." The man turned and headed for the windowed wall.

Rosen stumbled forward as he was shoved from behind. Nearing the windows, he saw something he hadn't noticed before—a door in the glass wall. Beyond it was a patio stretching the length of the suite.

"Open it," the woman said.

He hesitated, looking over at the man he called Scott. "Please. I realize it was just a test, but I wasn't going to say anything. I swear."

"Test? We didn't send the email, Larry," the man said. "Open the door."

"What? Then how did you—"

"You know we can do anything that needs to be done," the man said. "Now open the door or get shoved through it."

MILA STARED AT her monitor as the door for car number four remained open for several seconds, then closed again without anyone disembarking.

Where the hell is Rosen?

She stared at the screen, her mind racing through the possibilities until she snapped herself out of it, and slammed her computer shut. Whatever his reason for not showing up, the time for watching was over. Even if Rosen did show up, there was no way she'd meet with him now. The moment she set foot anywhere near that restaurant, she knew the remainder of her life would be measured in seconds.

THE DESTROYED

She shoved her laptop into her bag as she scanned the room to make sure she'd left nothing behind. She then moved to the door and carefully pulled it open.

The hallway was empty.

Wasting no time, she sprinted to the stairwell entrance and headed down.

The stairs let out in the back corner of the main lobby. She moved carefully through the doorway, knowing the man who hadn't hopped onto the elevator was around somewhere.

She was positive Rosen had no idea who he was supposed to meet, so his friends wouldn't know, either. But even if they saw her, they wouldn't know it was her. She had taken the extra precaution of changing her appearance as much as possible. She was dressed in jeans and a beige men's shirt. A brown baseball cap covered her hair, cut short a week earlier. On her face was a pair of non-prescription, wire-frame glasses. With her breasts wrapped tightly, she looked like a young man of no more than twenty-one, an age that was actually several years in her past. She was just another tourist: bland, and not worth a second look.

At least that's what she was hoping.

As she passed the reception desk, she finally spotted the other man. He looked even more intimidating in person than on her computer monitor. She'd seen men like him hundreds of times before. He was a pro for sure.

She forced herself to keep walking like she needed to be somewhere but wasn't in a hurry. When the man turned his gaze in her direction, she was sure she'd done something to tip him off. Fortunately, her old training took control, and she neither hurried nor slowed down, keeping the pleasant smile on her face as she walked right by the man.

Though she could no longer see if he was looking at her, she sensed that he'd written her off as no one important.

As she neared the front, she realized she'd been holding her breath and finally let it out.

The doorman noticed her approach and opened the door. "Have a good evening, sir," he said as she stepped outside.

She nodded her thanks, and began walking down the

sidewalk away from the hotel.

She'd made it. She was free. No, not free, she realized. Not until she got out of Tanzania.

Whoosh.

The sound had come from behind and above her somewhere. It was strange enough to make her turn to see what it was, but she'd barely started twisting around when the *whoosh* was replaced by a loud, wet smack.

On a portion of the sidewalk close to the hotel's front entrance lay the twisted body of a man.

Without even thinking, she ran toward him.

If he'd been a jumper, she would have expected him to be lying on his stomach, face smashed into the ground. Instead, he was on his back, his eyes open and staring blankly at the night sky, terror still etched on his face.

On Lawrence Rosen's face.

She knelt down beside the man she had tricked into coming to Tanzania.

He was dead; there was no question about that. His glassy eyes reflected images he would never see.

She looked up the building, but could see no obvious spot from where he started his fall. The thought that this was an accident didn't even cross her mind. Nor did she consider the possibility that he'd come all this way just to throw himself to his death.

Someone else did this.

The man and the woman who had been on the elevator with him.

Get out of here. Now!

She jumped up.

"Do you know him?"

It was the doorman. He and several others who'd been out front had begun gathering around the body.

She shook her head. "No," she whispered.

"Is he dead?"

She nodded.

A woman gasped, then an old man started reciting a prayer.

THE DESTROYED

"Please, everybody, stand back," the doorman said loudly, trying to take charge. "We must keep this area clear." He then spoke in Swahili, presumably repeating his warning.

But no one moved. Except Mila, who slipped unseen to the back of the growing crowd and disappeared into the city.

CHAPTER
TWO

WASHINGTON, DC

"THIS WAY," THE senator's assistant said.

He led Peter down a long hallway lined with dark wood. Hung along it were black and white pictures taken at various locations around the world. The senator appeared in every image, sometimes looking no more than thirty, and in others middle-aged. There was always someone else in the photo with him, shaking hands or smiling or just looking at something that was out of frame. Trophy shots. The powerful American helping those in need, especially if the need was military in nature.

The assistant finally stopped next to a closed door. He knocked twice, then turned the knob and ushered Peter inside.

"Senator," the man said. "Your guest has arrived."

A large man with a full head of hair that was now more white than blond pushed himself off a couch. The senator looked older and stockier than he did in most of the hallway pictures, but his eyes were still piercing, and there was no missing the aura of power that radiated from him. He held out his hand. "Peter. Good to see you."

"Senator Mygatt," Peter said as they shook.

As of just over a year ago, Christopher Mygatt was actually no longer a senator, but like many titles in Washington, his was one that would stick with him until he obtained a better one.

The senator turned to another man sitting in a chair next to the coffee table at one end of the large office. "You know William Green, of course."

"Yes," Peter said, nodding a greeting.

Green was a weaselly man who'd been in the intelligence business about as long as Peter had been. Peter had done everything he could to avoid working with the man, but a few times when he was running the now-defunct organization known as the Office, he'd had no choice but to associate with Green. No matter how simple the assignment had been, Peter always felt he needed a bottle of hand sanitizer nearby whenever he even talked to the man on the phone.

"Peter," Green said. "How are you coping?"

Keeping his tone neutral, Peter said, "Fine, thanks."

"Would you like something to drink?" Mygatt asked him.

"No, thank you."

The senator glanced at his assistant. "Some tea for me, if you would. William?"

"Coffee."

As soon as the assistant left, Mygatt motioned at the couch. "Please, join us."

Peter sat.

"So, I understand you've been doing some consulting," Mygatt said.

"Sitting behind a desk, making a suggestion now and then that no one listens to." Peter shrugged. "I guess you can call that consulting."

"I'd call that a waste of taxpayers' money," Green said.

Peter ignored the comment, and said to the senator, "I understand you're doing well, sir."

"Things are moving in interesting directions," Mygatt said.

"So it seems. If the rumors are true—"

The senator waved a hand in the air. "I don't deal with rumors. Only facts."

"And what are the facts?"

A mischievous smile crossed the man's lips. "Now, Peter. I also don't talk before it's time."

Mygatt was no longer a senator because he'd left to serve as his political party's committee chairman. Now that the presidential primaries were over and the convention was looming, there was talk that his sure-handed stewardship of the party might lead to something considerably more visible. Specifically the vice presidential spot on the upcoming ticket.

But Peter had his doubts about that. He was sure the vice presidency was not the kind of position Mygatt would enjoy. Too much ceremony and not enough action. He had a feeling there was another position or two the senator was eyeing. *Those* rumors, though not as vocal, had been circulating, too.

The assistant reentered the room carrying a tray with Green's coffee, and a teapot and cup for Mygatt. He set it on the coffee table, excused himself, and left.

"Peter," Mygatt said as he poured his tea. "I've asked you here because I wanted to discuss something you might be able to do for me."

"I thought it might be something like that," Peter said. "I'm afraid, sir, you've wasted your time. The contract I have with my current employer clearly states I'm excluded from doing work with private industry."

"Like no one ever cheats on the government," Green scoffed, himself a government lifer.

The senator raised his cup. "The project I have in mind might be better referred to as a favor."

Peter shrugged. "You can call it whatever you want, but I'm not the man you're looking for."

"Actually, you are," Green countered. "It's finishing something you were supposed to have completed a long time ago."

Peter frowned, and shook his head. "I have no idea what you're talking about, and quite honestly, I don't care. I have a job, and that's all I need. Thank you, senator, for considering me, but I'm going to have to pass." He stood up. "Now, if you'll excuse me."

"Peter," Mygatt said, his voice sterner than before. "Whether you help us or not, you're involved. Wouldn't you rather be in a position to control the situation than have to deal with the fallout later?"

Peter remained where he was, but said nothing.

"I'd like to show you something," Mygatt said. "If you want to leave afterward, you're more than welcome to do so."

"What is it?"

"Just sit. It'll only take a moment."

"I think I'll stand."

Mygatt laughed softly. "Fine. Then stand." He looked at Green. "Please."

Green picked up a remote control from the coffee table and aimed it at the television monitor on the credenza at the end of the sitting area. The screen flashed a vibrant blue before displaying a paused nighttime video.

"This is the main entrance to the Majestic Hotel in Dar es Salaam," Green explained. "I assume you've never been there."

"I've heard of it," Peter said. "New, right?"

"It just opened a month ago. Watch the area close to the building about fifteen feet beyond the entrance."

Green hit PLAY, and the still image began to move. People went in and out of the building in a steady stream—couples, a few men together, several men on their own—keeping the two doormen out front busy.

"Here we go," Mygatt said.

For a moment, there was nothing unusual, then something flashed down from the top of the screen and whacked into the sidewalk.

"Son of a bitch," Peter couldn't help saying.

Where seconds before people had been walking, a body now lay sprawled on the concrete, its arms and legs jutting out at impossible angles.

"Who the hell is that?"

Green paused the playback. "His name was Lawrence Rosen."

Rosen? The name sounded familiar. "A security guy, right? Does protection, things like that?"

"Very good. He went freelance a few years ago."

"So what was he doing in Tanzania?"

"Meeting someone."

"Looks like the meeting got cut short," Peter said. "Is there a point here?"

"Patience," Mygatt said. He nodded at Green.

The playback started up again. Most of the people closest to the entrance turned and stared in shock at Rosen's body. One person, though, ran out from the darkness on the far side over to the dead man. It was a guy who had left the hotel moments before, Peter realized, the one wearing a baseball cap.

The man knelt down beside the body, checked to make sure Rosen was dead, then glanced upward as if trying to see where the body had come from. Suddenly, he jumped to his feet, and within seconds had melted into the growing group of onlookers that had started to crowd around the body. As soon as he disappeared, Green stopped the video again.

"That's it?" Peter asked. "I still don't understand what I'm supposed to be looking for."

"The man in the baseball hat," Green said. "Did you recognize him?"

"No. Should I have?"

Green hit another button. "How about now?"

The hotel image was replaced by a close-up of the man in the hat from when he'd exited the building. The guy looked young, early twenties at best. A tanned Caucasian, maybe Latino. No way to tell for sure. He was wearing glasses and looked otherwise unremarkable.

"Still nothing?" Green asked.

Peter prided himself on his memory of names and faces. "I've never seen him."

Mygatt leaned forward. "Are you sure?"

The way the senator asked the question made Peter hesitate. "Who is he?"

"Show him."

Green once more did his trick with the remote. The shot on the monitor was replaced this time by a split-screen image. On both halves were identical close-ups of the man's face in front of the hotel. Then, while the one on the left remained the same, the one on the right began to change. The glasses disappeared first, then the hat. After that, the hair grew until it was past the man's shoulders, and went from sandy blond to dark brown. There was a slight altering of the cheeks and lips, and the eyes turned from brown to gray-green.

The man in the baseball cap wasn't a man at all. Worse, the woman underneath the disguise *was* someone Peter recognized. But that was…

THE DESTROYED

...impossible.

"So tell me, Peter," Mygatt said. "How is it that a dead woman is walking the streets of Dar es Salaam?"

Six years earlier, the Office had been assigned the task of terminating Mila Voss by Mygatt via Green. At the time, the senator was not yet a senator, but the deputy secretary of defense overseeing military intelligence. Green was his CIA liaison. Though the project was not without its problems, the mission had been completed, and Peter reported back to his clients that the courier Mila Voss had been eliminated.

Only it was clear now that the mission had not been as successful as he'd been led to believe.

"I...don't have an answer for you," Peter said.

"Convenient," Green spat.

"Peter," Mygatt said, his voice calm. "You need to find her for us."

"And while you're at it, maybe you should *finish* the job," Green threw in.

There was no way Peter could walk out now. The fallout from this could turn extremely ugly. As Mygatt had pointed out, his only chance at controlling the situation was to be involved. He nodded, and said, "I'll get back to you."

"Soon," the senator said.

"Yes. Soon."

"I have a man named Olsen who will be back later today," Green said. "We'd like him to assist you."

"That's not necessary."

Green leaned forward, glaring. "Considering what *didn't* happen before, I don't think you're in the position to determine what's necessary or not."

Mygatt stood up, a smile on his face. "Just consider him my personal contact, freeing you up to concentrate on the job at hand. I'm sure there won't be any problems."

Peter knew he had little choice. "All right," he said. "Do you have any paper?"

"On the desk."

Peter found a notepad and pen on the blotter, quickly wrote down an address, and handed it to Green. "That's to an apartment in Georgetown, a remote office I'll be using." He

28

turned his attention to the senator. "I need to finish a couple of things for my current employer so I can free up some time without them becoming suspicious. I'm sure you'll agree that we don't want anyone else looking into this matter."

Mygatt nodded. "That would be unwise."

Peter looked at his watch. It was nearing two p.m. "I'll be in Georgetown by seven. If this Olsen guy is here by then, send him over."

"See? I knew you'd want to take care of this."

INSTEAD OF CATCHING one of the available taxis at the corner, Peter continued on foot. Twice he doubled back, and three times he made sudden stops before crossing streets in the middle of the block, making sure he wasn't being followed. Not until he was positive he was clean did he finally hail a cab. Paranoia was part of his DNA, and explained why he lived as long as he had.

A simple phone call to the agency he'd been working with was all it took to get some time off. A family emergency, he said. He might be gone a week or longer. As he'd known, the man overseeing him didn't care. He'd be happy not to have Peter underfoot.

Peter had the cab drop him near a metro station, then took the train—changing lines twice—out to Arlington. While he did indeed have a fully equipped apartment in Georgetown, ready to use for any kind of special operations, it wasn't the only secret place available to him. Even in his reduced role within the intelligence community, he maintained over half a dozen different locations in the DC area alone.

The place where he was now headed was located in a walled-off, soundproofed section of a church basement that could only be accessed through an underground tunnel from a self-storage unit next door. He was the only one who knew of its existence, unlike the apartment in Georgetown.

Using yet another indirect route, he made his way from the station to the storage facility. The door to his unit was inside a covered hallway, itself accessed via a number-coded lock on the outside door. The code he'd been given was a generic one that all the tenants used, so it was impossible to know who punched it in. For that, the facility relied on a security camera mounted near the door. Peter wasn't worried about that, either. His years of working as a spook wrangler had given him a healthy sense of paranoia, so he never went anywhere without a portable electronic jamming device in his pocket. He switched it on before approaching the door, and knew that for the few seconds he was there, the camera would seemingly malfunction.

Inside, he made his way to his unit, and input the combination on the bottom of the lock. This didn't actually open it. Instead, it released a small panel on the surface that exposed a touch screen. He placed his left thumb against it, waited, and heard the faint click of the real lock on the inside of the door as it disengaged. The padlock remained closed, having already served its purpose. He pulled on it, and the door swung out.

The interior light came on as soon as the door was back in place. The unit looked pretty standard, albeit with only about half the amount of stuff it could have held. Peter moved around a couple stacks of cardboard boxes, and lifted a nearly invisible trap door in the concrete floor.

Forty-five seconds later, he was sitting in his safe room below the church.

Using one of the disposable phones he kept there, he called Misty first. She had been his assistant back in the Office days, and proved herself time and again as one of his most valuable assets.

"Misty?" he said.

There was a long pause. "What's wrong?"

"An old case has resurfaced. I need your help."

Another hesitation. "You'll have to get me out of my current gig."

"You're still at the Labor Board?"

"Yes."

"All right. I can do that. Finish out the day. You won't need to go back until we're done."

"When and where do you want me to report?"

"You remember the townhouse in Georgetown?" he asked.

"The one on the top floor?"

"Yes."

"I remember it."

"After work, go home, pack a bag, and head there." He paused. It had been six months since he'd checked in with her. "You *can* do that, right?"

"Are you asking if I have someone waiting for me at home?" She laughed. "Just Harry."

Harry was her dog, a little Westie that was getting up in years.

"Can someone watch him?"

"My neighbor. What am I supposed to do when I get to the apartment?"

"I should be there ahead of you. If not, just get everything operational and wait for me."

His next call was to the one man who could clear up what had gone down in Las Vegas the night Mila Voss was supposed to have died.

One ring, two. After the third, a recorded voice said, "Please leave a message."

"Quinn, it's Peter. I need you to call me as soon as you get this. Don't blow me off. I need to talk to you *now*." He gave the number of the phone and hung up.

He tried to remember the last time he'd spoken with Jonathan Quinn. It had been a while. Once the Office was disbanded, Peter had no longer been in a position to need the cleaner's talent for disposing of unwanted bodies.

While he waited for Quinn to call him back, he logged on to his secure computer, and started putting feelers out to some of the sources he had in Asia, seeing if anyone might have unknowingly worked with Mila.

At a quarter after four, his phone rang. Only Misty and Quinn had the number, so he snatched it up without looking at the display.

"Yes?" he said.

"You called?" Not Misty.

"Quinn?"

"Hello, Peter."

Not Quinn, either.

CHAPTER
THREE

BANGKOK, THAILAND

BROWSERS AND SHOPPERS and people who had nothing better to do crowded the sidewalk, checking out the stalls and tables selling charms and tokens and Buddhas by the bucketful. Though their number included more than a few tourists, most were Thai. The sellers who offered the best wares drew the largest crowds, sometimes making the sidewalk impassible for a minute or two.

On the street itself, cars were caught in a logjam, their pace even slower than that of the pedestrians—a few feet forward, stop, wait, a few feet more.

One of the taxis veered toward the curb. Before it had even stopped, the rear door swung open, and a *farang*—a foreigner—climbed out. Dressed in jeans and a black T-shirt, he looked like just another Westerner out exploring the sights of the Land of Smiles. But he hadn't come to Thailand for the culture. He was there for only one purpose.

Those on the sidewalk seemed to sense the difference in him. It wasn't fear he invoked, but something closer to determination, a sense of mission, causing Thais and tourists alike to move to the side so that his path was unimpeded.

The clouds that had been gathering above Bangkok all morning had finally blanketed the sky, and the distant rumble of thunder warned of a change ahead. Many of the street vendors began to double-check the canopies and umbrellas that covered their goods, and those who didn't have protection began packing up.

The smell arrived first. Rain on asphalt, perhaps a few blocks away. Then the initial drops began to fall. It started as a smattering, nothing more than a tease, but within seconds became a downpour, skipping all steps in between.

Tourists caught in the open rushed for cover, while the locals, who lived with the rain every day, went on with business as usual. The man in the black T-shirt continued walking as if the sun were still shining, and gave the rain no acknowledgment whatsoever.

It wasn't long before he came to the point where the road took a sharp turn to the right. Instead of continuing with it, he went left into a short extension of the asphalt filled with food carts, where cars were no longer welcome. Dozens of tables were set up under umbrellas and tarps, crowded with people enjoying meals and staying dry.

Vendors called out to the man, trying to entice him to stop. Each time he put his hands together in front of his chest and bowed his head slightly in a Thai *wai*, thanking them for the offer but never once slowing his pace.

At the back end of the food area was a permanent structure. Inside were more stalls, a mixture of food and T-shirt vendors and souvenir shops. This was where the majority of the *farang* tourists had taken refuge.

The man walked all the way through the building and out the other end, onto a covered ramp that led down to a dock. Beyond was the wide and mighty Chao Phraya, the river that sliced the city in half. Its brown water was littered with green patches of vegetation floating rapidly southward toward the Gulf of Thailand. Long boats and barges and small river ferries, unconcerned about the rain, continued to move up and down it.

On the covered part of the dock, several people waited for one of the ferries to arrive. The man could see it approaching from the north. Like the others that traveled between the piers, it was long and low to the water, with rows of seats along each edge, like a canopy-covered airliner missing the top half of its tube.

The man walked all the way down to the dock, and took a

position several feet from the others. He carefully scanned the river, noting at a subconscious level where each vessel was.

With a series of whistles from a man at the back of the boat, the ferry eased against the dock, then the motor was thrown into reverse to hold it in place. The whistler jumped off, and tied the vessel to the pier. As soon as he was out of the way, half a dozen passengers piled off, then those who had been waiting climbed aboard.

The only one who hadn't moved was the man in the black T-shirt. The whistler gave him a questioning look, wondering whether he was going to get on, but the man on the dock shook his head. Seconds later, with another whistle, the ferry took off.

As the man scanned the river, he resisted the urge to bend his leg. He knew the cramp he felt in his right calf was all in his imagination. He didn't *have* a right calf, only a high-tech prosthetic attached to the few inches that remained of his leg below his knee. The phantom pains and discomforts were more an annoyance now than anything. He'd taught himself how to deal with them, and knew how to push them from his mind. After a moment, the cramp went away.

From the south, the high-pitched sound of a motor rose above the other noises on the river. Not a longboat, not even a ferry. It was a powerboat that looked like it would be more at home on a lake in the States than here on the Chao Phraya. It was racing down the center of the river. Then, as it drew closer, it veered toward the dock, where its wake rushed toward the longboats tied up nearby, rocking them against the docks and causing more than a few angry shouts.

Not exactly subtle, the man thought.

It had almost reached the dock when it powered down and let the river's current bring it to a stop. There were two men on board. One hopped off the back and looped a rope around the end of a pillar.

The second remained at the controls. He looked over at the waiting man and smiled. "I believe you hired boat for day, yes?"

The expected question.

"That's right. You came recommended." The expected answer.

Once the man in the black T-shirt climbed aboard, the guy who'd roped off the boat untied it and jumped into the back.

"Can go under," the pilot said, pointing at the door to the lower cabin. "No rain, and have beer and food if you want. Can sleep also. Will take us a couple hours, I think."

"I'm fine here," his new passenger replied.

The pilot shrugged. "Up to you." The smile came out again. "Welcome aboard, Mr. Quinn."

"Thank you," Nate said.

THE RIVER TOOK them north out of the city, and away from the rain. After about an hour, they reached Ayutthaya—the capital of Siam in centuries past—and skirted around its southern edge until it bent northwest into the countryside.

Small villages and farms surrounded the river, quickly turning the craziness of Bangkok—and, to a lesser extent, Ayutthaya—into a distant memory.

After a while, the pilot said, "Not long now."

Nate nodded, his gaze fixed on the river ahead. Not for the first time, he played through his mind some of the possible scenarios of what was about to happen. This kind of thinking had been part of his early training when he was an apprentice cleaner to Jonathan Quinn.

It had been an invaluable tool. In a world where their job was to make bodies disappear, the ability to be flexible and immediately react to any situation was often the difference between success and becoming one of the bodies.

The problem with his upcoming meeting was that he'd already thought of at least a dozen ways it could go, and was sure there were at least a dozen others he hadn't even considered.

A few minutes later, the river bent to the right and straightened again. As it did, a temple came into view on the left bank about a quarter mile ahead. Like with all Buddhist temples in Thailand, the upside down, conical stupa—or, as the Thais called it, *chedi*—rose prominently in the middle of the temple grounds. This one, unlike some others he'd seen, was not covered in gold. Its pitted surface had been white once, but dirt and mold had worked their way into the nooks and cracks, dulling its long forgotten brightness.

The temple building itself was undergoing renovations. An intricate, clearly makeshift wooden scaffolding had been erected around most of the structure. A small group of men was spread out along it, working on the temple walls.

The boat's engine began to throttle back, and the man at the wheel steered the craft toward the small pier that served the temple. Through the bushes at the edge of the bank, Nate thought he could see movement on the temple grounds. When the boat was only a hundred feet away, three monks wearing bright orange robes, their heads shaved bare, stepped onto the dock and watched them approach.

The boat's pilot eased them forward, and with a perfect touch, brought the side of the vessel up against several old tires that buffered the dock.

"Wat Doi Thong," he said, announcing the name of the temple. "How long do you think?"

"I don't know," Nate told him.

"I don't want to spend night out here."

"Neither do I, but you're being paid enough, so if it happens, it happens."

Nate stepped onto the dock.

"Mr. Quinn."

Nate looked back. "Yes?"

"You like one of us come with you?"

"That won't be necessary."

The pilot seemed relieved. "Okay. No problem. We be here."

Nate walked over to the monks and gave them a deep *wai*. "*Sawadee, krap.*"

The monks returned the *wai* and the greeting, almost as one.

"*Khun phood phasa Angrit, dai mai?*" Nate said, asking if any of them spoke English.

The middle monk seemed to think for a moment, then said slowly, "Sorry. Only Thai."

Nate was about to call to the boat pilot and have him do some translating, when a new voice said, "I speak English."

A man was standing on the shore just past where the dock

ended. Nate was sure he hadn't been there a moment before. He, too, was wearing a saffron robe, but unlike the other monks, he sported a goatee and had a full head of black hair that fell almost to the base of his neck. On his exposed shoulder, Nate could see a tattoo of a tiger peeking up over the top, like it was ready to pounce off the man's back.

Nate walked toward him. "Great. I believe I was expected. My name's—"

"I know who you are," the man said. Surprisingly, though he looked Thai, he sounded as American as Nate did. "I'm afraid you've wasted the trip, though."

Nate stopped at the edge of the dock. "He's not here?"

"He's made it clear he has no desire for visitors."

"This isn't a social call."

"I'm sorry," the man said, then glanced at the boat. "If you leave now, you might get back to Bangkok before it gets too late."

Nate stepped onto the shore. "If he doesn't want to see me, he can tell me that himself."

A wry smile appeared on the long-haired monk's face. "That would be defeating the purpose, don't you think?"

"I don't care about the purpose. I'm not leaving until I see him."

"Then I think you should make yourself comfortable. You're going to be waiting a long time."

"Yeah?" Nate said, taking another step forward. "Well, I don't have time to wait, either."

The man laughed. "You're playing right into the American stereotype. Always in a hurry."

Nate walked up the short path, straight toward the monk. When he neared him, he said, "Excuse me."

The man, still smiling, stepped to the side, but just as Nate passed him, the monk grabbed him from behind and twisted him around, intending to knock Nate to the ground.

Nate was ready for it. Since the first moment he'd seen the monk, he knew the man would not simply back down. There was a roughness to him, a spark in his eye, and a set to his stance that spoke of a life not unfamiliar with violence.

Nate shifted his weight, bringing his shoulder under the

monk's chest then heaving him upward and tossing the man to the side. Freed, he continued toward the temple.

But the monk was not through with him. Before Nate had gone ten feet, the man came at him again, slamming Nate in the back and knocking him off the path into a knee-high, white stone fence.

Off-balanced, Nate jumped as best he could over the obstruction, scraping his left shin on the top, but maintaining his footing as he landed on the other side. He whirled around, sure that the monk would come at him again.

The man hit Nate in the chest like a linebacker, and together they fell onto the ground with a thud. A dull ache throbbed for a moment in the upper left of Nate's chest. About nine months earlier he'd been shot there. The wound had healed well, and he'd done everything he could to regain the strength he'd had before, but on occasion, the injury would still remind him of its presence.

The monk wrapped a leg over Nate's waist, and attempted to pin the cleaner in place. With all his strength, Nate pushed the man to the side and spun after him.

"Nate! Daeng! Enough."

Both men stopped struggling, and looked over at the man standing twenty feet away.

"Get up," Jonathan Quinn said. "You're making fools of yourselves."

CHAPTER
FOUR

STOCKHOLM, SWEDEN

IN THE EARLY hours of the morning on Mila's first day in the Swedish capital, she had set up a camera aimed at the door of an apartment building in Södermalm, an island neighborhood just south of the center of Stockholm. Over the next two days, she'd kept track of the comings and goings, something easily done given that the building only had three units.

But it was now the third day, the day she needed to make her move. She checked the video feed on her phone again. Still quiet. The most activity had been just after seven a.m., when two people had left within a few minutes of each other, but in the four hours since nine o'clock, the door had remained closed.

"Come on, you idiot," she whispered to herself. "You've got to eat sometime."

If the man she was waiting for didn't leave the building soon, she would have to find another place to watch from. She'd already been at the café longer than she should have been, having stretched her solo lunch to nearly an hour and a half. Every time her waitress walked by, the woman gave Mila a look that said, "You're still here?"

Mila picked up her coffee cup. At most it had two sips left. She took the first, thought *Screw it*, and drank it all. The last thing she wanted was for people to remember her, something that was probably too late in the case of the waitress. She put enough kronor on the table to cover the check and an appropriate tip, then left.

The place she was surveilling was three blocks away, a four-story building divided into three apartments—one on the ground floor, one on the floor above it, and the third taking up the top two. That top apartment was the one she was interested in.

The man who lived there was named Mats Hagen. He was a freelance tech, who, for a sizeable fee, could obtain almost any information a client might ask for as long as it was on a computer somewhere. When Mila had known him several years earlier, he'd been fairly new to the scene. He took on work wherever he could get it, meaning he was on the road most of the time. Since then, he'd apparently established a reputation that now allowed him to do most jobs from home.

After the fiasco in Tanzania, Mila had spent a sleepless night trying to figure out what her next move should be. If only she had been able to talk to Rosen. If she was wrong, she could fade back into her assumed life. If her fears were true, she would have to do something about it. But with Rosen no longer an option, she had to find someone else she could approach.

She did have the name of one of the other guards who'd been on the flight, but she'd already looked into him and discovered he'd moved up in the world in the years since, and would be extremely difficult to get close to.

She needed to find someone more accessible, which meant obtaining access to information she would normally be unable to get her hands on. That's when Hagen came to mind. She had never been a big fan of his. He always looked at her in a way that made her feel extremely uncomfortable. Once he'd even tried to put a hand on her ass, but she put a quick stop to that, and he never touched her again. All this made him the perfect candidate for what she needed.

She had caught the first available flight going north. After stops in Athens and Frankfurt, she landed in Oslo, Norway. From there, she took the high-speed train across the Norwegian/Swedish border to Stockholm, where she had now been for three days.

If Hagen stuck to the habits she'd observed previously, he would leave his place for a two-hour lunch at any moment. In fact, he was running late. That worried her. Maybe he wouldn't go out at all today. She could, of course, delay her plans, but she already felt like she'd been in Sweden too long, and the sooner she could get out of the country, the safer she'd be.

Her phone vibrated once, an alarm she'd created that was triggered by the motion sensor built into the video program. She glanced at the screen and saw that the door to the apartment building was open. Mats Hagen was stepping outside.

Finally.

As soon as she knew which way he was going, she altered her course, and less than a minute later was walking about two dozen feet behind him. As usual, he headed for the T-Bana station—Stockholm's subway—only a few minutes' walk from his front door.

She descended into the station a few seconds after him, used the seventy-two-hour pass she'd bought her first day there, and took up a position at the far end of the platform from where he waited. A train arrived three minutes later. She remained where she was as Hagen got on and the doors closed. Once the train started to speed away, she returned to the street.

She knew from the beginning that breaking into his place would not be easy. He was a pro, after all, and one who had more than a passing familiarity with technology. But even pros had weaknesses, especially geeky ones with obvious money to burn. Hagen's weakness was named Eva Stahl.

Mila had uncovered the woman while researching Hagen as she'd been waiting in the airport before leaving Dar es Salaam. The first night in Stockholm she confirmed Hagen's relationship with Eva. Knowing today would be the day she made her move, she had paid the woman a visit twelve hours earlier.

Getting into Eva's apartment had been a snap. Mila moved quickly through the flat to the bedroom where she found the woman deep asleep. A quick blast of a gaseous anesthetic ensured she'd stay that way for at least a few minutes longer. Then it was a simple matter of administering the shot at the back of the woman's knee where she'd never notice the mark.

Mila gave the drug five minutes, then tapped Eva on her cheeks until she opened her eyes. The drug had three effects: it removed any resistance to answering questions; the recipient would remember the episode as no more than a fading dream, if at all; and the unlucky person would feel ill for the next twelve hours, and more than likely spend the day in bed.

It took Mila less than three minutes to learn what she needed to know. She left the woman's apartment with the two keys and the security codes she would need to get into Hagen's place.

Now, as she approached his building, she donned a wide-brimmed hat that had been in her bag, a pair of sunglasses, and thin rubber gloves. Though she hadn't been able to spot it, she knew that Hagen would have installed a security camera somewhere out front. What she really wished she had was a disrupter that would scramble the camera's signal, but she'd been unable to get her hands on one. The disguise would have to do.

Keeping her head down, she walked up to the front door, punched one of the codes Eva had given her, and entered. There were three doors in the small lobby: two in front of her, and one to the right. The one on the right led to the ground-floor apartment. The other two opened onto private staircases, one leading to the second-floor residence, and one to Hagen's place. According to Eva, his door was the one on the left.

She found the hidden keypad, input the appropriate code, and entered. The staircase doubled back twice before reaching another door at the top. A third code plus the use of the keys and she was in.

As soon as she saw the place, she rolled her eyes. No way Hagen had done the decorating. She distinctly remembered him having no sense of style. His apartment looked like it had jumped out of a featured article in *Kick-Ass Homes Monthly*—metal and leather and wood and granite all blended together by someone who knew what they were doing. It was a guy's place, though not too "guy," the kind of apartment someone like Hagen probably thought would surely get him laid. Given his relationship with Eva, it had apparently worked.

Mila did a quick search through all the third-floor rooms, already knowing there was nothing on this level that interested her. What she wanted was in his private office, one floor up. The stairs were tucked out of sight behind a faux wall between the living room and the guest bedroom. The keypad where the final code needed to be entered was located behind a small panel in the hallway closet. Mila punched in the sequence, and went up the stairs.

Apparently, the designer who'd done the living space below had not been allowed to touch the upper floor. The space was one large room that extended the length and width of the building. One wall was covered with metal shelving units filled with computer parts—some small, some whole systems stretching back God only knew how long in computer history. At the front end of the room was a workbench, with all the tools and accessories necessary to build pretty much anything electronic Hagen might need.

Scattered throughout the space were several desks, each with a different type of computer on it. Piles of magazines, files, and manuals were spread across the floor. She counted three trashcans filled to the brim with empty Coke cans and food wrappers. Tucked in the back corner beside the stairs was a low-slung couch and a television monitor hooked up to every type of gaming console imaginable.

A geek's heaven.

She examined each of the computer stations, then picked the one she was most familiar with and sat down. Before waking it up, she removed a thumb drive from her pocket and stuck it into an open port. Though the monitor remained dark, she could hear the computer come to life, as the program that would hide her presence inserted itself into the machine's operating system.

Once it had taken charge, the computer dinged and the monitor faded on. She was now connected to the rest of the world in a way few people had ever been.

She navigated through several different restricted networks, finally discovering the picture of someone she remembered. A few minutes later, she had his name. From there, she was able to find a current address, and was surprised it was closer than she'd expected. Even more interesting was the fact he'd been involved in not just one aspect of what had happened to her, but two. As she was about to dive back in and see what else she could dig up, her phone vibrated once. She looked at the screen.

Oh, crap!

Hagen was standing at the outside door, holding a bag in one hand, and punching in the door code with the other. She checked the time. He hadn't even been gone forty-five minutes. *What the hell?*

She closed everything, forced the screen to go dark, and headed for the stairs. Her only chance was to reach the living area before he did and find someplace to hide until he went up to his office.

She was halfway across the room when she remembered the thumb drive. It was still in the back of the computer. She raced back, pulled it out, then checked her phone as she ran for the stairs. Hagen was no longer outside. Which meant he was heading up to the third floor at that very second.

She jumped onto the staircase, bypassing the first two steps, and raced toward the bottom. As she ran, she tried to recall if there was anyplace on the floor below where she could hide. She had a vague sense of a couple of locations that *might* work, but nothing solid.

When she reached the bottom, a part of her screamed for her to stop and listen to find out if Hagen was in the apartment yet, but she ignored it. If he'd come in already, so be it. She'd take him by surprise, then get the hell out of there before he could do anything. If he hadn't entered, she still had the chance to escape without him ever knowing she was there.

Pushing the door open, she prepared herself to hear Hagen yell in surprise, but there was nothing, no sound at all, just the dead air that had been there when she'd passed through earlier.

She looked left and right for anything she could crawl under or hide behind. There was a dark wooden cabinet in the corner that looked as if it had a little space behind it. But it would be tight—*very* tight—and if she didn't fit, she'd be caught in the direct sightline from the door.

Kitchen? No, the bag probably had food, so he might head straight there.

Outside the main door, she heard someone climb the last step and stop.

No!

Whipping around once more, her gaze fell on a door under

the staircase to Hagen's office. It was flush to the wall, designed not to be noticed.

As silently as she could, she hurried over, and pulled on the recessed handle. A closet, stuffed with jackets and a few boxes and bags. She jammed herself between the clothing, and pulled the door closed behind her. Two or three seconds later, she heard the front door open and Hagen's footsteps.

She'd made it. If she played it right, he'd never even—

Wait, was he wearing a jacket when he left? she wondered. *If he was, would he put it in the closet?*

She tried to recall what he'd been wearing as she followed him down the street to the T-Bana, but she couldn't remember.

Relax, it's a beautiful day. Plus, he's a Swede. If he doesn't have to wear a jacket, he won't.

She concentrated on the sounds coming from the other side of the door. Hagen seemed to be moving around near the kitchen. Then the noise faded, and for a few minutes she picked up nothing. With each passing second, her tension grew.

What are you doing?

Another half minute passed, then the sound of footsteps returned. Only this time, they were heading her way.

They became so loud, he had to have been passing right outside the closet. A second later a door opened, then steps again, but these rose above her as Hagen ascended the stairs to his office.

The same voice that had urged her earlier to wait did it again, but the part of her that still retained some of her previous training knew that the time to leave was *before* he got settled. For a minute or so, he would be moving around and less likely to hear any noise she might make.

The latter voice won out.

Just over a minute later, she was on the sidewalk, her pace a leisurely stroll, something that would not draw attention.

Something that took every ounce of her will to maintain.

CHAPTER
FIVE

WAT DOI THONG, THAILAND

AS NATE CLIMBED to his feet, Quinn turned and walked away.

"Truce?"

Nate looked back. The monk he'd been fighting was holding out his hand.

"You're not going to yank me back to the ground, are you?" Nate asked.

"Apparently we're fools, so no. I don't think that would be a good idea."

Nate shook the man's hand.

"I'm Daeng."

"Nate."

"I've heard about you."

"Can't say the same." Nate looked toward the spot where he'd last seen Quinn. "Where did he go?"

"I can show you," Daeng said.

"So now it's all right?"

With a shrug, Daeng said, "Apparently," then started walking down the path.

The main temple was at least three stories high. Through the large open door in front, Nate could see a partial view of a gigantic Buddha at the far end. Instead of going inside, though, Daeng led him around the building toward a much less assuming one set back amongst some trees.

As they walked, Daeng asked casually, "Which is the leg

you lost?"

Nate kept his expression blank, but couldn't help but feel uncomfortable with the fact that the monk apparently knew a lot about him. After a second, he said, "The right."

"How far down?"

"Just south of the knee."

"And everything below that is man-made. Amazing. The way you moved, I would have never guessed."

"Yeah, well, I'll never forget."

They walked the rest of the way in silence. Along the wall of the smaller building was an open door. Daeng went through first, and Nate followed.

The room they entered was obviously used for teaching. There was a portable blackboard at the front, and several rows of chairs with attached desks through the middle portion. At the back was a desk where Quinn sat, writing something in a black ledger-sized notebook.

While Daeng seemed content to remain near the door, Nate strode across the room, and stopped a few feet in front of the desk.

Always trim, Quinn looked even thinner than usual, but that, by far, wasn't the only change Nate could see. Quinn's hair had grown out, too, falling an inch or two below his ears. Nate guessed it had also been at least a week since his boss—or perhaps former boss, that was still unclear—had picked up a razor.

Without taking his eyes off what he was doing, Quinn said, "You shouldn't have come, Nate."

"I'm sure my showing up like this isn't a surprise," Nate said. "That woman, Christina—she must have told you."

"And I told her to tell you to stay away."

"Yeah. I got that message."

"And yet you're here."

"I'm here."

Quinn finally looked at him. "Okay, you've seen me. I'm alive. Now you can get back on your boat and go home."

"I didn't come here just to check if you were okay."

"I don't care why you came," Quinn said. "Please, Nate, leave. I don't want you here."

"Look, I've only come because—"

"Aren't you listening to me? I said, I don't care!" Quinn closed his eyes and seemed to be trying to get himself back under control. When he opened them and spoke again, his tone was level and calm. "I have work to do. Please respect that."

Out of the corner of his eye, Nate could see Daeng approaching.

"I'm not here out of disrespect," Nate said. "In fact, it's just the opposite."

Quinn let out a breath and shook his head. He looked at his watch and glanced over at Daeng. "Please escort him back to his boat. I'm late, or I'd do it myself."

"No problem," Daeng said.

Quinn headed for the door. Nate started to follow, but Daeng stepped in his way.

"I'm not leaving until you hear what I have to say!" Nate called out as he grabbed Daeng's shoulder and tried to shove the man to the side.

Daeng stood his ground. "Let him be."

Across the room, Quinn had just reached the door and was stepping outside.

"Mila Voss!" Nate yelled.

Quinn froze.

"She's why I'm here."

In a near whisper, Quinn said, "Mila Voss is dead."

"Then I guess someone needs to tell her that."

Quinn looked back into the classroom, his eyes fixed on Nate. After a few seconds, he shifted his gaze to Daeng. "Get him something to eat. I'll be back in a few hours."

He resumed walking away.

"We should talk now," Nate insisted.

"Relax, buddy," Daeng said. "Be happy he's not kicking you out. He'll be back. You can talk to him then."

Beyond the doorway, Quinn veered off to the right and out of sight.

As much as Nate hated to admit it, Daeng was right. At least now he knew Quinn would listen.

Daeng smiled, and slapped Nate on the shoulder. "You hungry?"

DAENG TOOK NATE to another building, where they found a kitchen manned by two older women and a girl who was probably no more than ten. The two men were each served a plate with rice and stir-fried vegetables.

Nate had been sure he'd have only a few bites, but quickly realized he was hungrier than he thought, and finished his meal before Daeng was even halfway done with his.

"You want more?" the man asked.

"No. This was fine."

For several seconds, the only sound was that of Daeng's spoon scraping across his plate.

"Where did he go?" Nate asked.

At first it seemed as if Daeng hadn't heard him, then the monk finished off the last of his vegetables and looked over. "You want to see?"

"Please."

THEY WALKED DOWN a road that led away from the river and into a countryside dotted with small fields. Though evening was approaching, in several of the fields families tended their crops. There were no big farm machines here. It was mostly bent backs and handheld tools and the occasional ox pulling heavier equipment. Scattered among the fields, some close to the road and others much farther away, were small houses where the farmers lived and kept whatever livestock they might have.

After the two men had walked for about ten minutes, Daeng moved to the side of the road and stopped.

"There," he said, pointing across the fields to the right.

For a few seconds, Nate wasn't sure what he was supposed to be looking at. The fields were no different than those they'd passed. Then he saw two figures standing together a couple hundred yards away. Nate couldn't make out any faces, but one looked to be a teenage boy, his brown skin darkened by his time spent under the sun. The other's face Nate didn't need to see. The hair, the clothes, the posture—Quinn.

Nate wasn't sure what they were doing, but it had something to do with working the field.

"Two weeks ago, the man who owns that farm broke his

leg in two places and injured his back in a motorcycle accident," Daeng said. "The people here aren't rich. He couldn't afford to hire anyone to take care of his crops, not if he wanted to feed his family, too. So it fell to his son, but the boy is fourteen and can only do so much. Every day for the last week, as soon as your friend finishes teaching his English lessons at the temple, he comes out here and gives the boy a hand."

They watched Quinn and the boy work.

"We should go back," Daeng said. "Better if he doesn't notice that we're here."

Nate nodded, though he was sure there was little chance Quinn hadn't already seen them. Nate was an expert at picking up small details, but he was nowhere near as good as his mentor.

As they walked back to the temple, Nate asked, "Why isn't your head shaved? Aren't all monks supposed to do that?"

"I'm not a monk," Daeng said.

Nate looked at him, confused.

Daeng smiled. "I *was*, but that was a long time ago. The other monks here allow me this honor when I visit."

"So you're kind of a pseudo monk."

"I guess you could call it that."

They walked quietly for a moment, the temple coming into view just ahead.

Nate said, "I'm guessing you've spent some time in the States."

"Have I?"

"Your English. You speak it like a native, and your accent is Middle America."

"Californian, actually."

"Really?"

"Hollywood High."

"You're kidding." Nate pointed at his chest. "Santa Monica High."

"Samo? Beach brat, huh?"

Nate nodded. "When I could be. So you were born in the States?"

Daeng took in a long breath. "No." He paused before adding, "Moved there when I was young. Came back here after high school."

There was obviously more to the story, but Nate knew Daeng had shared all he wanted to for now.

As they reentered the temple grounds, Daeng said, "Feel free to have a look around, or you can wait in the classroom. If you need me, I'll be in that center building over there." He pointed at a group of small buildings beyond the stupa near the river, then gave Nate a *wai* and walked off.

With little else to do, Nate decided to do a little exploring.

He was standing just inside the temple, his eyes fixed on the golden Buddha that dominated the room, when he heard someone enter behind him.

"Peaceful around here, isn't it?" Quinn said.

"It is," Nate agreed. "I can understand the appeal."

"Can you?"

"Of course I can."

"And yet, you're here to take it away from me." Before Nate could respond, Quinn said, "This isn't the place for us to talk."

Without further comment, he turned and walked outside.

THEY ENDED UP back in the classroom. Quinn closed the door this time, and once they were both sitting at one of the student desks, he said, "Tell me."

"Four days ago, I got a call—" Nate stopped himself. "*You* got the call. I returned it."

"From who?"

"Peter."

Quinn nodded as if he'd expected the answer.

"He wanted to talk to you, of course," Nate said, "but I told him you were unavailable, and if he had something to discuss, he should tell me."

"He must have liked that."

Nate smirked. "Oh, yeah. It definitely put him in a good mood. He said he needed to talk to you and only you. He had questions about an old case."

"Mila Voss."

"Yeah, but he didn't tell me that right away. Not until after I explained you were on a, um, sabbatical, and reaching you was not easy. That's when he insisted I find you, and tell you he wants to know why Mila Voss is still alive."

Quinn looked over at the wall, his expression unreadable.

"Since I didn't know where you were, I contacted Orlando," Nate said. Orlando was Quinn's girlfriend and sometimes partner. "She was reluctant at first to say anything. When I told her what Peter wanted, she said almost the same thing you did—'But Mila Voss is dead.' Only when *she* said it, I could tell she thought it was true. You, not so much."

Quinn hesitated, then said, "How is she?"

"Worried about you."

"She said that?"

"She didn't have to."

Quinn fell silent for a second. "Where was Mila seen?"

"Peter didn't say. Only that if I didn't find you as soon as possible, things could get very uncomfortable very fast."

Quinn's head drooped, and Nate thought he heard him whisper something. A curse, perhaps.

"Who is she?" Nate asked. It was something he'd been wondering since he'd talked to Peter. He'd asked Orlando, too, but she wouldn't tell him. She did finally say that Quinn was somewhere in Thailand, but she didn't know where specifically. She only had the name of a woman in Bangkok—Christina— and a code phrase that would let the woman know it was all right for her to tell Nate where Quinn was staying.

Instead of answering Nate's question, Quinn said, "Do you have your phone?"

"Of course."

"Get Peter on the line."

CHAPTER
SIX

MOST MORNINGS WHEN Quinn had woken during the past
few months, his only thoughts were of the classes he would be
teaching that day. He wished it was the same this particular
morning.

The previous fall, his work as a cleaner had nearly caused
the deaths of his mother and his sister. The safeguards he'd put
in place, the firewalls he thought he'd built between himself and
them, had all failed. If it weren't for his quick action and that of
some of his associates—most notably Nate acting as bodyguard
for Quinn's sister, Liz—his mother and sister would have died.
Nate had been shot in the process, and nearly died himself.

The realization that his work could so affect the ones he
loved shattered the illusion of the life he imagined he'd created.
He became mentally paralyzed, unsure if he could ever return to
the dangerous life he was so good at, especially if it meant the
innocents he cared about could be harmed.

For two months he did nothing but hole up at his house in
Los Angeles. He returned no calls, pursued no new jobs. The
easy assignments he'd already committed to, he gave to Nate.

It was a visit from Orlando that finally shook him loose.

"You don't have to do this anymore," she told him. "But
you also don't have to make any decisions now. You have the
luxury of time. Take as much as you want. I think you should go
someplace unfamiliar, where you can clear your mind. If you
want, I can suggest a few, and use some of my contacts to line
something up."

He thought about it overnight, and when he woke the next

morning with her in his arms, he said, "I want."

He wandered for a few weeks after that, first visiting his mother in Minnesota, then spending a week with his sister in Paris as they continued to try and rebuild a relationship that had been broken for so long. After that he headed to Thailand, where the mysterious Christina had sent him to Wat Doi Thong.

In the first few months at the temple, he'd continued to have the same dream every night—though dream was probably not the right term. It was more like a sleeping memory. A hospital room in London. Nate asleep on the bed, recovering from his wound. Liz sitting beside him, holding his hand, then turning to look at Quinn who had entered a few moments earlier.

"What?" she said in the dream, and in the memory.

He took a step forward. "How…how's he doing?"

Liz held his gaze for a second. "He was awake for thirty minutes. The doctors said that's a good sign."

In the memory, they talked about Nate—a neutral topic, less painful. But in the dream they would skip ahead, and he would find himself standing beside his sister as she asked, "Who *are* you?"

The question hurt more than she could have possibly realized. His fault, not hers. He'd hidden his true life from his family. Hell, he'd barely talked to Liz since she was a kid. He'd thought it was the right thing to do. He'd thought it would be best for her. But now it seemed so pointless, years wasted, the bond they once had destroyed. He wished there was a way to return to the relationship they'd had before, but as good as he was at visualizing all the scenarios in his work, he couldn't see the way back to that. "I…I just wanted to…I thought…I thought I was doing…" He fell silent, knowing no words would ever be adequate.

That was the moment Liz could have pounced, and rightly ripped him apart. But her face had softened, and she looked at Nate. "When he woke he asked about you and Orlando. He said you were the two people he respected most in the world." She turned to her brother again. "He said you always try to do the right thing."

Quinn didn't know how to respond.

Silence filled the room for a while, then she said, "I don't know how to feel. About you, I mean. I hated you for so long. I don't think I hate you anymore, but I don't know how I feel." A long pause. "That's the best I can do."

"It's more than I can ask," he said.

As he started to turn away, she put a hand on his wrist. He looked at her, and she at him. Then she fell against his chest, wrapped her arms around him, and cried.

He knew it didn't change what she had said. The ordeal she had just gone through had been intense, and the man she'd started to have feelings for was lying in the hospital bed beside her, a bullet wound in his chest.

Yet for those minutes he held her, it was like none of the mistakes he'd made mattered. "I love you, Liz," he wanted to say, but knew it would be too much.

He always wished the dream would end there, but it didn't. After they'd pulled apart, Liz had donned her coat of armor again.

"I'll need time," she said as he turned for the door. "Maybe forever."

That was where the dream ended.

But as the hot Thai months moved on, the dream came less and less, until he'd stopped having it at all. But the previous night, after Christina sent word that a man would be arriving to see him, the dream had come to him again, more vivid than ever. When he woke before dawn, his usual thoughts of English lessons and working in fields were replaced with memories of violence and death.

From the description Christina gave him, he knew his visitor was Nate. Yet when he saw his former apprentice, he was surprised. There was something older about Nate, his edges sharper and more defined. There was a confidence, too. While Nate undoubtedly had more to learn, he was now a professional who could stand on his own.

What Quinn also saw was a window into the world he was not yet ready to return to, a world he was unsure he would *ever* be ready for again. His assumption had been that Nate was there to lure him back. Nearly nine months was a long time to be away, so the attempt would not be unreasonable, but that didn't mean he had to agree to it. His plan had been to make it clear to Nate he wasn't going anywhere.

Then Nate had yelled out Mila Voss's name.

Mila Voss. Seen alive.

Dear God, what was she thinking?

Quinn could hear the call ringing on the other end as Nate handed him the phone. There was a click, and a familiar female voice said, "Yes?"

"Misty?" Quinn said, surprised.

A pause. "Quinn." He heard a smile in her voice before her tone turned serious. "I heard your father passed away last year. I'm so sorry."

"Thank you," he said. "I understand Peter wants to talk to me."

"Let me see if I can find him."

He was on hold for nearly three minutes before Misty came back on.

"Sorry for the wait. Connecting you now."

A double beep, then, "Jesus, Quinn. Where the hell are you?"

"Hello, Peter."

"Are you going to answer my question?"

"No."

"Haven't changed, have you?"

Quinn let that one pass without comment, wanting to get this over with. "I've been told we have a ghost."

"Would be nice if that were the case. Afraid this one's very much flesh and bone."

"Mila Voss."

"So it appears."

"Where was she seen?"

Peter briefed Quinn on the incident in Tanzania, and the discovery of a disguised Mila Voss hovering over a body on the sidewalk.

"Security detection software picked it up first, then matched it to a known photo. Ninety-nine-point-five-percent sure it was either her or her twin sister. But as far as we know, she doesn't have a twin."

"Who was the dead guy?"

"Not important."

Quinn knew that probably wasn't true, but he didn't push. "I'd like to see the footage."

"It's already uploaded. I put it on one of the servers you and I have used in the past. ADR-3."

"All right, I'll check it."

"Hold on," Peter said, sensing that Quinn was about to hang up. "You're not getting off that easy."

Quinn waited.

"You were the one who was supposed to have disposed of her body," Peter said.

"I was."

"So what happened?"

"The body I was given, I got rid of."

"Yeah, but was it dead when you made it disappear?"

"I don't typically dispose of people who are alive."

"And it was Mila?"

"You can read my report, Peter. It's all in there."

"I *did* read it. You were the one who ended up having to ID her. So, *was* it Mila?"

"I disposed of the body of a woman that was Mila's height, had her hair, wearing the clothes she had last been seen in, and dropped off at the hospital by the driver who'd picked her up at the airport. It sure as hell looked like Mila to me."

"So as far as you know, the body you got rid of was Mila's."

"Didn't I just say that?"

"Then how the hell is she walking around alive?"

"I was relying on the assassin for information. If I recall correctly, he had a spotter following her from the airport. Why don't you ask *him* if they fingered the wrong person?"

"Not a bad idea, except Kovacs was killed several months after that assignment. So that's not an option."

"Well, I'm not sure what else you want me to say, Peter."

Peter let out a defeated breath. "If it really is her, this is a total fuckup."

"The best I can do is look at the footage and tell you what I think. Other than that, I'm as much in the dark as you are."

"Honestly, I'm looking for anything that will help at this

point. If you find something, call me right back."

Quinn hesitated. "There's no computer where I am, so it could be a day or so before you hear from me."

"The sooner the better," Peter said, then hung up.

As Quinn handed the phone back to Nate, he tried not to think about how many lies he'd just told. What happened on this job in Las Vegas had gone against all his training, but *he* was the one who caused the job to go off the rails. *He* was the one who'd made the conscious decision to ignore the professional detachment he was usually so good at maintaining. He had hoped it would never come to this, but even then he'd known the secret of that night—that Mila Voss was still alive—would come to light one day.

That day had finally arrived.

Nate pocketed his cell. "Okay. I've done what I promised. I'll leave you alone now and head back to Bangkok." He held out his hand. "If you need me, you know how to reach me."

I'm not ready to go back, Quinn thought. *In a few more months, maybe. Not now.*

But he could no longer suppress the words whispering in the back of his mind. *"I'll make sure she stays safe,"* his old friend Julien had said. *"But if there comes a day that I can't, then it will be up to you."*

A pact, one that Quinn couldn't ignore.

He finally looked up, but didn't take Nate's hand. "It's too late to leave now. We'll get some sleep and head out in the morning."

"You're coming, too?"

"Yes."

CHAPTER
SEVEN

**SEVEN YEARS EARLIER
LUCERNE, SWITZERLAND**

"HE'S IN THE room," Henrik whispered over the comm in Quinn's ear.

Quinn touched the bag sitting on the floor beside him. It contained the tools he had predetermined would be needed on the job ahead. His current location was a little-used storage room in the basement of the Chateau Gallant Hotel in Lucerne, where he could remain out of the way until his specialized services were needed.

After consultations with Henrik, the team leader, when he'd first arrived, Quinn had been pleased to find out that the method chosen for the elimination of the subject would be mess-free. A powerful, quick-acting anesthetic would be released from a metal canister hidden behind the headboard as soon as the subject lay down for the night. Once he was under, Henrik would enter the room and administer the fatal dose of Beta-Somnol. Henrik and his team would then have five minutes to locate the documents the subject was supposed to be carrying before Quinn took over. If things went according to his plan, and they usually did, the body would be out of the hotel and on its way to its final resting place no more than seven minutes after that.

He glanced over at Julien. The larger Frenchman looked somewhat ridiculous in his coveralls, but it was better than dressing him as a bellhop. At his size—several inches over six feet and broad in both shoulders and chest—he would have instantly stood out to the hotel staff. It was less likely, though, that anyone would know all the maintenance personnel who might service the facility.

"Won't be long now," Quinn said.

"Good. I'm starving. Maybe on the way out of town we can stop for something to eat, *oui*?"

"How about we get rid of the body first and eat later."

Julien shrugged. "I do not think he will mind."

Quinn rolled his eyes, but gave no other response.

Over the comm, Henrik was giving the play-by-play of what was happening in the room. Apparently the subject was trying to get some work done before going to sleep.

Julien pulled out a deck of cards. "Some more poker while we wait?"

"I don't think so."

"I was lucky earlier. Don't you want a chance to win back what you lost?"

"I have a feeling you'll still be lucky."

"Luck, who knows where it lands? Sometimes good for me, sometimes good for you. You know this." He smiled. "Okay. This time we play just for fun, huh?"

Quinn was saved from declining again by Henrik announcing that the subject had finally decided to crawl into bed.

"All right. Looks like his eyes are closed," Henrik said. "I'm activating the gas." He was quiet for a few seconds. "He should be breathing it in right about…now." Another pause, this one for half a minute. "All right, we're going in."

There was the sound of movement over the radio, then the click of a door opening. That would be the room Henrik was using just down the hall from the subject. More movement, then another click.

"Okay, we're inside," Henrik whispered.

Quinn grabbed his bag and stood up. That was their cue.

"You're sure about not stopping for food," Julien said as they left the room.

"I'm sure," Quinn replied.

Julien frowned for a second, then suddenly brightened. "Maybe the target ordered room service and didn't finish. Can't let that go to waste, huh?"

"You can't be serious."

"If no room service, he must have bought some Swiss chocolate, don't you think?"

By the time they reached the door to the stairwell, Henrik had administered the Beta-Somnol, and the five-minute clock had begun. Based on their trial runs, it would take Quinn and Julien exactly four and a half minutes to get from their current position to the subject's door, providing them with a thirty-second cushion in case anything slowed them down.

Nothing did.

Quinn tapped the door twice, paused, then once more. He expected to see Henrik and the three men working with him standing nearby, ready to leave, when the door opened. Instead, all but the one who opened the door were still searching the room.

"Twenty seconds," Quinn said.

"We can't find it," Henrik explained.

"Doesn't matter. You're out by the deadline or you're moving the body yourself."

"I realize that," Henrik said. He pointed at the desk next to the subject's laptop. "They should have been right there."

"Maybe it's on the computer."

"No. Hard copies only. I was told they were concerned about having any of it in digital form."

"Did anyone lay eyes on it to be sure he had it?"

"Peter confirmed the handoff occurred, but he couldn't tell us exactly what the information was contained in," he said. The Office was the client on this job. "Both he and I assumed it would be in an envelope or file folder."

Quinn looked at his watch. "Five seconds. Are you staying or am I?"

Henrik frowned, then scooped the laptop off the desk and looked over at his men. "Grab his suitcase and shoulder bag. We'll search them again off-site."

Quinn grimaced. The bags were part of his disposal responsibility. He didn't like having pieces floating out there that could cause problems later. "You'll need to burn them."

"Don't worry. We will."

"You do it yourself."

"I'll see to it personally," Henrik assured him.

Reluctantly, Quinn nodded.

Henrik headed for the door. "Let's go. Let's go."

Before the team was even out of the room, Quinn and Julien began preparing the body for transport. Soon they were also leaving, carrying an aluminum-reinforced cardboard box that contained the subject. If asked, Quinn would simply say they were carrying a replacement duct for the heating system. But they made it through the hotel without any fuss.

They put the box into the dark green van parked downstairs, then leisurely drove off. As soon as they were out of sight of the hotel, Quinn moved into the back, opened the box, and began removing the clothes and all identifying items from the body. These, like the now-dead target, would be going up in flames. He had just pulled off the guy's undershirt and was reaching for the waistband of the pajama pants when he noticed a flesh-colored bandage on the man's torso, just below his ribs.

He pulled it off in case there was some sort of tattoo underneath that he hadn't been told about. No tattoo, but that didn't suppress his surprise. There was a bump under the skin, one-centimeter square. It was red with a fresh scab at one end that looked very much like it was covering an incision.

Quinn swore to himself, and for a second considered slapping the bandage back on. This wasn't his responsibility. The only thing he'd been hired to do was get rid of the body. Except, much to the disapproval of his old mentor Durrie, he'd never been one who focused solely on his job and ignored everything else. On this particular operation, he was fully aware that the main focus, beyond the subject's death, was to obtain a set of documents.

He grabbed a knife out of his kit, and cut around three sides of the square, turning the skin into a flap. Underneath was exactly what he'd been worried he'd find, a small container holding a stack of microphotographs.

The documents. Had to be. Old-school spy craft at its best. *Son of a bitch.*

With extreme reluctance, he called Peter.

"Don't tell me you've already finished," Peter said.

"Still in progress."

"Is something wrong?"

"Has Henrik given you an update?"

"Yes. Very disappointing."

"Maybe not."

After he finished explaining what he'd found, Peter sounded almost jubilant. "Oh, thank God! Good work. Really, really good work."

"I don't want to hold on to this. That's not my responsibility."

"Of course not. Stay on the line. Let me see if I can reach Henrik and arrange a handoff."

Henrik, it turned out, had followed protocol and gone to ground. It would be at least another twenty-four hours before he checked in again.

"Don't worry," Peter said. "I'll arrange an alternative. Tell me where and when."

DECIDING THAT THE photos were less a problem to be driving around with than the body in the back of the van, Quinn set a rendezvous time for after the disposal of his primary cargo.

Once that was done, Quinn and Julien took the van to the location Quinn had given Peter for the handoff—a darkened street a few blocks behind St. Leodegar's Church. As Quinn had planned, they arrived fifteen minutes early to do a quick reconnaissance on foot to make sure the area was clean.

"Five minutes," he said. "Then we're out of here." He'd already done more than his due diligence by reporting what he'd found and agreeing to the handoff. He wasn't about to risk his and Julien's lives by spending any more time in Lucerne than they had to.

Two minutes before his self-imposed deadline, they heard the whine of a scooter growing louder and louder as it neared their street, then stopping just around the corner.

The silence that descended was soon broken by the sound of footsteps echoing softly off the old stone buildings. A silhouette appeared at the end of the block, walking toward them. The person was no more than five foot three or four, and had a matching small frame. Despite the helmet, Quinn knew it was a woman. It wasn't just her size that gave her away; it was how she walked in the confident yet natural way only a woman could achieve.

"Beautiful night for a stroll," she said as she neared, her voice distorted somewhat by the helmet.

"Could be warmer," Quinn replied, completing the on-the-fly recognition code Peter had come up with.

She reached up and pulled her helmet off, releasing a torrent of thick, shoulder-length hair. Even in the darkness, Quinn could make out her face well enough. His first thought was that she was probably Eastern European. She had the slightly Asiatic eyes and high cheekbones that graced the faces of many Slavic models. If it weren't for her height, she probably could have been one, too.

"Mila," Julien said, surprised. He smiled and threw his arms open wide.

The woman grinned and let the big Frenchman envelop her in a bear hug. When he finally pulled back, he held her in front of him, a hand on each of her shoulders as he looked her over.

"How have you been?"

"Good," she said.

"Keeping busy?"

"Yes. Thank you for passing my name around." Not Eastern European. American. Unless she'd worked her ass off getting rid of any trace of an accent.

Julien scoffed. "Please. It's what we do, huh? Help each other out?"

"Not everyone thinks like you. I mean it—thank you."

"Are you guys finished?" Quinn asked.

Julien threw an arm around the woman's shoulder, and turned her to face Quinn.

"Have you met Mila Voss yet?" he asked.

"Uh, no. But apparently you have."

Julien laughed more loudly than Quinn would have liked, given the supposed secrecy of their meeting.

"Of course, I know her," Julien said. "I got her into the

business." He leaned forward, his volume dropping only a few decibels. "We were together for a while. You know—young woman, Paris, a handsome man like me. It was only natural."

The woman looked embarrassed. Quinn couldn't tell whether it was because she regretted her relationship with Julien, or because she didn't want that to color Quinn's professional opinion of her.

"Julien, please," she said. She patted him a few times on his ribs, and pulled out from under his arm. "We talked about this, remember?"

"What?" he asked, then his smile faltered a bit. "Quinn's different. He's not going to care."

She sighed.

"Okay, okay," Julien said. "*Je suis désolé.*" He looked at Quinn. "Some things are apparently better left unsaid."

"I'm going to have to agree with you on that," Quinn said.

"Let's start again, *d'accord?* Jonathan, this is Mila Voss. Courier extraordinaire. Mila, this is the legendary Jonathan Quinn."

She held out her hand. "Pleased to meet you."

"You, too," Quinn said. "Now, if you guys don't mind, maybe we can get this handoff taken care of and get the hell out of here."

"Of course," Mila said.

"I have a great idea," Julien said. "Quinn and I are going to grab a late dinner after this. Maybe you can join us?"

Quinn was about to tell Julien that was a bad idea when Mila said, "Thank you, but I've been instructed to deliver this without delay. Maybe some other time."

The Frenchman looked disappointed.

"Sure," Quinn said quickly. "Some other time." From his pocket, he pulled out the envelope he had put the microfilm into, and gave it to her. "That's it."

"Thank you," she said. "I'll, uh, just be on my way. It was good to meet you, Mr. Quinn."

"Just Quinn is fine. Good to meet you, too, Mila."

She gave Julien another hug. "Be safe, okay?" She hesitated before adding, "I still worry about you."

"No need to ever worry about me. I will live forever. *I*

worry about *you*."

She hit him on the arm as she pulled away. "Find a good woman and settle down. That's what you need to do."

"Is that an offer?"

She shook her head and laughed to herself as she walked away.

Once she disappeared around the corner, Quinn said, "You're still in love with her."

"I'll always be in love with her," Julien replied wistfully. Then, in a tone of recharged energy, said, "I will always be in love with any woman who shares my bed. Why would I invite them there otherwise?"

Quinn saw right through the lie of the second part, but he could tell the first was one hundred percent true.

CHAPTER
EIGHT

LONDON, UNITED KINGDOM

MILA'S HAIR WAS now black. Technically, it was the wig that was black, but she'd learned many years ago that to really sell a disguise, you had to make it your own—*be* a woman with black hair, in this case.

She was dressed in a conservative gray business suit, and carried over her shoulder a brown leather briefcase. Tinted glasses helped hide her still youthful face, and high heels made her seem taller than she was.

She had taken the Victoria line of London's Underground from Oxford Circus all the way out to Tottenham Hale. From there she transferred to a regular passenger train out to Waltham Cross Station, and then grabbed a cab into neighboring Waltham Abbey.

It was early yet, only ten thirty, and while many of the shops were already open on Sun Street near the old church, the shoppers had yet to show up in any kind of numbers.

As she walked down the middle of the walking street, she could feel the eyes of those in the stores looking out at her, wondering who she might be. That was fine. It didn't matter if they remembered the black-haired businesswoman who looked like a lawyer or stockbroker or some other high-powered type. She wouldn't be that person for long.

Her destination was a half block before the end of the street, a small suite of offices on the upper floor of a building, above a pub called Sir David. The door to the offices was off to the side, allowing the pub to have as much front real estate as possible. There was no sign next to the door, nothing to indicate what kind of business was beyond. There was only a cream-colored plastic box with a speaker on top and a button on the bottom that Mila pushed.

The speaker crackled to life.

"Yes?" a male voice said.

"I have an appointment," Mila replied, her voice low so that it wouldn't carry down the street.

"Ms. Carter?"

"Yes."

"One moment."

As the speaker went dead, the front door lock clicked. She grabbed the handle and pulled it open. Carpeted stairs rose through a narrow, dingy passageway to another door at the top. Just before she reached it, it opened.

"Come in," the man standing on the other side said.

She covered her hesitation with a smile. The information she'd uncovered in Stockholm had been right. It *was* him.

The six years since she'd last seen him had not been particularly kind to the man. He looked older, *much* older, and favored a hip as he backed out of the way so she could enter. She had expected some change, of course. According to what she'd learned, he'd been forced out of the business because he'd contracted lung cancer, and while surgery and chemotherapy treatments had put it into remission, it was obvious his illness had taken a huge toll on him.

"I assume you're Mr. Johnston," she said.

"I am. Please, this way."

She sensed no recognition in his eyes, but given her disguise and the fact that she supposedly died just hours after the only time they had ever met, it wasn't surprising.

He led her through two rooms, stuffed with old books in boxes and on shelves, to an office at the back.

"Make yourself comfortable," he said, motioning to the guest chair in front of the desk. "Would you like some tea?"

His English accent amused her. It was good, but she knew he was as American as she was.

"Not right now, thank you," she said as she sat.

"You won't mind if I have some, I hope."

"Not at all."

Johnston walked over to a hot plate on a cabinet in the corner, and picked up the teakettle. Once he'd filled a cup, he carried it back to the desk, stirring constantly, and sat down in his stuffed leather desk chair.

"You're right on time, Ms. Carter. I appreciate that."

"Time is not something to be wasted."

"Very true." He smiled and took a tentative sip of tea.

"In the interest of *time*, perhaps we can get right to business? You said you had one of the books on my list."

"I do."

He stood again, and used a key to unlock a nearby cabinet.

If he'd actually figured out who she was, this was the moment he'd make his move, and retrieve not a book but something more lethal. She slipped her hand into her shoulder bag, encircling the grip of the pistol inside, and pointed it at the retired spy.

Since his body blocked her view, she couldn't tell what was in his hand until he turned around. At the sight of the book, she released her gun.

He set the Steinbeck on the desk in front of her. On the worn dust jacket was printed *The Grapes of Wrath* and the author's name. Below this was a faded illustration of a man in overalls looking down into a valley at several trucks heading, presumably, to California.

"Viking Press first US edition, 1939. I'm lucky enough to have two copies, but this is the one in the best condition."

"Good." She pretended to examine the book. "And the others on the list?"

"I have leads on the Maugham and two of the Greenes. Perhaps next week. The Hemingway is proving to be more difficult than I expected."

She shrugged. "No matter. It's not the books that are important."

The man looked at her for a moment. "Pardon? I must have misunderstood you."

She reached into her bag once more, and this time pulled

out the suppressor-enhanced pistol, aiming it at the man's chest. "I don't think you misunderstood me at all, Agent Evans."

His eyes narrowed. "Who sent you?" he asked, all traces of his English accent gone.

"No one sent me."

"No one?"

"I came on my own."

He examined her face, confused. "I don't know you."

"Actually, you do." She removed the glasses and pulled off the black wig. From his continued look of bewilderment, she could see he still had no clue. "How about this? Las Vegas in May of 2006? You weren't there, but you were the one who hired me to take a package there. Surely you haven't forgotten that."

For several seconds he just stared at her. Finally he said, "Not possible. Mila Voss is dead."

"Come now. You handed me the package yourself. In a hotel room in Arlington, remember? The ugly orange bedspreads, and the lime-green carpet? You rushed me out. I thought at the time it was because the room was too disgusting to remain in, even for you. But I think you just wanted to make sure I didn't miss my flight."

The blood drained from his face. "Dear God. We...we were told you were dead." He paused. "I had nothing to do with it."

"Really? How did they come to think I was going to be a problem that had to be dealt with? It was because of the Portugal trip a month earlier, wasn't it? Turns out *you* were the agent in charge of that. I don't remember you. I'm sure you weren't on the plane."

"I...I was in Lisbon."

"That explains it. So what? Did one of your men tell you they thought I needed to be looked into?"

"It wasn't like that. I had to report it to my superiors. What they decided to do wasn't my call. It came from the top."

She removed a newspaper photo from her pocket and set it on the desk. Tapping it, she said, "From the Lion?"

Though his agent instincts were undoubtedly rusty, Evans was almost able to pull off keeping his face blank. But she saw it, just for a second, an instant of shock in his eyes that confirmed she was right. The Lion was indeed the same man in the picture, the one behind it all.

She *had* been right to come out of hiding.

Evans leaned back in his chair, his hands falling to his sides.

Mila had been so focused on what she had just learned that it took a second to register that Evans had moved. She jumped up, her gun in front of her. Evans was already twisting to the side, bringing up a gun hidden within the back of his chair.

His pistol cracked once, the bullet flying past her head and lodging in the wall behind her. Two spits through her suppressor kept him from pulling his trigger again, both her shots catching him high in the chest.

"You asshole!" she said.

She wasn't an assassin. No matter how dangerous it would have been to leave him alive, she hadn't wanted to kill him. The information was all she came for. If the Lion found out from Evans that she was alive, so be it. She'd still have the upper hand.

She eased over to the window that overlooked the walking street. While her shots had been muffled, his single one had not. But there was no one rushing toward the building, and no one standing by the front door pushing the intercom button. The books, she realized, had probably absorbed much of the noise.

She looked back at Evans. "Asshole," she repeated. "Why did you do that?"

Three minutes later, a girl in jeans and a dark green tank top descended the back stairs of Johnston's Rare Books Finding Service, and turned down Darby Drive. Her mousy blonde hair was pulled back in a single ponytail that went halfway down her back. She knew those who saw her would think she was just a teenager enjoying the sunny day.

If only.

CHAPTER
NINE

THAILAND

FOR MONTHS, QUINN'S daily routine had been up before dawn, breakfast, meditation, three classes in the morning, lunch, two classes in the afternoon, work on the temple—Quinn was paying for the renovations himself—dinner, read, then sleep. Any deviations, such as helping Ton and his family with the farm, were only extensions of the other things he was doing. In the half year since he'd arrived at Wat Doi Thong, he had never traveled more than a few miles away.

Prior to leaving that morning, Quinn had apologized to the head monk for his abrupt departure, and promised he would be back as soon as possible. The money for the restorations, he assured the man, would continue to be available. His only request was that someone be sent every day to help Ton in the fields. The monk assured him that would happen.

Now he sat in the back of a speedboat with Nate on one side and Daeng on the other, heading for the chaos of Bangkok and the rest of the world. He had known he would have to reemerge one day, but in his mind it had been in the distant future.

Mila had forced the issue. The question was, why? Why had she come out of hiding?

No, he corrected himself. His only question should be: What would he have to do to get her to disappear again?

Mila, what the hell is going on?

DURING THE VOYAGE, Daeng made a call and arranged for them to be picked up at Thewes Pier, just north of the Rama VIII Bridge in Bangkok. When they arrived, they found a black sedan with tinted windows waiting for them.

The driver was on the large size for a Thai man. He was bald like the monks back at Wat Doi Thong, though Nate doubted he'd ever donned the orange robes. By the deference he displayed, it was clear Daeng was his boss.

"Someplace with a secured Internet connection," Quinn said to Daeng as he climbed into the backseat with Nate.

"No problem," Daeng said, getting into the front passenger seat. "I'll take you to my place."

They drove through Bangkok for twenty-five minutes before stopping in front of a high metal gate in the middle of a dirty white wall. The driver pulled out a phone and made a quick call. Seconds later, the gate was pulled open from inside.

The world within the walls felt like it had been transported from somewhere outside the city. The vibrant greens and reds and yellows and purples of the vegetation looked almost unnatural. It was a jungle, controlled, well taken care of, but a jungle nonetheless.

The house was located near the very center. It, too, was different from anything else Nate had seen in the city, a beautiful two-story home constructed of glass and metal that would have fit in nicely next door to Quinn's place in the Hollywood Hills.

The driver parked in a designated area not too far beyond the gate, and they all climbed out.

"While I'm getting some lunch together," Daeng said as he led them inside, "you can use one of my laptops. There's one on the kitchen bar."

"Thanks," Quinn said. "Will it track what I'm doing?"

Daeng bowed slightly. "There's tracking software on all of my computers, but it can be easily turned off."

"Good. I'd like you to do that."

The interior of the house was surprisingly spartan, given how the outside looked. Utilitarian furniture that was nice but not expensive, a few photographs and a handful of paintings on the white walls and that was about it. There were none of the touches a designer might have added, and nothing beyond the paintings and photographs that could be considered decorative. The only lavish item was a waterfall built into the wall in the foyer. It would have probably been beautiful but it wasn't running, and there was no water in the small pool at its base. Through the windows of the living room, Nate could see a grass area in back where at least a dozen kids were playing while four or five women watched.

The kitchen was off to the left and opened into a dining room with a simple wooden table long enough to seat twenty people. Between the two rooms was a raised bar with a closed computer on top.

Daeng tapped away at several keys then took a step back. "All set."

Quinn immediately got on, and Nate moved in behind him.

ADR-3 was one of dozens of remote servers Quinn, Nate, and Orlando used when necessary. They were all owned by companies that had no idea part of their computer storage space had been usurped for private use.

Using the appropriate login and password, Quinn quickly found the file Peter had uploaded and copied it onto Daeng's machine.

While they waited for the transfer, Nate said, "You want to tell me who this Mila Voss is now?" He'd tried asking a few times on the boat, but Quinn had said nothing.

Nate thought he would get the same non-response as before, but Quinn said, "She was a courier."

"A courier? Was she supposed to have been killed in action?" While the majority of the time a courier's job was a piece of cake, it could also be extremely dangerous. Mostly they traveled alone, and there was always the danger of someone wanting the packages they carried.

But Quinn said, "She wasn't on an assignment at the time. Well, I guess technically she was, but…"

Nate frowned. "So…someone ordered her killed. That's why you were there. To get rid of her body?"

A pause. "Yes."

"And yet she's alive."

Quinn made no reply.

A few seconds later, the download finished. Quinn opened the file and hit PLAY.

The first part started with a man falling to his death in front of a building. This was soon followed by the arrival of another man wearing a baseball cap. Both Nate and Quinn watched with trained eyes as the second man checked the body for any signs of life, then got up and disappeared into the crowd.

The second part of the video was a split screen showing the man in the cap on both sides, then one side morphed into an image of a woman while the other remained unchanged.

Quinn hit PAUSE.

"That's her?" Nate asked, surprised by the transformation.

Quinn nodded.

"So she *is* alive."

Quinn closed the computer. "That was never an issue."

"You mean you *knew*?"

"Of course I knew."

"But you told Peter she was dead."

"I told Peter I got rid of a body."

"You made it pretty clear you thought it was her."

Quinn remained silent for several seconds, then said, "If I'd told him the truth, Mila wouldn't have lasted another twenty-four hours."

"Wait. I just want to get something straight. Did you know she was alive *before* you disposed of the body? Or was it something you realized after?"

Though Quinn said nothing, the look on his face was answer enough.

"Are you kidding me?" Nate said. "How many times have you hammered into me the importance of integrity? Of maintaining an excellent reputation? You were hired for a job that you lied about. Not just today, but back then, too."

"Life isn't always so black and white."

Nate stared at his mentor. "That's not how you trained me."

"Training's what gets you by until you have enough experience to know where you can bend the rules."

"So this is one of those rule-bending situations? That's a pretty damn big bend."

Quinn stood up and glanced at Daeng. "Where's the toilet?"

"Through the living room, and down that hall," Daeng said. "Second door on the right."

Without looking at Nate, Quinn left.

Nate chastised himself. He had no idea what the extenuating circumstances were with this woman, and knew he was in no position to judge Quinn's actions. Chances were, he would have done the same thing. He was just surprised, that's all.

"How about a beer?" Daeng asked, holding out an opened bottle of Chang.

"Thanks," Nate said, taking it from him. He drank deeply then set the bottle on the counter.

Daeng nodded in the direction Quinn had gone. "Your friend—he's searching."

Nate picked up the beer again. "Searching?"

"When a soul gets unhinged, it is very difficult to return it to where it should be."

"His soul is unhinged?"

"What would you call it?"

Nate shrugged, but said nothing. The truth was, it was a pretty accurate description. Having his family threatened had obviously sent Quinn reeling. But his mother was fine, as was his sister. Nate knew that firsthand. He'd been with Liz a few weeks earlier.

Outside, one of the kids screamed, then laughed. Nate turned to see a small boy running across the lawn with three other chasing him. "Are any of those kids yours?"

Daeng shook his head. "No. I don't have any."

"Oh. I just thought…" He trailed off, unsure what to say next.

"They're Burmese," Daeng said.

"I'm sorry?"

"The children. The women, too. They're Burmese."

"Refugees?"

"Yes."

"I thought the situation in Burma was getting better."

"Yes, but it still has a long way to go.", He looked out the window. "They've been in camps in Thailand for years. Most of those kids have never even been in Burma."

"They live here with you now?"

Daeng shook his head. "Only visit. When I can, I have some of them smuggled down here, so they can have a little time away from the camps. They'll have to go back soon."

Nate looked out at the kids again, wondering, not for the first time, exactly who Daeng was.

Before he could ask anything more, Quinn returned.

"Thank you for delivering the message, Nate, but it probably would be best if you went home now," Quinn said. "What I need to do next will be best handled on my own."

"Look," Nate said. "If I sounded disrespectful, I'm sorry. I didn't—"

"That's not it at all. You said what you needed to say. The questions you asked were ones *I* would have asked in your place. But this is something you shouldn't be involved in. It happened before you were around so you're untainted. Go. Get out of here. I don't need you."

"Damn," Nate said, a mischievous grin on his face. "Sounds like you're breaking up with me."

From the look in Quinn's eyes, it was obvious he didn't see the humor in the situation. As he was about to say something, Nate held up a hand, stopping him.

"I don't care when this thing happened. I'm pretty sure you're going to need some help, so I'm not going anywhere."

"This isn't your—"

"You can kick me out, but I'll just follow you. And I'm good now, too. *Real* good. You know you won't be able to lose me."

"I can't ask you to get involved."

"You're right. But I can volunteer. And I do."

Quinn looked at him for a moment longer, then his gaze strayed to the bottle of Chang on the bar. He turned to Daeng. "Please tell me you have more of those."

THE PROBLEM WAS, Nate was right. Integrity *was* the backbone of being a good cleaner.

A cleaner's job was to make bodies disappear, or, at the very least, make it appear as though the victim died by some other means than the real one. With full access to the scene of the event, a cleaner was entrusted with evidence that would not only put the actual killers in jail for the rest of their lives, but the clients, too. A sloppy cleaner could accidentally leave some of this behind, whether at the scene or the place they got rid of the body or someplace else entirely. An unscrupulous cleaner could purposely do the same. Soon word would get out about those types, and work would dry up if the cleaners in question weren't killed outright. Integrity, performing to a higher standard, playing straight with clients—these were the things that kept work coming in.

With Mila, Quinn had broken that code.

When he had stood in Daeng's bathroom after walking out of the kitchen, rubbing his face with his hands, he knew he couldn't put Nate in a situation that might ruin his future. Was he surprised when Nate refused to walk away? No.

What he actually experienced was relief, and that just made him feel worse.

"So, what's the mission?" Nate asked, quickly glancing at Daeng and back at Quinn. "Or…?"

"Daeng's already agreed to help me," Quinn said.

"Wait. You didn't want me tainted, but you're not worried about him?"

"I worry about everything, but Daeng's as stubborn as you are."

Nate shook his head, then shrugged. "All right, then, I'll ask again. What's the mission?"

"Simple. We find Mila."

"And then?" Nate asked.

"We cover her tracks and make her vanish again."

"What if she doesn't cooperate?"

"Then we'll have to figure out a way to convince her."

"You're running this show," Nate said. "If that's what you want to do, that's what we do."

"Thanks," Quinn told him, meaning it.

"When do we start?"

"Now." Quinn held out his hand. "I need to borrow your phone."

QUINN CARRIED NATE'S mobile into the living room. He selected a name from Nate's contact list, then hit CONNECT. Once he did, he had a sudden urge to hang up as quickly as possible, but instead he raised the phone to his ear.

One p.m. in Bangkok meant it was eleven p.m. in San Francisco the day before. Would she still be up? Or would he wake her? It had been three months since he'd last talked to her. *No*, he realized. *Four. Oh, God.*

Orlando answered after one ring. "Did you find him?"

She obviously thought Nate was calling. "He did."

He wasn't sure how to read the pause that followed. Anger? Disinterest? Annoyance?

"Hey," she finally said, that single syllable adding nothing to his understanding of what she might have been thinking.

"I...I'm sorry. It's been a while."

"It has."

She is not *making this easy.*

"I...I just..."

"Are you calling to chat? If you are, you're doing a pretty bad job."

"No. I, um, need your help."

"Of course you do." She paused. "Mila Voss, right?"

"Yes."

"Figured. I've already pulled everything together I could find so far. I'll email it to you."

"Thank you. Peter put a video up on ADR-3, security footage of Mila showing up at a hotel in Tanzania. There's a dead guy in the shot, too. Peter didn't tell me who he was. I was wondering if you could find out? Maybe even see if there's a connection between the corpse and Mila?"

"I can try," she said, sounding somewhat resigned. "You know, I met her once."

"You did?"

"She was working on an assignment that ran in tandem with something Durrie and I were on." Quinn's late mentor had once been Orlando's boyfriend, not to mention the father of her son, Garrett. "I liked her. I was sad when I heard she died."

"She didn't die."

"So I gather. You had something to do with that?"

"Yes."

Nothing for a moment, then, "I'll find out what I can and get back to you."

"I...I miss you," he said, but his words fell on dead air. Orlando had already hung up.

CHAPTER
TEN

IF HE COULD have run flat out, Quinn would have, but it was out of the question. A warm, beautiful Friday night along the Las Vegas Strip meant the crowds were even more massive than usual. The best he could manage was to weave in and out of the waves of people that seemed to be throwing themselves in his way every few seconds.

Once, in a rare moment when a stoplight ahead had halted traffic, he moved out into the road and made a full block in the same amount of time it had taken him to travel a quarter block earlier. Ahead, he could see the Lux casino, and, across the street, the faux cityscape and scaled-down version of the Empire State Building in front of the Manhattan Hotel, his destination.

"She's been spotted," Jergins had said over the phone. "They're converging there now."

Spotted? *How?* Of course there was no way he could ask the team leader, so Quinn had gotten off the call and headed straight for the Strip.

At the moment, he was on the wrong side of the street, but that would be rectified when he reached the pedestrian bridge that stretched from the Lux to the second-floor entrance of the Manhattan.

"Hey, watch it!" a man said.

"Sorry," Quinn replied, knowing his apology had probably been lost in the hum of the crowd.

THE DESTROYED

Foot traffic thickened as he neared the Lux, his pace dropping to what could best be described as a quick walk. The pedestrian overpass was maybe a block away, but damn if he couldn't buy a break in the crowd.

"Excuse me," he said, pushing forward. "Excuse me, excuse me."

"Hey, we're all going somewhere, buddy. Why don't you cool it a bit?"

Quinn looked at the man, his face hardening into an expression that had made violent men back down. The other man's eyes widened, then looked away as if he'd never seen Quinn.

The quick encounter only heightened Quinn's self-anger. The civilian crowd was not fair game. His response to the man had shown weakness, not strength.

He didn't let it stop him, though. He couldn't afford to do that.

Finally, he reached the escalators that led up to the elevated walkway. It, too, was crowded with people, so he could only stand there as it slowly rose to the top. The inaction momentarily allowed him to wonder once more what had gone wrong.

The assassin and his spotter should have been at the Planet Hollywood Hotel waiting for Quinn's confirmation from the hospital, not at the Manhattan. But instead, Kovacs and his man had *found* her. How?

As he reached the top of the escalator, he pushed the question aside and made his way across the bridge. He slowed to a walk just before he reached the hotel door, and entered right behind a group of guys barely old enough to buy a drink. Now that he was inside, running would only draw attention, and not just from those he was coming to stop. Casino personnel would not be keen on someone turning their establishment into a racecourse.

He walked past the pretzel stand and straight over to another escalator. This one took him down to the casino floor. Spread out before him were dozens of tables where guests were playing blackjack and mini baccarat and roulette and craps and Let It Ride, apparently enjoying handing over their money to the dealers.

Once he reached the bottom, he made his way past the central bar, and the faux Manhattan streets with their full restaurants and shops. Finally, he reached an unmarked door tucked away where most visitors would never see it.

He tried the handle.

Locked.

That wasn't a good sign. He'd manipulated the lock himself so that it would only seem to be engaged, but if pushed and turned the right way, the door was supposed to open. Unfortunately, no matter how much he pushed and turned, it wasn't budging.

He glanced around, made sure no one could see what he was doing, then pulled out his lock picks. It still didn't open. Someone had jammed it closed from the inside.

There were two other ways to the area beyond that door; neither was convenient. The least inconvenient was via a service elevator and a maintenance-access hallway located over fifty yards from his current position.

Seeing no other options, he headed in that direction. The elevator was beyond a set of doors that could only be opened via a security card issued to hotel staffers. That wasn't a problem. He had his own copy.

The problem turned out to be waiting for him on the other side of the door. It came in the form of a big beefy security guard with a wry smile and superior look in his eyes.

"Can I help you, sir?" the man said.

"Maintenance elevator?" Quinn asked, not missing a beat.

"And why would you need that?"

Quinn looked at him like he was an idiot. "To do some *maintenance.*"

The left side of the guy's mouth rose even higher. "Perhaps you should come with me first."

Even though he knew there was little chance of it working, the maintenance ploy had been worth a try. Quinn acted like he would cooperate. As he came abreast of the guard, the man said, "Keep going. There's a door at the end of the hall. We'll—"

Whatever else he was going to say was lost in the expulsion of air that rushed from his lungs due to Quinn's unexpected gut punch. Even before the guard's wind was completely knocked out, Quinn had twisted the man's arms behind his back, and quick-walked him down the hall to the maintenance elevator. Using his foot, Quinn pushed the call button.

The doors opened just as the security man started to get his breath back. Thankfully, the car was empty. Quinn forced the man inside, and did the same toe trick on the button for the lower basement.

"What the hell do you think you're doing?" the guy sputtered.

"Kicking your ass."

Quinn shoved the man's arms upward.

The man screamed and moved forward, trying to alleviate the pain. That was exactly what Quinn was waiting for. He pushed hard on the guy's back, ramming the guard's face into the side of the car with a loud smack.

"Fuck!" the guy yelled.

"Want me to do it again?"

"No, man. No."

Something dripped on the floor. Blood, probably, but Quinn saw no need to check. There was a soft *bong*, and the doors opened again.

The lower basement was not a place most people went. Maintenance only, mainly pipes and electrical systems and the kind of things no one ever thought about. Quinn pushed his companion out of the car and took a look around. Off to the right were two large storage rooms he had checked out on his initial recon. He used his free hand to open one of the doors then shoved the guard inside.

"I don't know who the hell you think you are, but you're in a shitload of trouble," the man said.

"You couldn't be more right about that."

He shoved the guy's arms up even higher, then rammed the man's head into the wall. The security guard dropped to the ground, unconscious.

"I'm sorry," Quinn said. "You should have just pointed me to the elevator and kept walking."

He jammed the lock as he went out and shut the door. Even if the guy did wake up soon, he'd have a hard time getting it open.

Without giving the guard another thought, Quinn took off, sure that he was already too late. He worked his way through the labyrinth of the lower basement until he reached the small, closed-off hallway.

Like the door he'd tried on the main floor, this one was locked, but this time he was able to pick it open. The dark hallway beyond had mainly been used when the hotel was being built. Now its only real purpose was as an unintentional shortcut to a group of storage rooms that had a separate stairwell and elevator.

Quinn used the light on his phone to navigate to the other end where a second door—this one unlocked—led into the back of one of the storage rooms. Whoever had packed the place had the foresight not to put any of the wooden crates that took up a majority of the space all the way against the walls. What had been left was a two-foot gap. Quinn had to shimmy sideways down it until he reached the slightly less narrow walkway running through the middle of the room.

When he reached the storage room door, he withdrew his SIG Sauer P226 and attached a sound suppressor to the end of the barrel.

He stepped into the corridor.

There were seventeen separate rooms down here. The one Mila should be in was marked 21AY. It was six down and on the other side.

Quinn padded quietly along the cement floor, his head cocked, listening for any noise ahead.

Reaching the door to 21AY, he slowly opened it, and stared in surprise at what he saw inside.

CHAPTER
ELEVEN

SAN FRANCISCO, CALIFORNIA

ORLANDO LOVED QUINN. There was almost nothing he could do that would change her feelings. She even understood his self-imposed exile. Hell, she'd helped him set it up, putting him in touch with Christina in Bangkok in the first place.

He had been so damaged when he left, she wondered if he would ever recover. She wished she could do more for him, but Quinn wasn't wired that way. Maybe in time she could help, but this first part, this finding himself again, had to be all him.

Why she'd acted annoyed with him when he called, she didn't know. Perhaps it was just the way she thought most people would act in a similar situation, and she'd just fallen into it naturally. Perhaps, subconsciously, she'd wanted him to know his recovery wasn't just about him. She was here, too, waiting for him, hurting for him.

Whatever he would discover at the end, she didn't care. If he wanted to get out of the business entirely, and leave the world of secrets behind, she was fine with that. If he wanted to stay, take on some more work, she could handle that, too. She just wanted him to get to a point where he could decide which it was going to be.

Now this business with Mila had forced itself into his recovery. What his role in it was, she didn't know. But she *was* worried it would prevent him from finding his peace again.

Her biggest concern at the moment was the fact he hadn't worked in nearly nine months. Sure, he was good, the best probably, but was he sharp enough at the moment to return to the field? What if this business with Mila got him killed?

That was the one outcome Orlando dreaded over all others.

There was no question in her mind she would do everything she could to help Quinn, to give him what he needed, to hopefully keep him safe.

She had watched the video Peter had uploaded more times than she probably needed to. The raw, stark security footage was devoid of emotion, and, because of that, oddly riveting. Empty concrete one moment, distorted bag of guts and bones the next. Even seeing the man in the baseball hat check the body—knowing it was actually Mila—was fascinating.

The whole thing was a mix of the surreal and the hyper-real.

When she finally forced herself to quit watching, she turned her attention to identifying the dead man. The news reports were useless. In the initial articles she found, the police were quoted as saying the name of the victim was as yet unknown. Follow-up reports yielded the same. The only things the police would say were that the man was Caucasian, had no ID, and had jumped.

The first part, yes. The second, perhaps. The last, she didn't believe at all.

After three days, there were no additional reports. The world had moved on to other, more pressing news. A foreigner committing suicide off a new high-rise hotel might be bad for business, but it didn't hold the public's attention for long.

The killer would know his name, of course, but she was willing to bet that someone in official authority knew who he was, too.

To see if she was right, she hacked into the Dar es Salaam police network, and scrounged around for any information concerning the incident. The problem was, Swahili was not one of the languages she knew, so she had to rely on the date and the phrase "Majestic Hotel" to guide her.

Still, it didn't take long to uncover the report. Scanning through it, she looked for any names that she could use as touch points for further searches. None stood out. The only thing she could find were three references to another number that had a similar pattern to the incident's case number. Some other event that might be tied to this one?

She dug deeper into the system, looking for a case that matched this new number. At first, she came up with nothing. Not willing to give up so easily, she opened a program she'd written herself. She called it the burrower. It was a worm that could dig its way through an entire system, looking for whatever specific word or phrase or pattern she instructed. While it was fast, because of the size of the police network, it could take several minutes to complete its task.

Orlando input the number she'd found, started the program, then got up to refresh her cup of tea.

The water on the stove was still warm enough that she didn't need to heat it again. As she poured it into her cup, she wondered about the assignment to eliminate Mila. Had Quinn known she was the target? Why was she still alive? Surely the gunman hired for the job had been more than a match for an unsuspecting courier.

Unless she was more than a simple courier.

Orlando realized she didn't know much about Mila. She hadn't lied when she told Quinn she'd met her before, and she *had* liked her, but after that she had only heard the girl's name in passing and had never seen her again. As far as she could remember, Quinn had never once mentioned Mila Voss.

She was carrying her cup back to her computer when she suddenly stopped mid-stride. What if Quinn and Mila had been more than just coworkers? Mila had certainly been a beautiful woman, and probably could have attracted any man she wanted.

Orlando shook her head. *No, not possible. He would have said something.*

But, as she returned to her desk, she wondered if he really would have said anything. He *was* the master of walling things off, and any relationship with Mila would have occurred in those years Orlando and Quinn hadn't been talking to each other.

It certainly would explain why he might have covered up her death. Of course, that opened up a whole other mess of problems. What about the shooter? Wouldn't he have known that the woman he'd been sent to kill was still breathing? Was he in on it, too? And if Quinn were having a relationship with Mila, why would he have even been included on the job to take her out?

Orlando decided she needed to find out more about the events surrounding the not-so-well-executed death of Mila Voss.

She sat back down and checked the burrower. Not only was it done, it had found what she was hoping for. The number was indeed another case file. Its prefix, though, was apparently only used for a special set of cases that could be accessed solely by the very top level of the force's administration. The files for these cases were kept behind an additional password-protected firewall. The people who set up the system were good, just not as good as Orlando. Using another of her self-written programs, she was soon through the wall.

The file was interesting. The majority of it was written in Swahili, but there was a name listed that was most definitely not Tanzanian: Martin Langenberg. Was it the name of the dead man on the sidewalk? She looked for other information that might be useful, and turned up two additional names that sounded Tanzanian—perhaps witnesses or the officers who had worked the case—and one phone number in Dar es Salaam.

She checked the time. It was after midnight. Doing a quick calculation, she determined it would be late afternoon in Dar es Salaam. She picked up her phone and dialed the number.

The person who answered did not speak in Swahili, or even in English, but in Dutch. "Martin Langenberg's office. May I help you?"

While Dutch *was* one of the languages Orlando knew, speaking it was not one of her favorite things in the world. It was full of hard sounds that made her feel like she was doing permanent damage to her mouth and throat. Which was the main reason she couldn't speak it with a native flair like she could French or Vietnamese or Korean.

"May I speak to Mr. Langenberg, please?" she said.

"He is in a meeting. May I ask who's calling?"

"I'll just call back."

She hung up before the woman could say anything more.

THE DESTROYED

A Dutch-speaking office in Dar es Salaam. *Interesting.* The obvious guess was something oil-related.

She pulled up one of her favorite search engines and typed the phone number into it.

No listing.

There were a couple other legitimate places she could try, but she decided to go right to the source. She found a proven hack posted on one of the specialized message boards she belonged to, and used it to enter the Dar es Salaam phone company's database. The number was listed to a Karas Holdings.

That didn't tell her anything.

With an annoyed grunt, she dove in further.

An hour and a half later, she stood up and stretched. She'd found what she was looking for, only it was more than she expected, in a very troubling way.

Karas Holdings was a front for an organization known as REJ, who, in turn, worked almost exclusively for the CIA. She had dealt with REJ before—both she and Quinn had done jobs for them. Martin Langenberg, according to her sources, was the REJ agent overseeing operations in Africa.

Using this info, she did a surgical hack into the REJ server, looking only for anything dealing with the dead man in front of the Majestic Hotel.

She found a single document for the transfer of a body. According to the description, the body had fallen from a great height, and it was recommended that the casket remain closed.

There was a name, too.

Lawrence Rosen.

It didn't take much work after that to compile a partial bio for Rosen, more than enough to know there was absolutely no way he had jumped. Rosen was a security operative. Freelance now, though a few years earlier he'd been a civilian employee within military intelligence. He was a connected man living in Dubai who undoubtedly had many enemies.

In Orlando's line of work, believing in coincidences was a quick way to an early death. Rosen and Mila had both worked in the intelligence world. The fact that he died and she'd been the first to his side could not be put down to chance. There was a connection.

What, Orlando didn't know.

CHAPTER
TWELVE

BANGKOK, THAILAND

THAILAND WAS NOT where they needed to be. There was no question in Quinn's mind that by the end of the day they'd be on a plane heading out of the country. The only thing holding up their departure was that he had no idea where they should go. Hopefully, whatever Orlando found out would point the way. While they waited to hear back from her, there *was* something he needed to do, a thank you that was best delivered in person.

The first time he met with Christina had been in her large apartment in the center of the city. This time, though, Daeng took them via the SkyTrain to a restaurant just off of Sukhumvit.

Christina was sitting at a table in the far back corner of the patio. A tall, blonde, Caucasian woman, she had been in Bangkok since near the end of the Vietnam War. Why and how she had come to Thailand as a young adult, Quinn didn't know, and never asked. It wasn't his business. He was also unsure hold old she was now—late fifties, early sixties. Someone who didn't know anything about her background might guess her age to be anywhere between fifty and seventy.

Two Thai men were standing a few feet behind her on either side, while two others were stationed at a table a dozen feet in front of hers.

As Daeng, Quinn, and Nate walked toward her, Daeng said

something to the closest bodyguards. They both nodded a greeting and let the trio pass without incident.

"Mr. Quinn," Christina said, a subtle smile on her lips. She then looked at Nate. "And you must be Nate." She motioned at the empty chairs around her table. "Would you gentlemen like to have a seat?"

Quinn and Nate took the two chairs across from her, while Daeng selected the seat nearest her.

Christina touched Daeng's arm. No words passed her lips, but the look she gave him was like one a mother might give to her adult child. When she looked back at Quinn, she said, "Have you enjoyed the countryside?"

"I have."

"I'm glad to hear it. I can see it has already done much for you."

"It has."

"So, what brings you back to Bangkok?"

Quinn hesitated, then said, "I unexpectedly find myself with something I must do. Unfortunately, this means I have to leave. I plan on coming back, but I'm unsure how soon that will be. Not long, I hope." He paused. "The reason I wanted to see you today was to thank you. The temple was exactly what I needed. You couldn't have made a better choice."

"It was my pleasure. I'm glad it worked out."

"If you're ever in need of me for anything, call," he said.

Her smile grew as she reached over and took hold of his hands. "And I thank *you* for that." When she let go, she looked at him and Nate. "Something to drink? Or to eat? They make a wonderful curry here. One of my favorites in the city."

"Thank you, but no," Quinn said, standing. "Some other time."

"Of course."

He hesitated. "There is one thing."

"Yes?"

"I would appreciate it if someone could keep an eye on the temple renovations. I've made sure they have enough money to do what needs to be done, but I worry the work might slow in my absence. The monks are very forgiving, so might not always push when they need to."

"It won't be a problem. Daeng can keep an eye on things."

Quinn and Daeng exchanged a look, then Daeng said, "I'll be going with him."

"You will?"

"Yes."

Quinn knew that Daeng didn't work *for* Christina, just occasionally *with*, but from the beginning Quinn had sensed Christina's protectiveness of the former monk.

"I'll check on the temple myself, then," she said.

"You don't need to do that," Quinn told her. "One of your people could make the trip."

"It will be my pleasure."

AS THEY WALKED back to the SkyTrain station, Nate whispered to Quinn, "Are you sure it's a good idea to bring him with us?"

"We could use his help."

"Sure, but how well do you know him?"

"Well enough."

"That's not really an answer."

Quinn glanced at him. "Do you trust me?"

"Of course."

"Okay. I trust Daeng. So that means you can trust him, too."

Quinn made it clear that was the end of the conversation. It didn't help Nate, though. Daeng was still an enigma to him. There was the Daeng who fought with him at the temple, the Daeng who showed him Quinn working in the fields, the Daeng who owned a large home in the middle of Bangkok where he played host to Burmese refugees, and finally the Daeng who was obviously connected to the mysterious powerbroker Christina.

He couldn't make all the pieces fit. Not the best position to be in, he thought, especially if they found themselves in serious situations that required Nate to trust Daeng completely.

He also wasn't happy with the way Quinn had shut him down. It was almost as if he was an apprentice again, and he most certainly was *not* anymore.

For the last six months, he had been a full-fledged cleaner, running Quinn's business on his own. Well, with the occasional assist from Orlando, but the point was the same. He'd been operating successfully outside Quinn's authority for half a year. So just because Quinn was reverting to old habits didn't mean Nate had to.

He reached out and grabbed his mentor by the shoulder, turning him around. "I need more than just your word."

Anger flared in Quinn's eyes, but Nate didn't back down.

"You've been gone since last year," Nate said. "I've seen what you've been doing with your time, and that's all well and good, but I've been *working* since the moment you left. My instincts and skills are sharp. Can you say the same about yours?"

Quinn stared at him for a second, then said, "Don't ever touch me like that again."

"And don't treat me like a kid. I'm here. I *will* help you. But I'm not your damn lackey. You want me to treat you with respect? Then treat me with the same."

"You guys coming?" Daeng called out. He had stopped a couple dozen feet down the sidewalk.

Nate held up a hand, indicating for him to wait a moment.

"So?" he said to Quinn.

The fire in Quinn's eyes waned. He took a breath. "Daeng's a good man who has seen a lot of other good men die and decided he wasn't going to stand for it any longer. I've seen the things he's done, the help he's given his people—"

"Those Burmese kids? I thought he was Thai."

"His mother was Burmese, his father Thai. For a long time he's been involved behind the scenes in the struggle between the Burmese people and their government. You can trust him, Nate, and we could use his help. *I* could use his help." He paused. "Just like I could use yours."

Nate snorted softly and looked away for a moment. When he turned back, he said, "All right. And for the record, my help is never a question."

As they began walking again, Nate sensed that Quinn wanted to say something more. He looked over, but his mentor shifted his gaze away and remained silent.

THE CALL CAME only seconds after they'd hopped on the SkyTrain. Nate handed Quinn the phone. The display read:

ORLANDO.

"Hey," Quinn said.

"I have something for you. Well, more than one thing," she told him. Though he'd been hoping otherwise, the tone of her voice was basically the same as on their previous call.

"The dead man in Tanzania?"

"His name was Lawrence Rosen. Does that ring a bell?"

"Rosen? Yeah, I've worked with him before. Military intelligence guy, right?"

"Was. Went freelance a few years back," she said. "Is there any reason Mila would have something to do with his death?"

"None I can think of, but I guess it's possible." The scene in front of the Majestic Hotel flashed in his mind. "In the video. When she was looking at him, she seemed—"

"Surprised when she saw who it was?" Orlando said.

"Exactly."

"Have you ever heard of someone named John Evans?"

"Evans?" He ran the name through his mind. "There was someone involved in the Las Vegas job named Evans, if I remember correctly. Don't know his first name, but he was the one Mila picked up the package from before flying out, I believe. Why?"

"Twelve hours ago there was a report out of London about the murder of a man named Bernard Johnston. Mr. Johnston was the owner of Johnston's Rare Books Finding Service. He was also a retired American agent whose real name was John Evans. Witnesses say they saw a beautiful dark-haired woman go into his offices a few hours before his body was found."

"Any security footage of her?"

"Nothing that I've been able to uncover."

"You think it was her?"

"When I read the report, I wasn't sure, but I wasn't aware of the connection you just told me about. So there's a chance."

"Did anyone see her leaving the building?"

"No one," she said. "There's something more."

"What?"

"I can't give you an exact number, but just from an initial check, Evans and Rosen had worked together several times in the past."

Quinn fell silent. Though he didn't want to believe it, all his instincts were saying that the dark-haired woman was Mila. But why kill this Evans guy? That didn't sound like her, even if she was desperate.

"Where did this happen?"

"In his shop in a small town northeast of London. I assume you want to go there. If you want, I can arrange your flight."

A memory played through his mind.

"It's a lot to ask, I know," Julien had said four years earlier. *"But someday things may change, and I need to make sure it will still be there if they do."*

"No," Quinn told Orlando. "Rome."

"Any particular reason?"

"London will put us behind her."

"And Rome will put you in front?"

"That's what I'm hoping," he said.

"All right. Rome. How soon do you want to leave?"

"As soon as we can get out. We'll head to the airport now," he said, then added, "Three tickets."

"Three?"

Quinn got Daeng's pertinent information and gave it to Orlando. "Thank you," he told her after he finished, then, "I'm sorry."

"You said sorry already. What's this one for?"

"Falling off the face of the earth."

A quick, spontaneous laugh escaped her lips. Not derisive, just surprised. "You idiot. Don't you know if you did that, I'd be right behind you?"

It felt like the first time in forever he could breathe again. The weight of her perceived condemnation had been pressing down more heavily on him than he'd realized.

"I'll text you your flight info," she said, and hung up.

CHAPTER
THIRTEEN

WASHINGTON, DC

"YOU'RE SURE?" PETER asked.

"As sure as I can be," Lee told him. "The breach originated from Mats Hagen's townhouse in Stockholm."

"No chance it was just routed through there to throw us off and incriminate him?"

"If it was, I haven't been able to pick up any trace beyond there. If you ask me, that's where it started."

"Doesn't make a hell of a lot of sense," Peter said. "Check it again."

"I've already checked it three—"

"Check it again."

Peter walked out of the room that had been set up for Lee to use in the Georgetown apartment. Lee was the best computer expert available on short notice. Peter had hired the kid before, and knew Lee was more than competent. Still, the person he wished he had sitting in that room was Orlando. If *she* told him the breach had originated with Hagen, he would have believed it from the first. But she hadn't even answered his call.

That Hagen might have been the one who hacked into the highly secure military intelligence system wouldn't have been particularly earth-shattering news. There could have been a dozen or more explanations for it—all, no doubt, tied to a client's request. Leaving his digital fingerprint *was* surprising, though, and so was the file he'd looked into. Peter could think of only one person who would have any interest in them.

Mila Voss.

The Georgetown building the townhouse was located in was a throwback to an older time. While larger structures with fifty or more units had sprung up around it, it had survived with only eleven apartments, two on each floor. What the other residents didn't realize was that the two at the top had been joined together to form a single flat.

There was one highlight of the place that only Peter and Misty knew about. The two top-floor apartments had originally come with trap doors in the hallway ceilings that led up to storage areas. Peter had removed the trap doors, and converted the space into a two-room safe house, complete with an insulated floor to cut out any sound, and a secret entrance that even the best in the business would have a hard time finding. With enough supplies, someone could stay days or even weeks in the room without detection by anyone who might enter the main apartment.

The room had been used four times in the past, but it had been more than three years since its last long-term occupant. There were times when Peter would use it for a few hours to work in peace. It was a great place to think things through and work out strategies. Exactly the kind of place he could very much use at that moment. Unfortunately, that option was not currently open to him.

Right on schedule, Scott Olsen had shown up the evening after Peter's conversation with Mygatt and Green. Peter had welcomed the saccharine-smiling son of a bitch into the townhouse, and shown him to the office the two of them would be sharing. The safe rooms upstairs, he did not mention.

For two hours he'd had to endure the man's questions before Olsen left for the night. In the days that followed, there was no telling when Olsen would drop in or how long he might stay. Sometimes it was only an hour in the afternoon, other times it was all day.

When Peter arrived that morning, he'd been hoping that Olsen wouldn't show up until at least one p.m. That way, he could get a little time upstairs, and try to get a handle on what was quickly becoming a shitstorm. But when he walked in the front door, Misty, who was always the first one in, nodded toward the back and mouthed, "He's here."

Peter sat through another hour of questions and ideas. Finally, Olsen's cell phone rang, giving Peter the break he desperately needed. He got himself a cup of coffee, then checked in with Lee and found out the origin of the computer breach Green had discovered the day before. He then stopped by Misty's desk, briefed her on what Lee had said, and asked her to find out what was going on with the team that was being pulled together in Europe.

Unable to delay his return any longer, he steeled himself and headed back to the office.

Olsen was still on the phone. "No, no. Of course we wouldn't do that."

Peter sat down, and signed back on to his computer. Instantly, a message popped up from Misty.

> **Michaels says he's all set. He and his team are on standby in Brussels. Orders?**

At the other desk, Olsen said, "Listen, he's here now. Why don't I call you back in a bit?...Okay."

Peter began typing a response.

> **Tell them we're a go. Need to get to—**

Olsen hung up his phone and fixed his gaze on Peter. "Have you figured out where it came from yet?"

Peter continued typing.

> **Hagen's place immediately.**

"Well?" Olsen asked.

Peter hit SEND and looked up. "The breach appears to have originated in Stockholm."

Olsen frowned. "Stockholm's a big city. I assume you've narrowed it down a bit."

Patience, Peter told himself. "We believe a computer

belonging to a man named Mats Hagen was used."

"Who's he?"

"A freelance tech and hacker."

On Peter's computer, another message from Misty appeared.

Ok. Calling him now.

"You don't seem convinced," Olsen said.

"It strikes me as strange that someone with his skills would be sloppy enough to leave clues behind that allowed us to trace the intrusion back to him. I think the last thing we want to do is jump to conclusions."

"But you said that's where the breach came from. Did it or didn't it?"

Peter fought to keep a frown from his face. "I believe it did."

"Okay, then. I assume you have a plan."

"Of course," Peter said.

After the silence stretched out for several seconds, Olsen said, "The idea here is that you keep me in the loop. Remember?"

"I remember. I have a team on the way to Stockholm right now." A bit of a lie, but they'd be on the way soon enough.

"When will they get there?"

"We should know something in a few hours."

"You don't have anyone closer?"

Peter took a breath and stood up. Heat began to radiate from his bald scalp, and he knew from past experience that he was probably turning red. "I'm sure there are people closer we could hire, but I only work with those I know I can count on. It was *my* understanding from the senator that he expected this situation to be handled with extreme sensitivity. So being able to trust whoever we put in the field would seem to be an important thing, don't you think?"

Instead of waiting for an answer, he walked out of the room.

THE DESTROYED

MICHAELS AND HIS men took the first flight they could from Brussels to Stockholm, arriving just a little over an hour and a half after taking off. They picked up their rental car and headed straight for the Södermalm neighborhood where Mats Hagen lived.

Upon arrival, Michaels and his second-in-command, Alder, took a walk around the block, and used a portable heat-sensing device to determine if anyone was in the target apartment. It turned out there were two people present. Though the device couldn't determine identities, odds were one of those present would be the man they'd come to see.

Since it was still relatively early, Michaels placed Alder and the other two men on his team—Janick and Sterns—strategically along the street. He then climbed back into the rental to give Hagen and his neighbors time to settle in for the night.

Over the next two hours, the street went from mostly quiet to dead still.

Michaels touched the earpiece he was wearing, activating its microphone. "Janick, let's see what our friends are doing."

"Copy," Janick said.

Janick had been given possession of the heat sensor, and charged with the task of periodically checking Hagen's flat.

There was a delay of about twenty seconds before Janick said, "They're in bed."

Finally, Michaels thought. "Okay. Everyone hold tight. Won't be long now."

He turned off his mic and called Peter.

"They're finally asleep," he reported. "We're going to wait forty-five minutes, then go in."

"Excellent," Peter said. "Let me know—" A voice in the background cut him off. "Hold on."

It sounded like Peter put his hand over the phone. Michaels could hear voices but nothing distinctive.

When Peter came back on, he didn't sound pleased. "Can you go in sooner?"

Michaels was surprised by the question. "Only if we don't care if they're in a deep sleep or not."

Another muffled conversation, then, "Do you feel that's

important?"

"Peter, what's going on?"

"Just answer the question, please."

"All right. Yes, it's important. You want the guy alive. There's a lot better chance of that happening if he's struggling to wake up, as opposed to jumping right out of bed because he hasn't fallen asleep yet. There, does that work for you?"

"Just a second."

A third conversation ensued. It quickly became clear to Michaels that someone else was trying to call the shots.

"Okay, proceed with your plan," Peter finally said. "Report in as soon as you have him."

"Should we be worried about this job?"

Peter paused. "*You* shouldn't be."

The line went dead.

MATS HAGEN FELT the bed move. Probably Eva getting some water. A herd of horses was quieter sometimes. He turned on his side and tried to recapture the dream he'd been having.

It was about the girl who worked at the coffee shop around the corner. In his dream, he'd found himself alone in the kitchen with her as she started to take off her clothes. It was a poor substitute for real sex, but Eva had made it clear he wasn't getting any tonight.

"My stomach still bothers me," she'd said. "I just want to sleep."

He told her that was fine, mostly because he'd had a vision of being puked on mid-thrust. That was enough to turn anyone off.

A groan, soft and distant but urgent. Part of his dream? *Coffee girl calling me back.* At least she wasn't going to say no. *Baby, here I come. You're going to love—*

"Get up."

The voice was most definitely *not* part of his dream. It wasn't Eva's, either. Hagen's eyes failed to open the first time, but on the second try, they did.

A man stood near the bed, silhouetted by the light filtering in through the window.

A man?

THE DESTROYED

Hagen sat up with a jolt, his hand automatically moving toward the hidden compartment in his headboard where he kept an unregistered Beretta pistol.

"I wouldn't move another inch," the silhouette said.

How in God's name had they gotten in without him knowing? His alarm should have gone off. He should have had plenty of warning.

"So you are Mats Hagen." A statement, not a question. The man grabbed Hagen's arm and yanked him to his feet. "Come on."

As Hagen stumbled around the end of the bed, he saw Eva near the wall. Another man was holding her from behind, one of his gloved hands over her mouth. Her terror-filled eyes implored her boyfriend to do something.

But what could he possibly do? These guys were bigger than he was, and obviously armed. *His* gun was still sitting in his hidey-hole. Which, on further consideration, was probably not a bad place for it to be. If he'd pulled it out, he probably would have been dead by now.

The man pushed him all the way into the living room, where two more men were waiting.

This was seriously not good. They were obviously pros, which meant there was a very good chance they were sent by someone he'd worked with before. He tried to think of anyone who might have been dissatisfied with his work. There were a couple minor things, but nothing worthy of this kind of reaction.

Or maybe it wasn't a client, but someone affected by the work he'd done for someone else.

"Look, I don't know who you are or why you're here, but whatever the reason, I'm sure we can work it out. Maybe there's someone I can talk to?"

"I'm glad to hear you say that."

The man shoved him in the back again. Hagen's initial thought was that they were heading for the front door. Perhaps they'd take him down to a waiting car, and then who knew where after that. But instead of the door, the man reoriented him toward the stairs that led up to his office.

A) He should have expected that, and B) *oh, shit*.

He had far too much sensitive information up there. His only chance at keeping them from finding anything damaging would be if he could reach his kill switch. It would trigger the automatic corruption of all his drives, rendering each completely unrecoverable. It would be a huge blow to his business, but it would be worse if the info got out.

When they reached the bottom of the stairs, he said, "What exactly are you looking for? If you tell me, I can—"

"Up," the man ordered.

"All I'm saying is, if you give me a little hint, I can help."

The man yelled toward the hallway. "Number Three."

"Yes?" one of the men answered.

"A warning."

A warning? Hagen glanced around. The only man not in the stairway with them was the man holding— "Wait," he said. "Wait, wait!"

Eva screamed in pain.

"Stop it!" Hagen yelled. "Stop!"

"Up," the man behind him said.

This time Hagen did as he was told. When he reached the top, he didn't wait to be ordered to open the door. He turned the knob and rushed in. The kill switch was only a few feet inside, disguised as part of a poster frame hanging on the wall. His hope was to get there and push it without the man realizing what he was doing, but he'd barely crossed the threshold when he saw that no matter how fast he might have moved, it wouldn't have mattered.

The poster was no longer on the wall. In fact, none of his artwork was. Each had been pulled down and thoroughly inspected. The kill switch was lying on the floor, its wiring pulled out and its case smashed. It was clear the men had gone through all his computers, too.

A chair from his main desk was sitting in the middle of the room with nothing else around it, like an electric chair waiting for its next client.

As if to reinforce this image, the man shoved Hagen toward it. "Sit."

After he sat, he asked, "Okay, now what?"

Saying nothing, the man walked over to the computer

station nearest Hagen. He turned the monitor so it could be seen from the chair. "You said you wanted to talk to someone."

He hit the trackpad, bringing the screen to life. On it was a head-and-shoulders image of a stern-looking bald man. At first, Hagen wasn't sure if it was a still or video, but then the man spoke.

"I have a question for you, Mr. Hagen."

"Who are you?"

"You can call me Peter."

The name in conjunction with the voice clicked something in Hagen's mind. "You're…you're in charge of…the Office. That's right, isn't it? Or, I guess, *were* in charge."

"Yes."

Hagen felt a surge of hope. This was a misunderstanding. Had to be. "We've worked together before. You know me. I was under the impression you were happy with my performance."

"This has nothing to do with any interactions you and I may have had in the past."

More confused than ever, Hagen asked, "Then what?"

"Your intrusion two days ago."

"My what?"

"We want to know who hired you."

"Who hired me for what? I don't know what the hell you're talking about!"

Peter stared at him, his lips sealed.

"Hired me for *what?*"

The punch in the gut caught Hagen completely off guard. The man who'd brought him up had moved over to the side opposite the computer, so Hagen's focus was in the other direction when the blow landed.

He doubled over, groaning, his hands gripping his stomach.

Computers were always something that came easy to him. It was why he'd fallen into that profession. One of the other things he liked about his line of work was being exposed to the intrigue while experiencing none of the danger.

Apparently, he'd been misleading himself.

Once he caught his breath, he pressed his forearms against

his thighs and tried to straighten up. Pain radiated out from his stomach, almost causing him to collapse again, but he gritted his teeth and held on. He said between stinging throbs, "I don't know...what...you're talking...about. What...is it you...think...I've done?...Just tell me. Maybe...I can...figure out what...happened."

The way Peter looked at him made Hagen think he was about to be hit again, but then the former head of the Office said, "One twenty-three p.m. local time, you hacked into a secure US governmental system and accessed files you should've left alone."

"One twenty-three? Not possible. I go out to lunch every day until at least two." He paused, thinking. *Two days ago.* He didn't go out that long then. He had an urgent project he was working on, so had only been away long enough to pick up his lunch and bring it back. When had he returned? "Wait. Two days ago I *did* come back early, but I'm sure it was later than 1:23." He thought some more, then said, "I have a receipt from my lunch. And you can check the T-Bana computer system to see when my monthly pass was used. I'm sure there's no way I could have been here at 1:23!"

"If not you, then who? Someone used your system."

"Impossible. My alarm would have gone off."

"It didn't go off tonight, did it?"

"No," Hagen admitted. "Okay, so I guess someone might have been able to bypass it, but there's something we can check."

"I'm not interested in stall tactics, Mr. Hagen."

"I'm not stalling." Hagen glanced at the man in the room with him. "I put a security camera outside that covers the entrance. You can access it through that computer over there. The footage gets stored on a dedicated drive and stays there until I run out of room. That usually takes about six months."

The man looked at the computer screen. "What would you like me to do?"

"Check it," Peter said.

Following Hagen's instructions, the man located a listing of the footage, then turned the screen so it could be seen by both Hagen and, via the other computer's camera, Peter.

"Looks like the camera was activated seven times between noon and two," the man said.

"Play them," Peter ordered.

The first two events were people leaving through the front door. The third was of a man walking up and knocking. When no one answered, he left. The fourth was Hagen leaving the building. This came at five minutes to one.

"See," Hagen said. "I told you I wasn't here."

"Keep playing them," Peter said.

The fifth showed a woman wearing a wide-brimmed hat entering. She kept her head down so it was impossible to see her features. This occurred at 1:10.

"I don't know her," Hagen blurted out.

The next image came up—Hagen again, returning.

"What's the time?" Peter asked.

The man studied the image, then said, "One twenty-seven."

"See? I was right!" Hagen said.

"The camera's clock could be off," Peter suggested.

"No way. It's synced with my computers, which are synced with the network. That time's actual."

"There's still two more," the man reminded them.

Peter nodded. "Let's see them."

The next was of one of the two people who'd left earlier coming back. The final was the wide-hat woman again, her face never once turning toward the lens.

"Oh, my God," Hagen said. "She must have still been here when I came back." He looked at Peter. "But…but you do see. It wasn't me."

Peter remained silent.

Hagen grew nervous again. "That wasn't me! I wasn't here!"

"No," Peter said. "You're right. It wasn't you."

Hagen's shoulders sagged as he let out a relieved breath.

"But there is still the fact that whoever that woman is, she was able to get into your apartment and use your equipment as if she had a key to the place."

"What? No. I don't know who that was! I don't! I swear I don't!"

PETER WAS TIRED of hearing Hagen's whines. He knew very well that the Swede had no idea who the person was, but his machines *had* been used, and that was a problem.

"There is very little room in our world for mistakes," Peter said. "And no room for someone who doesn't learn from them. I believe a lesson is in order."

"No! No! That's not nec—"

Peter cut the connection. Michaels would know what to do. If Hagen decided to stay in the business, he would undoubtedly be working from a fortress in the future.

"So?" Olsen asked. He was sitting off to the side so that the camera wouldn't pick him up, but at an angle that allowed him to watch what was going on.

"It was her," Peter said.

"Are you sure?"

"Do I have proof, you mean? No. But it was her. The size is right, and she's the only one who would want to get into that file."

Mila Voss, again.

Something ticked at the back of his mind. He brought up the file on her removal operation—still labeled COMPLETED—and searched the background information until he reached the part he was looking for. Just as he remembered. But was it worth checking out? With no other leads, what choice did he have?

He made a mental note of the particulars, then exited the file and stood up.

"I'm going out for a smoke," he told Olsen. "That is, if you don't mind."

"I wasn't aware that you smoked."

Peter pulled the half-used pack of cigarettes out of his pocket, and jostled one out. "Not as much as I used to, but sometimes...well..."

"Fine, but don't be long. I want you here when I call the senator with an update."

Peter left the room without another word.

"I'll be right back," he said to Misty. He then silently communicated to her that she was to contact him if Olsen followed him out.

Before he even reached the sidewalk the cigarettes were back in his pocket. It had been over ten years since he'd actually lit one, but he'd purchased the pack that morning, knowing it would provide the opportunity for a little alone time if needed.

Once outside, he went left to the end of the block and ducked into a bar around the corner. There were only a few customers in the place, none of whom even glanced in his direction. When the bartender saw him, he merely gave Peter a nod of recognition then went about his business.

Peter walked clear through to the back, and entered the bathroom. It was a single-occupant setup, so he locked the door, pulled out his phone, and called Michaels.

"Are you still with Hagen?" he asked.

"We're just emphasizing a few points," Michaels replied. "Should be done soon."

"Wrap it up. There's somewhere else you need to be," Peter said, then gave Michaels his new instructions.

CHAPTER
FOURTEEN

ROME, ITALY

THE FLIGHT FROM Bangkok took about eleven hours, touching down at Fiumicino Airport outside Rome just before ten p.m. local time.

A cab took them to a hotel Quinn knew about, not far from the reason they had come to the city. So far, neither Daeng nor Nate had asked him, why Rome? Daeng because that just seemed to be the way he was, and Nate because he had worked with Quinn long enough to know when to ask questions and when not to. That was why Quinn's earlier confrontation with his former apprentice had been so surprising. Sure, Nate had stood up to him once or twice in the past, but Quinn had always won. Nate was obviously not content to let that happen anymore.

Though it hadn't been part of Quinn's plan—what little plan he'd had when he'd gone into his self-imposed exile—his absence had apparently provided the final push Nate needed to move beyond his training phase. Quinn had called him an equal before, but their relationship had still been largely defined by their teacher-student past.

Clearly that was over.

The St. Apollina Hotel was in a quiet part of the city filled with old apartment buildings and shops that closed early every evening. The hotel was a small, family-run business with a dozen or so rooms. A call before leaving the airport guaranteed that a room with two beds and a couch would be held for them.

"Don't get comfortable," Quinn said once they were in the room. "There's a place near here we need to check. Wash up, do whatever you need." He glanced at his watch. "Let's say ten minutes, okay?"

It only took six before they were heading out again.

They walked up the hill for several minutes, over three streets, then up again for another two and a half blocks.

"There," Quinn whispered, nodding at a building just down the street and on the other side.

It was a four-story stone building that looked to be at least a hundred years old. While obviously maintained, it looked tired, like it just wanted to take a nap. There was a central, unlit entrance at street level, and six windows each on the floors above it. Light shone from a window on the third floor, but the others were all dark, their occupants either asleep or not home.

"The apartment we're interested in is on the second floor in the back," Quinn told them.

"Anyone inside we need to worry about?" Nate asked.

Quinn shook his head.

"What's the play?"

Quinn looked up and down the street. It was quiet, no one else out. "Daeng, find someplace to hide where you can keep an eye on things. If anyone is even just walking by, let us know."

"Got it," Daeng said.

Quinn looked at Nate. "You and I are going to take a look around."

NATE FOLLOWED QUINN across the street to the old wooden door that served as the building's entrance. Instead of a keyhole they could pick, there was a numbered security pad for residents to punch in a code. It seemed out of character for the building, but not for the times.

With the right equipment, they could bypass the pad and release the lock, but equipment was something they were currently lacking. Nate was about to suggest they look for an alternate way in when Quinn simply punched in five numbers on the pad.

As the door lock released, Quinn said, "You going to open

it?"

Shaking off his surprise, Nate grabbed the handle and pulled it open. "You want to tell me how you knew that?"

Quinn's only response was to squeeze by Nate into the building.

They found themselves in a rectangular-shaped central lobby that seemed to go all the way to the rear of the building. Nate counted four doors, two on either side. Beside each was a doorbell button and a small nameplate. In the center of the room was a staircase that rose to the next floor. As far as he could tell, there was no elevator.

Quinn had said the apartment was on the second floor, so Nate headed for the stairs. But Quinn walked past them toward the back. Feeling like he was becoming a semipermanent resident in the world of confusion, Nate adjusted his path and followed.

At the rear, a doorless entryway led to a smaller room with a closed metal door mounted in the outside wall. As Quinn pulled it open, warm night air rushed in.

"Don't let it shut or we're locked out," Quinn said.

As soon as Nate had control of the door, Quinn headed out into a small exterior space that was surrounded on the other three sides by the neighboring buildings. Walking slowly, he gazed at the stone-covered ground. There seemed to be no apparent pattern to his wanderings, but then he suddenly stopped and crouched down. Gently, he touched one of the stones, then looked at the wall of the closest building. Rising, he walked over to it, tapped a couple of the bricks, and pulled one out.

It was too dark for Nate to see what his mentor was doing with the brick, but within seconds it was back in place, and Quinn was heading toward him.

"What was that all about?" Nate asked.

"Come on," Quinn said as he moved past him into the building.

Quietly, they made their way up to the apartment on the second floor. Nate glanced at the nameplate. It was blank.

"My lock picks are still in L.A.," he said.

"Don't need them." Quinn opened his palm and showed

Nate three keys.

So that's what had been hidden in the brick, Nate realized.

Quinn used them to unlock the two deadbolts and the handle lock on the door, then pushed it open. Once it was wide enough, he whispered, "Don't touch anything. We're just making sure no one's been here already."

"You mean Mila?"

"Yeah."

Nate nodded, and they stepped inside.

As he started to move further into the room, Quinn held out a hand, stopping him. There was an alarm panel on the wall near the door. On it, a dull white light glowed bright then dim, bright then dim. Quinn opened a panel, and again punched in a number without any hesitation. The light faded off.

He took a moment to scan the room. "Okay. This way."

Being at the back of the building meant little light filtered into the apartment from outside, making it hard for Nate to get a sense of the place. He could see the shadows of chairs and tables, and could even make out a bookcase running along one of the walls, but the details were lost in the darkness.

Quinn led him through the main living area, a dining room, and past a large kitchen. When they reached the back hallway, he stopped. With no windows, it was even darker than the rest of the place.

He signaled for Nate to stay there, then headed toward the rear of the apartment alone. Though Nate wasn't particularly fond of being left behind, it was sound strategy. If someone was in the back, Nate would be the safety valve in case Quinn couldn't deal with him.

A little over a minute passed before Quinn called out, "We're clear."

When his mentor rejoined him, Nate said, "Whose place is this?"

Quinn looked like he didn't want to answer for a moment, but then he said, "Julien's," and started walking toward the front door.

The name caught Nate off guard. He stood there for a second, then hurried to catch up. "*French* Julien?"

"Do you know any others?"

"No. But…my God, this place has been empty since…"

"Yeah, it has."

In Paris the previous fall, Julien had been helping Nate get Quinn's sister Liz to someplace safe, and had ended up dead for his efforts. Nate had been the one to find his body. Which meant it was unlikely anyone had set foot in the apartment since before then.

As Quinn crossed the room, Nate said, "Wait. What does Julien have to do with finding Mila?"

"Maybe nothing."

"Quinn, stop."

Nate's mentor hesitated and turned back around.

"I appreciate that this isn't easy for you," Nate said. "But you're hurting my ability to help if you don't tell me what's going on."

He could see Quinn struggling with how to answer. Finally, his mentor said, "Mila and Julien were friends."

"*Good* friends?" Nate asked.

"At one time. But they were always close." Again, he paused. "Julien would have done anything for her."

So that's why Quinn needed to help Mila. He owed Julien a debt he could never repay. Nate owed him, too, for that matter. Helping Mila had to be an attempt to help offset some of the imbalance.

"Is there a reason she would come here?"

"Perhaps."

"But why?"

"Because he left it to her."

"He left his apartment to a dead woman? Can you even do that?"

Quinn sighed and closed his eyes for a second. When he opened them, he said, "He left it to me, all right? But *for* her."

"Oh," Nate said. "But it's still a long shot that she'd come here, don't you think?"

"There's something of hers here, something Julien was holding for her."

"What?"

"I don't know. I just know she hasn't been here yet. I left a tell on the brick with the key."

"You think whatever he was keeping for her has something to do with why she came out of hiding?"

"I have a feeling it does."

"But you don't know what it is," Nate said.

"It's not my business."

Nate ran everything through his mind, then said, "Okay, so we should probably set up a watch," Nate said. "The three of us can rotate."

"Yes," Quinn looked relieved. "Definitely."

"In the apartment or not?"

"I don't want to scare her off."

"All right, so not. What's our time window?"

"If she doesn't show up in the next forty-eight hours, she's not coming."

"I'll take the first shift," Nate said. "You can go back to the room with Daeng and fill him in."

Quinn started to protest, but then caught himself and nodded. "I need to put the keys back first. If she comes and finds them gone, she'll take off before we can get to her."

Four minutes later, Nate stood alone in the darkened entrance of a building across the street, images of Julien replaying in his mind. If the Frenchman would have helped this Mila Voss woman, then that was all Nate needed to know.

He was all in.

CHAPTER
FIFTEEN

THE FLIGHT FROM Los Angeles to Las Vegas took less than an hour, the flight attendants barely having time to serve drinks and collect the trash before strapping back in for landing. Quinn had been through McCarren Airport many times, so he was able to quickly navigate through the terminal and to the parking structure where he found the promised car exactly where he'd been told it would be.

The drive to the Planet Hollywood Hotel on the Strip was quick, and soon he was heading up to the room number he'd been given. When he reached it, he knocked on the door, and took a step back. As soon as he heard someone approaching on the other side, he looked up at the tiny camera temporarily mounted high above the door, and waved.

Pointing out to those inside the hotel room that he knew the camera was there was probably unnecessary, but he couldn't help it. He saw every detail, and since he'd never worked with these people before, it was a good way to let them know that right up front.

The door opened and a small guy in a light gray suit peeked out. "Can I help you?"

"I'm expected," Quinn said.

The man made a show of scrutinizing Quinn's face, then opened the door all the way. "Come on in."

THE DESTROYED

The room was a suite with a sitting area straight in from the door, a bar off to the right, and a dining area to the left. Beside the guy in the gray suit, there were four other men present. Two were also wearing suits, though in black, while the remaining two were dressed in buttoned shirts and slacks. They were all seated around the dining table, with several pieces of paper scattered in front of them.

One of the suitless guys stood up as Quinn came in. "You must be our cleaner."

"I am."

The guy held out his hand as Quinn neared. "Perry Jergins. I'm team leader."

"Jonathan Quinn."

They shook.

"It's a pleasure to meet you, Jonathan."

"You can call me Quinn."

"All right, then. Let me introduce you around." He turned back toward the others. "Okay, we got Whit Kaufman, Leo Kovacs, Maurice Danner," Jergins said, pointing individually to the men sitting around the table. "And Cary Hills is the one who opened the door for you. This here's Quinn, our cleaner."

Quinn exchanged nods and hellos with the other men.

Jergins waved at the chairs. "Have a seat. We were just going over the details. I'll bring you up to speed, and you can let me know if you need anything specific. We'll have you out of here in no time."

"Sounds good."

The plan was pretty straightforward, which pleased Quinn. All too often, planners tried to get fancy when there was no reason for it. Quinn believed those people were attempting to live up to the James Bond vision of their world. Bond was enjoyable enough on screen, but if any of that happened in real life, those involved would find themselves not only out of work but rotting away in a prison somewhere. Or dead.

The operation's target would apparently be tricked into coming to a room in the hotel. When the target arrived, the assassin, Leo Kovacs, would already be inside, waiting. Since this wasn't an operation in which the subject needed to be interrogated first, Kovacs would eliminate the person immediately. Once this was done, he would text Quinn, who would then move in and get rid of the body.

"It's a no-brainer," Jergins said. "The target has no idea, so there'll be no problems getting her into the room."

Her, Quinn noted, not that it made a difference. It was just that the majority of bodies he dealt with were male.

"The other guys are here just to get things set up. By op time, all three will be well out of town. Since mission specs call for this to be *very* low profile, I'll be running backup myself. Given the circumstances, I should be more than enough."

Kovacs picked up one of the papers and laid it in front of Quinn. "This is a layout of the room," he said. He pointed at a spot next to the bed, around the corner from the door. "I'll be here so I won't be seen when she comes in."

"What are you planning to use?" Quinn asked, hoping like hell he wasn't going to say gun or knife. If so, Quinn would lobby hard to cover the termination room with plastic sheeting ahead of time. Otherwise, a mess like that would be a huge pain in the ass.

"Poison from a needle on the back of a ring. All I have to do is grab her and stick her anywhere. Paralysis is almost instantaneous. Death comes a few seconds later."

"Do you expect her to fight back?" Again, Quinn was concerned about a mess, though straightening out a room or dealing with anything that might get broken was a lot easier than getting blood out of the carpet.

"A little," Kovacs said. "She has some training."

"A pro?"

Jergins grabbed a small stack of stapled papers and tossed it to Quinn. "Here's her info if you want to take a look."

Quinn reached down to pick up the report, planning on tossing it back and saying that wasn't necessary, when the picture on the top page caught his attention.

Eastern European-looking face. Shoulder-length brown hair. Slight frame.

Mila Voss.

He acted like he was reading the paper, but in reality he was fighting to keep any emotion from showing on his face. Once he felt he had control, he flipped through the other pages, looking for any information that might tell him why she'd been targeted for death. But, not unusually, no cause was mentioned.

As if disinterested, he set the papers back down and turned to Kovacs. "You're right. A little trouble maybe, but not much. I'll make sure I have access to spare fixtures or anything else that might need to be replaced. But if you can avoid any breakage, I'd appreciate it."

"Don't worry. I won't let it get that far."

Jergins took over and talked about the basic setup. Quinn listened and nodded in all the right places, but barely heard any of it.

"For you," Jergins said, slipping two hotel key cards across the table.

Quinn pushed thoughts of Mila to the side as he picked up the keys and tried to focus. One had a slight notch along one edge as if someone had banged it against the corner of a table. Otherwise, the two keys were identical. He knew one would be to the room Mila was to be killed in, and one would be to the room where he would be expected to wait until he was needed, but which was which and what were the room numbers? Had Jergins already told him and he hadn't heard?

He held up the one with the notch. "And this one is to…?"

"The job site on the seventh floor."

Quinn nodded, and glanced down at the table. "Do you have a floor map? I'd like to see exactly where it is in conjunction with exits and other rooms."

"Yeah," Jergins said. "There's one here somewhere." He started looking through everything. "Whit, down by you."

Kaufman picked up a piece of paper and handed it to Quinn. Kovacs leaned over so he could see it, too.

"There," the assassin said. He pointed at the room marked 739. Then he touched 753, a little farther down the hall. "And that's your room. But one floor up, of course."

"Sure. Thanks." Rooms 739 and 853. He burned the numbers into his memory.

Jergins wanted to go through the plan one more time. Quinn said that was a great idea, and once again listened without hearing, all the while wanting to rush out of the room.

When they were finally done, he said his goodbyes, then

forced himself to walk leisurely through the suite and into the hotel corridor. During the full ten minutes it took him to reach the street, he refrained from doing anything that would seem out of character. There was just no way to know if someone might be watching him, someone who may have realized he actually had a connection to the target.

One thing was for certain—the Office had no idea Quinn even knew Mila. Peter would have never given Quinn the assignment.

Mila, what the hell did you do?

As he moved south down the Strip, he worked through all of his options. Being the professional he was and with his outstanding reputation, he knew he should ignore the fact that he'd learned the target's name and just do the job he was hired to do. He wasn't the guy pulling the trigger, after all. In his capacity, he could at least see to it that her remains were treated with respect.

But as noble as that might be, it rang hollow when considering he was in position to stop it from happening at all. Doing so, though, could mean putting his own life in danger, not to mention jeopardizing his career. If he did intervene, he would have to be exceedingly careful.

Are you really considering this? You'll have to pull it off without screwing up everything else. Is that even possible?

Though he currently had no answers to those questions, he realized there was one thing he could do. Granted, if he did nothing else, it would be a passive-aggressive approach to solving the problem. But it was a start, and hopefully he would come up with a more definitive plan prior to Mila's arrival at Planet Hollywood.

He ducked into a casino and found as quiet a spot as possible near some unused slot machines at the back. Even though it was after midnight in Europe, he made the call anyway.

"*Oui*," a deep baritone voice said.

"Julien, it's Quinn."

"Quinn, my friend. *Comment ça va?*"

"I'm fine. Thanks. Are you free right now?"

"You have a job for me?"

"I do."

"I have something I'm supposed to do that starts on Sunday."

"Can you get out of it?"

Julien was quiet for a moment. "I suppose. Is this a good job?"

"I'm sure you won't want to miss it."

"Where?"

"Las Vegas."

"Vegas? I have not been there in many years. I like this idea. When do you need me?"

"Tomorrow, as early as possible."

"Tomorrow for me? Or tomorrow for you? It's already Saturday here."

"Tomorrow for me. Today for you."

"I don't know if I—"

"Find a way, Julien," Quinn said, his tone dead serious. "I *need* you here."

The humor that normally ran through Julien's voice vanished. "Let me see what I can do."

"Thank you."

Quinn hung up and made a second call. "Jergins? This is Quinn."

"What's up?" the team leader asked.

"I've been giving it some thought, and I think I'm going to bring in a man to help out. It'll just keep things smoother."

"Sure. Do you have a name?"

"Not yet. I'll make some calls."

"All right. As soon as you know who it is, let me know. Peter wants a listing of all those involved."

Having zero intention of actually doing that, Quinn said, "No problem."

CHAPTER
SIXTEEN

ROME, ITALY

IT HAD BEEN a quiet night outside Julien's apartment building. Quinn had taken the second shift, the hardest because it split sleep time in half, or it would have if he had actually fallen back to sleep when he returned to the room. Eventually, he gave up trying and went out for a long walk around the city.

When he returned, Nate was dressed and about to head down for the breakfast that came with the room.

"You going to go relieve Daeng after you eat?" Quinn asked.

Nate gave a hesitant nod, and said, "I have someone I need to meet first."

"Oh? Who?"

"If you haven't noticed, we're a little equipment shy. I thought it'd be good to gear up a bit."

Of course, Quinn thought. "Bianchi?"

"No. He's out of the business."

"What?"

"Heart attack."

"Dead?"

Nate shook his head. "Just scared the hell out of him apparently. He left the city and moved in with a daughter somewhere in the south."

In the past, Quinn would have been up on news like this, but during his exile, the world had moved on. "Who took his place?"

"Several players have stepped up, but none to Bianchi's level. The guy I'm seeing is named Nicholas Giacona. I used him once before. Seems okay."

I used him once before? Quinn was surprised. Nate had apparently been busy while he was gone. "You want me to come along?"

"Sure. You can help carry the bags."

THE TAXI DROPPED them off two blocks from their destination. The area was crowded with cafés and shops and other businesses, but at this early hour, it was only the cafés serving breakfast that were open.

"It's up this way," Nate said.

Though he'd been to Giacona's place only the one time, he remembered the route well. He led Quinn to the end of the block, through a narrow alley, then half a block down the next street before stopping in front of an unmarked door next to a butcher shop. On the wall near the jamb was an intercom. Nate pushed the button.

"*Sì?*" a male voice said through the box.

"*Buon giorno,*" Nate said. "I have an appointment."

"*Signor* Quinn?"

"*Sì,*" Nate said quickly, fighting the urge to look at his mentor.

The door buzzed and he pulled it open. On the other side was a scuffed-up hallway that ran the length of the building. There were several doors along it, all closed.

As they neared the back, Quinn said, "Are you going to explain that, or—"

The door at the very end opened, and a fiftysomething Italian guy with a goatee and salt-and-pepper hair looked out. "Quinn. Good to see you again."

Nate picked up his pace, and extended his hand. "I appreciate you getting up so early, Nicholas."

As they started to shake, Giacona noticed Quinn for the first time. "Your friend, who is he?"

"This is Jonathan. We're working together."

Giacona eyed Quinn for a moment. "If you say he's okay,

fine."

"He's okay," Nate said.

The arms dealer nodded. "Then come in, come in." He waved for them to follow him and disappeared inside.

Before they could step through the doorway, Quinn grabbed Nate's arm and pulled him back a few feet. "Why's he calling you Quinn?"

"Later," Nate said.

"Does he think you're me?"

"I said later." Nate had known this was something that would eventually come up, but he couldn't worry about it. He'd done what he had to do.

They passed through the doorway into a workshop that took up half the space of the ground floor. There were lathes and drill presses and hydraulic metal cutters and several other machines Nate didn't even try to figure out. To most of the world, Giacona ran a small but efficient machine shop that specialized in repairs and customized metal work. To those in Nate's and Quinn's world, he was a local supplier who was building a reputation as an expert in all things hard to get.

"Your call surprised me," Giacona said. "I didn't realize you were in town."

"A last-minute thing," Nate told him.

"Something I should know about?"

"Is it ever?"

That elicited a laugh from the Italian. "I always like to ask. So, what is it you need today?"

Fifteen minutes later, they left with three SIG Sauer P226 pistols—Quinn's weapon of choice and one Nate was growing fonder of—extra clips and ammunition, a couple miniature remote video cameras with built-in wireless connectivity, a compact set of short-range bugs and tracking devices, six sets of communication gear, and, as a last-second request from Nate, a set of lock picks. Everything fit nicely into a single, medium-sized duffel bag.

"Okay, it's later," Quinn said once they were on the street.

Nate looked around to make sure no one was nearby, then focused on his old boss. "He called me Quinn because I *am* Quinn to him, and to several others, too."

"Others? What are you talking about?"

"After you left, we still had calls coming in, jobs that wanted only Quinn."

Quinn's eyes widened. "You...pretended to be me?"

"I had to keep things going. I didn't know if you were coming back or not, but if you were, I thought it would be better if your reputation didn't tank completely while you were gone. So, yeah, I told people I was Quinn, not Jonathan Quinn, just Quinn. And you know what? I took jobs, did them, and never once had a complaint or problem."

"What if I don't return? You'll just go on being Quinn?"

"I haven't thought that far ahead. I've been doing this *for* you. Holding things together for *you*. If you can't see that, it's not my problem."

Nate started walking again. He didn't want to talk about this anymore. His anger was unfair, he knew, but he couldn't rid himself of it. No matter how much he knew that Quinn's disappearance had been necessary, he was having a hard time forgiving his mentor for basically abandoning him.

A few seconds later, he heard steps behind him, but didn't turn to look. Then Quinn drew abreast of him, and they walked in silence to the end of the block where several taxis were parked.

"Nate," Quinn said before they climbed into one of the cabs.

Nate turned.

"I..." Quinn paused, his head twisting to the side as if frustrated. Finally he looked back. "I'm not sure what to say. It seems every time I...I open my mouth, I..." He stopped again. "I wanted to forget about the world, isolate myself and clear my head. The thing is, I didn't think about the world continuing on without me."

"Yeah, well, that's what happens."

"I have no right to be angry about any of it, but that doesn't mean I won't react without thinking again."

"So are you apologizing for now or the future?"

"Both, I guess."

"I'm not going to let you off that easy," Nate said as he opened the cab's door. "We'll take it on a case-by-case basis."

"Sure. I can live with that...Quinn."

Nate rolled his eyes. "Oh, is that an attempt at humor? You know what? Maybe you *should* call me Quinn from now on."

"Don't press your luck," Quinn said as he climbed into the car.

USING PAPERS THAT identified her as a German elementary school teacher, Mila crossed the English Channel on a ferry, then took a train from Belgium across France and finally to Milan, Italy. For a brief time, she considered taking the train all the way to Rome, but when she read in the *International Herald* that a Mr. Johnston, a book dealer outside London, had been discovered murdered in his office, she decided that a less public entrance to the Italian capital would be prudent.

She knew the police would not be after her. There was no way they would ever figure out that the former spy's death had come at her hands, but those she was actually tracking down might be able to figure it out. Best to do everything she could to avoid detection. So she appropriated a car and drove south to the Italian capital.

Of course, going to Rome was in itself a risk, but not going had never been a choice.

She knew Julien was dead. The fact that he'd stopped checking in with her every few weeks had been the first indication something was wrong. Even in the assumed life she had been living in Canada, she had secure ways of checking in on her old world. That's how she learned that he'd been murdered on the streets of Paris. It had almost been enough to push her out of exile and go in pursuit of his killers, but the more she looked into things, the more she'd realized that there was a very good chance his killers had already been dealt with. That was enough for her to crawl back into her hole and pretend to be someone she'd never wanted to be.

It was a story in a magazine that made her realize her time in exile was at an end. She knew if the Lion was indeed behind the incidents in 2006—something now confirmed by the late John Evans—she had to do something.

Once Evans had given her the answer she'd been looking

for, she knew it was time to go to Rome and retrieve what was waiting for her in Julien's apartment. Another part of her also saw the Rome trip as a too-long delayed pilgrimage, a chance for her own private memorial service for the man who had loved her unconditionally, despite the fact that as a couple they could never make it work.

Thinking about him again—his big meaty hands, his always-smiling face, and that mane of hair she kept trying to get him to cut—made her catch her breath, and see the road through tear-filtered eyes.

Damn you. Damn you for dying, she thought.

She reached Rome midmorning, and fought traffic across town to the neighborhood where Julien had lived. As much as she wanted to drive down his street, she resisted. Best if she came at it quietly and on foot, so she could observe things before getting too close.

She parked the car seven blocks from the apartment, within sight of a Metro station. If the wrong people found the vehicle and knew she'd been in it—something she was sure was next to impossible—they would hopefully assume she'd jumped on the subway.

From the bag that held her few remaining possessions, she pulled out a scarf and sunglasses and donned them as she headed in the opposite direction of the station.

"YOU SEE THAT guy?" Daeng asked over the radio.

"Which one?" Quinn said.

He and Nate were hiding in the maintenance room in the basement below Julien's apartment, watching a video feed from one of Giacona's cameras that Nate had set up to monitor the street. Daeng was positioned on the roof of the building across from Julien's, so he didn't need the camera.

"The one who just walked by your friend's place," Daeng said.

"I see him."

"That's his third pass since seven a.m."

Quinn watched the man disappear from frame. "Probably just lives in the neighborhood."

"Perhaps. But he was wearing a suit earlier. Now he looks

like a tourist. Is it possible this woman is working with someone?"

"Anything's possible," Quinn said.

"We don't both need to wait here," Nate suggested. "I could follow him."

"If he comes by again, maybe."

Over the next several minutes, only a handful of people walked by, then Daeng said, "New contact."

Quinn studied the screen, but saw no one. "Where?"

"Coming from the north on foot. A woman. She's wearing a scarf, so I can't see her hair. Also wearing big sunglasses."

"How tall?"

"One hundred and sixty centimeters."

Around five foot three, Quinn thought. The right height.

"You should be able to see her in just a second," Daeng said.

True to his prediction, the woman soon appeared on screen. She was wearing pants and a loose-fitting shirt that made it difficult to judge her shape. She also had a small canvas backpack slung over her shoulder.

As she neared Julien's building, her head swiveled slightly side to side, and her pace slowed. Then, with a surprising suddenness, she cut to her left, moving quickly to the door. There was no hesitation as she punched a code into the security pad.

"It's her, isn't it?" Nate asked as they watched her enter the building.

"It's got to be," Quinn said. "Daeng, stay where you are in case we're wrong."

"Got it," Daeng said.

They headed out, Nate carrying the bag they'd received at Giacona's. Inside were a few of the items they thought they might need. At the top of the basement stairs was a door. Quinn and Nate moved up to it, but didn't open it. On the other side was the back room with the door that led out to the rear patio where Julien's keys were hidden. If the woman *was* Mila, that would be her first stop.

Quinn turned his head and listened, but could only hear the distant whine of a motor scooter on the street out front.

Ten seconds passed, twenty, then thirty. He was starting to think that maybe they'd been wrong, when all of a sudden there was the sound of someone in the hall beyond the door. Only the person wasn't exiting the building into the courtyard, but coming back in from it. Quinn realized she must have made her way through the lobby and gone outside before they'd even reached the top of the stairs.

Beyond the door, the steps receded toward the front of the building, then faded away.

"Anyone just leave the building?" he asked Daeng.

"No one."

The person had gone upstairs.

Quinn waited an additional fifteen seconds, then eased the door open. Silently, he and Nate moved down the hall to the stairs. Pausing at the bottom, he listened again, but could hear nothing from above. He did a quick time estimate in his head. If it was Mila, she would have gone one floor up, down the hall to Julien's door, listened for anyone inside, then used the keys to enter. He guessed it would have taken her forty-five seconds at most.

He counted off a full minute in his head, then nodded at Nate.

Into his mic, he whispered, "We're going up."

"Copy," Daeng replied.

They stayed at the edge of the stairs to keep any noise to a minimum, and made their way to the top. The common hallway on Julien's floor was empty. Staying in the lead, Quinn approached Julien's door.

From somewhere deep inside the apartment, a floorboard creaked.

Quinn glanced at Nate and pointed at the door, indicating she was there.

He put his hand on the knob and tested it. Locked, but only the handle. She hadn't engaged the deadbolts, probably because she didn't want them to trip her up if she had to get out of the flat in a hurry.

He moved out of the way and let Nate set to work on the lock with the new set of picks. Twenty seconds later, Nate opened the door, peeked inside, and nodded. Silently, they both entered the apartment.

Quinn glanced at the alarm panel, noted it had been disarmed, then scanned the room. The living and dining areas were both empty, as was the kitchen. He walked slowly toward the hallway with Nate following a few steps behind.

"Our walking friend is back," Daeng said just as they reached the kitchen. "He's not alone, either."

Quinn paused.

"Three men. They're walking fast, coming from the north." There were a few seconds of dead air before Daeng added, "They're heading into the building. No question."

Stealth was no longer an issue.

Quinn looked at Nate. "Door." He ran toward the hallway and called out, "Mila!"

Behind him, he could hear Nate engage the deadbolts and start to pull something across the floor toward the door.

"Mila, it's Quinn. We've got to get out of here!"

He stepped into the hallway.

"Stop right there. I'm armed."

It was Mila, all right. Though he hadn't heard her voice since that night in Las Vegas, it was the same.

"There's a team headed into the building right now, and I'm guessing they're here to get you."

"How do I know that's not why *you're* here?"

"It's me! Quinn! I'm here because I want to help."

He took another step forward.

"Stop!" she yelled. "Maybe you're Quinn. Maybe you're not."

"Just let me turn on the light, okay? So you can see it's me."

"Don't! Even if you are, I don't know whose side you're on now."

From behind Quinn, Nate whispered urgently, "I hear them in the corridor."

"Who's that?" Mila asked.

"He's with me. My partner. I came here to warn you that people know you're alive and are looking for you. But it sounds like they just found you."

"I don't need your help."

He could hear her move again, but couldn't see her. He took another step deeper into the hallway. "Mila? Please."

Nate rushed up to him. "They're trying the door. They'll be inside in seconds."

"Mila?"

Nothing.

"Mila?"

The only answer he received was the sound of the front door shattering.

CHAPTER
SEVENTEEN

"I DON'T NEED your help!" Mila yelled at the guy claiming to be Quinn. She shut the bedroom door and shoved a chair under the handle.

There were two windows in the room. One was narrow and too small for even her to fit through. The other was Julien's emergency escape exit. Anyone else who looked at it would see a window in a frame that had been painted over so much it wouldn't open. But a switch would release the frame and allow the whole thing to be shoved out or pulled in. The problem was, Julien had only shown her the switch once, and she couldn't remember where it was.

The man called out her name again. She ignored him and searched along the wall for something that would trigger her memory.

A sudden, muffled crash caused her to whip around. It could have only been someone breaking through the *front* door. Maybe he'd been telling her the truth. Maybe there *were* others.

It didn't matter. Others or not, she had to get out of there now.

Where the hell is that damn switch?

As she desperately tried to find the window release, she heard the spit of a sound-suppressed gun, followed quickly by several more shots.

Where are you? Where are you? Where—
Hold on. What was that?

She moved her gaze back a few feet. She'd been looking at a bookcase, then the top of the dresser. There'd been something, something that had seemed familiar.

There!

She rushed over to the dresser. On the wall just above it were several framed photographs. They were all shots Julien had taken around Rome. It was a specific one that had drawn her attention—an image of a fountain in a small plaza where two kids were jumping in the water.

"See," Julien had said. "To play like this is an escape to a different world. Simple, huh?"

She lifted the picture off its hook. Behind it, recessed into the wall, was a plastic switch that looked like it might turn on a light.

As she started to reach for it, there was a second crash. Not the front door this time.

The door to her room.

QUINN TWISTED AROUND in time to see the front door fly inward on its hinges.

Both he and Nate pulled out their guns at the same time, and aimed them toward the still-unoccupied opening. Quinn didn't like this one bit. Based on the conversation he'd had with Peter, it was clear the former head of the Office had been charged with finding Mila, so it didn't take a genius to figure out that whoever had just busted down the door was probably working for him. Mila was a loose end on a termination Peter had ultimately been responsible for. That meant it was a mess he'd want to clean up before anyone else found out.

"We can't let them see us," Quinn whispered. "I don't want anyone knowing we're here."

"Do we take them out?"

"Not if we can help it." That would cause even more problems.

"I'm heading your way," Daeng said over the comm.

"No," Quinn said. "We don't know where they all are, so someone might be watching the entrance. You're no use to us dead."

"Neither are you."

Someone moved a few inches into the doorway and tried to look in. Quinn let off a warning shot, hoping that would delay them long enough so that he could figure something out. Instead, it elicited a round of blind fire into the room.

Not wanting the strike team to just rush in, Quinn and Nate shot back.

"We need to get in the bedroom," Quinn whispered.

"You hold them. I'll get us in."

As Nate ran back to the closed bedroom door, Quinn let off a couple more shots. How much longer they could keep the others out of the apartment, he didn't know, nor did he have any idea what he'd do if they came in.

Behind him, there was a loud crash, followed quickly by a second one.

"Come on," Nate whispered.

Quinn sent three more rounds through the apartment then sprinted to the back end of the hall.

The door to the bedroom had been cracked nearly in half. Nate pushed it and the chair that had been jammed under the knob out of the way.

"Stop," Mila said as Quinn and Nate rushed in.

She was by the dresser, holding a pistol. Both men halted a few feet inside the room.

"It *is* you," she said.

"Of course, it's me," Quinn replied. "But we can say hi later. Right now, we've got to get out of here." In the apartment, more bullets smacked into the walls. Soon the others would realize the return fire had stopped and they'd rush in. "If we can get to the kitchen, we can get out the window and drop down to the courtyard."

She seemed to be contemplating something, then said, "You'd better not be lying to me."

"Lying?" Nate said, annoyed. "Those aren't rubber bullets they've been shooting at us."

Mila lowered her gun. "We don't need the kitchen."

She reached over and flipped a light switch that had been oddly installed inside a wall divot above the dresser. From the left came the faint sound of metal moving against metal.

"You want out, follow me," she said.

She hurried over to the larger of the room's two windows and pushed on it. It moved several inches. She pushed again, and this time it popped out of the opening, and fell out of sight. A few seconds later, there was the crash of glass as it hit the ground. Mila was already climbing through the opening.

Daeng's voice suddenly cut over the comm. "I'm on the street. Do I come in or not?"

"Clear out the hotel," Quinn said quickly. "We'll meet you at the emergency rendezvous point."

"Are you sure?" Daeng asked.

"Yes."

Daeng hesitated. "All right. You *will* make it, right?"

"That's the plan."

Nate nodded toward the window. "Go with her. I'll buy us a little time."

Quinn went after Mila and stuck his head out the window. The space outside was a narrow gap, not much more than six feet wide between adjoining buildings. On the ground below was the shattered window. Unfortunately, there were no exits at either end, just walls that would trap them there. Behind him, he could hear Nate shoot off a couple of rounds.

"This way!" Mila called out.

Quinn looked up. She was a floor above him. Her feet were on Julien's building while her hands were pressed against the one on the other side of the gap. She was working her way toward the roof two more floors above. It wasn't exactly the best escape route ever, but better than any of their other choices.

Quinn moved out and joined her. He'd made it about half a floor before Nate exited the apartment and started climbing behind him.

There was no question they were in a race against time. If the others stuck their heads out the window before the three of them reached the top, it was all over.

Hand, foot, hand, foot, up, up, up.

Quinn kept glancing down at the opening into Julien's apartment.

Any second now.

He was so focused on watching for the danger below that he wasn't paying attention to his own position. As he reached up, he found nothing for his hand to grab on to.

The top! Dammit!

He tried to snag the edge, but his balance was off and he started to swing to the side. Suddenly, a hand thrust out and grabbed his wrist, steadying him.

"I got you," Mila said.

He clamped on to the lip of the building and let his feet drop against the wall so that he was dangling high above the ground. Pushing up with his arms, he swung his legs over the edge, and rolled onto the safety of the roof.

"Thanks," he said to Mila.

She grunted in response as she moved a few feet away, her gaze suspicious.

Quinn glanced back into the gap just in time to see Nate grab for the top. He guided Nate's hand up, then hooked him beneath the arms and pulled. As he did, a head appeared out of Julien's window. The man looked down first, then twisted around and looked toward the sky.

"Hang on," Quinn said, yanking as hard as he could.

Just as Nate cleared the edge, two bullets slammed into the wall inches from where he'd been.

"Had to leave the bag," Nate said.

"Don't worry about it."

Nate glanced around. "Where's the girl?"

"What?" Quinn twisted around, his head jerking side to side.

Mila was gone.

Near the middle of the roof was a small structure that undoubtedly served as roof access for a set of stairs. But using them would be suicide. They were on the building *right next to* Julien's. Trying to leave from it would be a foot race they'd lose for sure. He couldn't imagine that Mila hadn't realized that, too.

He stood up and quickly scanned the surrounding roofs. "There," he said with relief.

She was one building away and preparing to hop across to the roof of another.

He sprinted after her, with Nate only a step behind him. They jumped to the next building without breaking stride.

"Wait!" Quinn yelled.

Mila didn't even look back.

The next gap was wider. They had to stop, back up a bit, then make a run at it and jump. By then, Mila was already on the adjacent roof, but instead of continuing on, she headed for the building's stairwell door.

"Mila, no!"

Again, she acted as if she hadn't heard him.

"I got her," Nate said.

In a burst of speed, he raced past Quinn, jumped the next gap, and made a beeline for the access door Mila had just gone through. As Quinn ran after him, he could hear sirens heading in their direction. Someone had called the cops. Normally, that would have been a problem, but in this case, unless the ones shooting at them were complete idiots, they would be forced to make themselves scarce. Anything that accomplished that would be a good thing.

He rushed through the door and onto a small landing, quickly grabbing the handrail to keep from losing control. He'd expected to hear the steps of the other two pounding down the stairs somewhere below him, but what he heard instead were the unmistakable sounds of a struggle.

He found them lying on the third-floor landing. Nate was behind Mila, his arms wrapped tightly around her, and his legs entwined in hers so she couldn't kick out. That wasn't stopping her from trying, though, or from attempting to head-butt him in the chin.

"I could use a little help," Nate grunted as Mila jammed her head back again.

"You can let her go," Quinn said.

"Are you sure?"

"She's not going anywhere." To make certain of that, he blocked the flight of stairs leading down.

Mila went on struggling as if she hadn't heard Quinn.

"Relax," Nate told her.

As he let go, he scooted away to avoid being hit. She rolled onto her hands and knees, and jumped to her feet.

"Get out of my way!" she yelled at Quinn.

He held his ground. "We're not going to hurt you."

"Then why did your partner tackle me?"

"Wasn't exactly something I wanted to do," Nate said,

standing.

Quinn could see several red marks on Nate's neck and face, and what looked like teeth marks on his hand. He focused on Mila.

"What the hell were you thinking showing up again? You're going to get yourself killed for sure this time."

Her jaw clenched, she said, "I don't care. I don't have a choice."

"What are you talking about? Mila, do you want to really get killed this time?"

She stepped toward him and tried to push him to the side, but he wouldn't move. "Please. Get out of my way."

"I can't."

"Move!"

"I can't."

"Why the hell not?"

"Because Julien's not alive to save you from yourself. It's my job now."

WHEN THE CALL came in, both Peter and Olsen were in their shared office.

Peter checked the ID.

"Is it them?" Olsen asked.

Peter nodded, then picked up the call. "Report."

"The team we'd designated Group C turned out to be a direct hit," Michaels said.

"Is that so?"

"They led us to an apartment, and a little while later, the woman arrived."

Peter knew Julien and Mila had been close, and that Julien had lived in Rome up until his death. Where, exactly, Peter hadn't been able to find out. It had been a risk to send the team there, but it'd been the only lead Peter had. After that it had been up to Michaels to find out who else might be working in the city, and perhaps helping the woman. Peter was happy it had paid off.

"Did you get her?"

Michaels hesitated. "No."

Peter forced himself not to look at Olsen. "Go on."

"We gave her some lead time, then followed. When we broke down the door, we ended up exchanging fire with the two men we've apparently been tracking. Unfortunately, they made their escape through a back window. And…"

When his team leader didn't go on, Peter said, "Michaels?"

Though he could hear the other man breathing, Michaels still said nothing. That's when Peter realized the man must have information he wanted to give Peter, but wasn't sure he should be relaying it over this call. Peter said, "It's clear—to me, anyway—that they've been working together."

It wasn't quite standard code, but Michaels got the message. "I'm only talking to you?"

"Right," Peter said.

"Okay. I got a glimpse of the guys with her. They were a couple dozen feet above me, and backlit by the sky, so not easy to get a good read on them, but…"

"Yes?"

"I can't be sure, but one of them stuck his head over the edge of the roof, and, well, I think it might have been…Quinn."

Quinn? What would Quinn be doing in Rome with a woman he was supposed to have disposed of years ago? "Is that a positive?"

He could hear Michaels take a breath. "Sixty percent, maybe. I wouldn't put it much more than that."

Low, but still more than Peter liked.

"I can tell you one thing," Michaels said. "The apartment belonged to the Frenchman. There were pictures inside of him, some with the woman, some without."

"Where do you think…she is now?" He almost said "they," but caught himself at the last second. For the time being, it was better if Olsen was unaware of Quinn's involvement, at least until Peter knew more.

"I'm sorry. I don't know. The police showed up so we had to pull out before we could locate her again."

"How long ago was this?"

"Just a few minutes."

"She can't be far, then. You need to find her."

"Understood," Michaels said.

As soon as Peter hung up, Olsen asked, "They missed her?

How?"

In the time it took Peter to pick up his empty coffee cup and stand up, he considered his options and came up with a course of action. "Apparently she wasn't alone. She and her companions were able to get away."

"Who was with her?"

Peter shook his head. "The team wasn't able to get a visual on them. No way to know."

"So they've lost her?"

"For the moment." Peter headed for the door.

"You're awfully calm about this," Olsen said.

Peter paused. "It's only a matter of time before we find her again."

"That'd better be true. Otherwise this will all fall on you."

CHAPTER
EIGHTEEN

WHEN QUINN SAW Julien exit the terminal at McCarren Airport, he hit SEND on his phone, shooting off the text he'd written ahead of time.

The Frenchman stopped and pulled out his own cell. After reading the message he'd just received, he casually turned away from the line of taxis, walked over to the crosswalk, waited until traffic had stopped, and made his way onto the bridge that led to the parking structure.

Quinn lowered his binoculars and started the car. He arrived at the exit to the stairwell just as Julien came up the final step. The Frenchman threw his bag into the trunk, climbed into the front passenger seat, and they took off.

"I did not know I was so important," Julien said, then let out a low, full laugh. "A personal pickup?"

"I had a little time."

"*Merci beaucoup.*"

Quinn nodded, but said nothing else as they exited the parking garage.

"I'd forgotten how brown it is here," Julien said as they drove toward the Strip.

"It *is* the desert."

"Sure, but you don't think about that when you think about Vegas."

"Maybe *you* don't think about that. I do, every time. Looks better at night, I guess."

"The neon," Julien said, excitement in his voice. "Yes. I remember." He paused. "So, do you think there will be any time to do a little gambling?"

"Probably not."

Though Quinn had told himself when he asked Julien to fly out that he was still unsure what he was going to do about Mila, the truth was, the moment Julien became involved, the future was set. Quinn could no longer pretend there were any other options. There was only one road they could go down now.

He pulled into a gas station near the Strip, and parked off to the side. For a few seconds he stared out the window, then he turned to Julien.

"What is it, my friend?" the Frenchman asked.

"I had an ulterior motive for having you come out here."

Julien nodded. "I thought there might be something. The notice was very short, and..." He shrugged. "I'm sure you could have found someone closer who could do whatever you needed done. So, is there a job, or is this something else?"

"There is a job *and* it's something else."

"Two things?"

"One thing that's both."

One of Julien's eyebrows shot toward his hairline. "Now you have my interest."

"You're going to wish that wasn't the case."

QUINN LAID IT all out for him, going step by step through Jergins's plan, and ending it by telling Julien who the intended target was.

The Frenchman became uncharacteristically quiet. He stared out the front window, but Quinn was sure he wasn't seeing the backs of the casinos a few blocks away.

Finally, Julien said, "Mila?"

"Yes."

A slow turn back to Quinn. "This isn't a mistake? Maybe someone who looks like her?"

Quinn didn't answer. In their business, mistakes

concerning other operatives were exceedingly rare.

"I…I can't believe it." The words were a whisper.

"What I don't know, and couldn't risk asking anyone, was why?" Quinn said. "Do *you* have any idea why someone would want to terminate her?"

Fifteen seconds passed, then half a minute, Quinn's friend once more lost in his thoughts.

"Julien?"

Julien looked at him with a start. "I'm sorry. What?"

"Why would someone want to kill her?"

His friend seemed to consider the question. "I don't know."

But Quinn could see Julien *did* know, or at least it looked like he did.

"Is this why you wanted me here?" Julien asked, a barely noticeable shake in his voice. "To be the one who buries her?"

"Don't be an ass, Julien. Of course that's not why."

"Then what?"

"What do you think? I'm giving you the chance to save her."

"How are we going to do that? If I warn her not to come, that will only delay her death for a day or maybe a week. Even if she goes underground and stays there, they won't give up until they know she's dead. That's how this works."

"That's true, but there might be another way."

Julien stared at Quinn. "What way?"

The plan had come to Quinn the night before as he'd tried to sleep. Since then, he'd been punching as many holes in it as he could, then patching them with solutions. The plan still wasn't perfect, but it was a hell of a lot better than burying Mila later that night.

"First off," Quinn began, "she still needs to come to Vegas."

CHAPTER
NINETEEN

ROME, ITALY

THE FIRE THAT had been in Mila's eyes suddenly cooled, but the anger was still there, even stronger than before. "Don't you dare bring up Julien," she said. "He would have never gotten in my way!"

Quinn held his ground. "He would if he thought you were about to do something stupid."

"You have no idea what I'm doing."

"Big picture? You're right. I don't. But in the here and now?" He gestured at the stairs behind him. "You go down these, and walk out of this building, you don't think there's a good chance the others will see you? And when they do, do you really think you'll be able to get away again?"

In her glare, he could see she knew he was right, but she kept her lips pressed tightly together.

"You want out of here alive," he said, "you'll follow my lead."

She looked away, thinking for a second, then turned back and said, "Fine. You're the pro. Get me out of here."

Quinn shot Nate a quick glance. "Check the street."

Nate nodded, and headed up the stairs.

"Stay right with me," Quinn told Mila.

He led her back to the roof, and over to the rear of the building, where he quickly took in their options. In the direction they'd been headed, they could only go for another four buildings before reaching a street corner and running out of roof. Each of those buildings presented the same problem as the one they were currently on—the only exit would be to the same street Julien's building let out on.

What he really wanted to do was get to one of the buildings behind them that would provide access to the next street over. There would be far less commotion there, and a trio of strangers in a city always full of visitors would go unnoticed. The problem was that the space between the two rows of buildings was, for the most part, too great to jump. There *was* one gap between a pair of back-to-back buildings that they might be able to cross. Unfortunately, it was two buildings on the other side of Julien's, and would force them to retrace their steps.

"The cops aren't here yet," Nate said, jogging up to them. "But they're getting close. A minute or two at best."

Quinn nodded. "All right. This way."

He started back the way they'd come.

"Wait," Mila said. "Why are you going that way?"

"It's our best chance."

"Julien's place?"

"No. Beyond it."

She looked dubious.

"We're at a dead end here," Nate said, obviously coming to the same solution Quinn had. He pointed toward Julien's building. "If we want to get away unseen, then that's the only choice we have."

She looked behind them, then back in the direction Quinn wanted to go. "Dammit," she said, still looking less than convinced. "If we're going to go, let's go."

They started running—Quinn in the lead, Mila in the middle, and Nate bringing up the rear. As they reached Julien's roof, sirens echoed up the buildings as what sounded like a dozen police cars turned onto Julien's street. Within seconds the cops would be making their way into the building.

Two roofs past Julien's, Quinn stopped.

"What now?" Mila asked.

He pointed at the apartment building behind them. "We jump."

Mila looked at the space between the roofs. "Isn't that a bit wide?"

"Ten feet, maybe eleven. Take a decent run at it, you'll make it with a couple feet to spare."

"If I don't trip and fall first."

Quinn looked at her, incredulous. "You came out of hiding, made yourself a target, something you *knew* would happen, and you're worried about a ten foot jump?"

"If I'm going to get shot, fine, but I'd rather not kill myself if I can help it."

But before Quinn could say anything more, she repositioned herself and ran hard toward the gap. At the edge was a six-inch brick retaining wall. She timed her stride so that her final step hit the top of that wall, and pushed outward, flying over the gap and landing, as Quinn had predicted, several feet beyond the edge of the other roof. But instead of stopping when she landed, she kept running and headed for the roof-access door.

"Mila!" Quinn yelled as he moved back to give himself enough running room.

Nate was already heading toward the edge. He leaped to the other side and took off after her.

Without hesitation, Quinn made his run, hitting the retaining wall at almost exactly the same spot Mila had. When he reached the other roof, though, his foot slipped and he began to fall. Curling into a tuck, he forced a roll, then popped to his feet. The other two had already entered the stairwell, leaving him the only one outside.

He raced over to the small hut-like structure and pulled the door open.

Behind him he heard someone shout in Italian. He glanced over his shoulder as he passed inside, and saw two cops on Julien's roof, looking in his direction. As the door closed, he could see the cops heading in their direction.

Great.

Running down the stairs, he could hear Nate and Mila farther below.

He activated his comm. "Nate, we've been seen. Cops on the roof heading this way."

There was a moment's delay, then Nate's voice came huffing back. "Got it."

CHASING A WOMAN down a staircase was not Nate's idea of fun. Doing it twice in the span of five minutes—even less awesome.

The first time, when he caught her in the other building, she'd put up a good fight, getting in a few punches and eventually biting him in the hand before he was able to subdue her. This time, her head start had been longer, and while he had cut the distance between them, she was still a whole flight ahead. If she was able to make it outside before he reached her, his chances of catching up to her would plummet.

He could see her turn down the final flight below. Knowing he had little choice, he jumped forward, sailing above the stairs, and barely missing the final riser as he hit the landing. She glanced back, surprised. He was less than half a flight away from her now.

Taking the remaining steps three at a time, he raced after her. When she reached the bottom, she jerked open the door, but before she could run through, he grabbed her arm.

She tried to pull from his grasp. "Let me go!"

"*Che succede?*" The male voice had come from the entranceway to the building.

"Let me go!" Mila yelled again.

Suddenly a man of about fifty appeared just on the other side of her. He looked surprised, then determined. "Stop!" he said to Nate, his accent heavy.

He reached over and tried to pry Nate's hands loose. As he did, Mila twisted, and the light windbreaker she was wearing fluttered open. Nate spotted the end of an envelope sticking out of an inside pocket, and made a quick decision. At the same moment he let go of her, he grabbed the envelope and stepped back into the stairwell.

When she realized what he'd done, she said, "Give that back."

"Stop fighting with us. We're only trying to help."

The middle-aged man pointed at the envelope. "Not you. Her."

148

"*Non sono affari tuoi,*" Nate said to the man, telling him it wasn't his business.

"*Perchè la stavi afferrando?*" the man asked, wanting more explanation.

Mila looked at Nate for a second, then at the man. "*Lo e il mio amico stiamo solo discutendo. Non c'e' bisogno che lei si metta in mezzo,*" she said. It was just an argument, and his help wasn't needed.

"*Sicura?*" he asked.

"*Si. Scusi il disturbo e grazie per aver cercato d'essere d'aiuto.*"

Looking confused, the man shook his head and walked off.

Once he was gone, Mila said, "Give me back the envelope."

"No," Nate replied. "Not until Quinn says it's okay."

She looked over Nate's shoulder. "Tell him to give me back my envelope."

Nate could hear Quinn descending the final steps behind him. "We can figure that out later." He pointed up toward the roof. "You hear that?"

Faintly from the top of the stairwell came the sound of someone heading down.

"It's the police," Quinn said. "We need to keep moving."

Mila kept her hand held out to Nate. "It's mine. Give it back."

Nate folded the envelope and stuffed it in his pocket. "As Quinn said, we can figure that out later."

Anger clouded her face.

Quinn grabbed her arm and pushed her into the entrance hall. "We don't have time for this right now."

The room was wider than the one in Julien's building but basically the same design. Quinn kept a tight hold of her arm as they walked to the front door.

The man who'd tried to stop Nate was standing off to the side, a phone held to his ear. By the way he kept giving them sideways glances, Nate knew he was talking to the cops. Then the man did a stupid thing. He moved his phone away from his ear, and held it so its camera was pointing at the three of them. Now Nate had no other choice.

While Quinn and Mila continued toward the door, Nate

veered over to the man and yanked the phone out of his hand.

"Sorry. You won't be needing this anymore," he said. He thought about saying it again in Italian, but it was clear from the look on the guy's face that the message had been received.

As Nate turned for the door, he looked down at the phone. Just like he'd thought, on the screen was a picture of himself, Quinn, and Mila. The man had been in the process of texting it to someone. Nate deleted the text and pulled out the phone's battery. He stuffed the phone in one pocket and the battery in another, then opened the door and headed outside.

Quinn and Mila were walking down the sidewalk, already a building and a half away.

Nate was only two steps past the door when—

Thup.

The sound of a bullet through a suppressor.

Instinctively, he dropped to the ground and pulled out his gun.

Behind him the door to the building opened. Before he could look back and shout a warning, there were two more *thups*, then the crumpled *oomphs* of bodies falling on concrete.

Somewhere ahead there was a scream.

Then a car door slammed, and an engine roared to life.

That was the point when he raised himself to his knees. The two injured men behind him wore police uniforms. One was unconscious but the other was rolling back and forth, groaning.

Nate shifted his gaze to where he'd last seen Quinn and Mila. Where the two had been standing, one lay sprawled on the ground.

Quinn.

On the street a sedan was speeding away. Nate got a quick glimpse of its license plate, automatically memorizing its number, but knowing it wouldn't matter. The car, undoubtedly with Mila inside, was surely stolen.

He jumped to his feet and ran over to his mentor. There was blood on the sidewalk and all over the upper part of Quinn's shirt. The bullet had hit near the base of his neck just above his clavicle, both entry and exit wounds no more than an inch from each other. As ugly as it was, it could have been a lot worse if it had been just a bit to the right, where it would have pierced his windpipe and shattered his spine.

People were starting to come out of their homes to see what had happened.

Nate knew he had to get Quinn out of there *now*. He looked down the street. Two cars were heading in their direction. The first was a taxi with a passenger, the second a sedan with a couple of kids in back.

Nate lifted Quinn to his feet, and dragged him into the street just in time to get in front of the taxi. The driver had no choice but to stop. He gestured angrily and honked, but only once. The gun in Nate's hand convinced him another blast of the horn was unnecessary.

Nate locked eyes with the passenger in back and motioned with his pistol for him to get out. The guy seemed glad to do so, and within seconds was running in the other direction. The driver seemed slightly more hesitant to leave.

Nate took a step closer to the car and motioned again. The cabbie apparently felt his loyalty to his taxi had been fulfilled. He scrambled out the door and followed after his passenger.

Nate quickly maneuvered Quinn into the backseat, did what he could to tie off the wound using Quinn's shirt, then climbed behind the wheel and pressed the gas pedal to the floor.

CHAPTER
TWENTY

A CLEANER WHO knows what he's doing always has a variety of contacts in the places he has worked: suppliers of weapons, local talent, information sources, and—though hopefully seldom needed—someone who could provide discreet medical services. On his previous job in Rome, Nate had been given the number of a Dr. Pelligrini, but had never had the need to call it.

That fact had just changed.

The phone rang four times before a man sounding hurried answered. "*Sì?*"

"I'm in need of a second opinion on a hairline fracture," Nate said in English, reading the phrase from the notes on his phone.

The doctor paused, then gave him an address with instructions on where to park behind the building, and what to do when Nate got to the door. The man hung up.

As much as he didn't want to waste the time, Nate knew they had to switch vehicles before they arrived at the doctor's place. By now police all over town would have been notified to look for the cab. The last thing he needed was for it to be found parked at the medical facility where Quinn was being treated.

He called Daeng, brought him up to speed, and agreed on a quiet place to meet not far from their hotel.

Nate reached the rendezvous point three minutes later, but Daeng wasn't there yet.

"Come on, come on, come on."

He looked back at Quinn. His mentor was still unconscious, the makeshift bandage soaked with blood. Nate reached back and grabbed Quinn's wrist, checking the pulse. Weak, but steady.

Just then a Volkswagen Golf hatchback with Daeng behind the wheel screeched to a stop next to the taxi.

Working quickly, the two men transferred Quinn to the VW's backseat.

"You want me to drive?" Daeng asked.

"I'll drive," Nate said.

Daeng got into the front passenger seat and twisted around so he could keep an eye on Quinn.

Nate took the quickest route to Dr. Pelligrini's office. The narrow alley that ran behind it was easy enough to find, though the white door the doctor had mentioned was more a faded yellow.

Nate jumped out, knocked three times on the door as he'd been instructed. For several seconds nothing happened, so he repeated the sequence. This time, just as he finished the last knock, the door opened, and a short, thin, balding man with tired eyes looked out.

"Dr. Pelligrini?" Nate asked.

"Yes," the man said. "You're the one who called?"

Nate nodded, and led the doctor over to the car. Daeng had already opened the back door.

Dr. Pelligrini took one look at Quinn and said, "Quickly. Bring him inside."

Draping Quinn's arms around their shoulders, Nate and Daeng carried him inside to a small examining room near the back door.

"Are you here alone?" Nate asked. The office was quiet and he'd seen no one on the way in.

"My nurse."

"Trustworthy?"

The doctor scoffed as he started peeling the bandage off Quinn's neck. "Of course. She's my wife."

Once the cloth was removed, blood welled in the wound.

"How long ago did this happen?"

"Less than fifteen minutes."

"Do you know his blood type?"

"A-positive," Nate said.

"Are either of you A-positive?"

Nate and Daeng shook their heads.

"Don't you have any here?" Nate asked.

"Yes, we have it, but I like to replace, you understand?"

"Mine might not be the same," Daeng said, "but you're welcome to some of my B."

"I'm happy to donate, too," Nate said.

The doctor looked over at them. "I need some space. There's a room down the hall where you can wait, but find my wife first and send her in here."

"I'd rather stay," Nate said.

"No. Out of the question. I must operate, and cannot have you here. You think I'm going to hurt your friend?"

"No, but—"

"Of course I'm not. Now, go, please. I need to get to work."

Reluctantly, they left.

"I should move the car," Daeng said.

"Good idea."

While Daeng did that, Nate found the doctor's wife—an unsmiling woman about the same age as her husband—behind a desk in a room near the front of the office. Once she was on her way, he went into the small waiting room, and made the call he'd been dreading.

"Nate?" Orlando said. Her momentary surprise switched instantly to concern. "What's going on?"

"First off, he's alive."

"What happened?"

"He's been shot, but it's not life threatening," he said, then described where the bullet hit. "I've already brought him to Dr. Pelligrini. He's prepping him for surgery now."

"How the hell did he get shot?"

"Ambush. I can give you the details later, but right now I've got to take care of a few things."

"What are you talking about? You're staying there!"

"I can't."

"Why not?" It was more accusation than question.

"Mila," he said. "Someone took her."

"I don't give a damn about Mila."

"Do you think Quinn would want me to stay here? He came here *because* of her. If he wasn't hurt, he'd be doing everything he could to find her. But since he can't, I'm sure he'd want me to do it."

"You *can't* leave him alone."

"What choice do I have?"

"What about the other guy?"

"Daeng? I'm going to need his help."

"For God's sake, you have to stay until he's at least out of surgery! Mila Voss can wait that long."

"I don't know if that's true."

"I. Don't. Care."

He closed his eyes. "Okay, okay. We'll stay until the doctor's done, but the second he is, we're leaving."

"Fine. But you keep tabs on him even then. You understand me?"

"Yes."

"And if *anything* changes, I want to hear about it."

"Don't worry, I'll call you."

"MRS. VU! MRS. Vu!" Orlando called out as she rushed out of her office on the second floor of her home in San Francisco.

"Yes?" the Vietnamese woman called up from downstairs. She and her husband helped Orlando around the house, and took care of her son Garrett when Orlando was on one of her frequent business trips.

Orlando stopped in the doorway to her bedroom. "I have to go on a trip. I'm not sure how long I'll be gone."

"When will you be leaving?"

"As soon as I'm packed," she said. It would take her only a few minutes since she always kept bags at the ready. "Please ask your husband if he could drive me to the airport."

"He'll be waiting."

Orlando retrieved the bag she wanted, threw in a couple of extra items she thought she might need, grabbed her laptop out of her office, and headed downstairs. True to his wife's word, Mr. Vu was waiting by the front door, keys in hand.

"Another trip," he said as he helped carry her bags out to the car. "Will you be gone long?"

Whether it was really there or not, she sensed a quiet rebuke in his voice. She knew he thought she traveled too much, and was away from Garrett more than she should be. Or maybe that was something she was just putting on him, her own concerns reflected in his innocent questions.

She pushed the thought from her mind. There was no way she could stay home today. While Garrett was her everything, Quinn was her everything else. And Garrett was doing okay, school going fine, no particular attitude issues. Quinn, on the other hand, was lying on an operating table, a gunshot wound just inches from his heart *and* his head.

There was really no question where she needed to be.

THE NEXT CALL came much sooner than Peter had expected, no more than six or seven minutes after the first.

"We got her," Michaels said.

Peter could feel Olsen's expectant gaze on him, but he kept his expression blank. "Yes," he said into the phone. "Finding her is our top priority, so any reasonable expenditure is approved."

Michaels got the message loud and clear. "I'll call back in five."

"Even twice that amount would be acceptable."

"Ten, then," the operative said and hung up.

"All right. I'll expect an update soon," Peter said into the dead air, then hung up.

"What was that about?" Olsen asked.

"I thought you were listening. Should have been pretty clear."

Olsen stewed for a second. "They need to spend some cash."

"You *were* listening."

"What are they going to spend it on?"

"That wasn't specified. They just needed to know what they were authorized to do."

Olsen frowned as he looked back at his computer. "That kind of thing should have been set up ahead of time. You don't really run the tightest of ships, do you?"

Peter rose from his chair. "I'm not running a ship at all.

I'm running a real-world-adapt-when-necessary operation. If you don't like it, you're more than welcome to take over."

He picked up his pack of cigarettes and headed for the door.

By the time Michaels called back, he was once again locked in the bathroom of the bar around the corner.

"You have her now?" he asked.

"Yes. I arranged for the use of a safe house south of the city." He then told Peter what had happened. When he finished, he paused before saying, "The guy with her was definitely Quinn."

"The one you *shot?*"

"Yes. My order was for a warning shot, but…"

"But what?"

"My guy's adrenaline was running a little high. He pulled it, and the bullet hit Quinn somewhere near his throat."

Peter was stunned. "Is he dead?"

"We didn't stay to find out."

"Well, find out now!"

"I'll get right on it. What do you want us to do with the girl?"

What, indeed? That question had been swirling around Peter's head since Michaels first called. Knowing now that Quinn was definitely involved didn't make coming up with an answer any easier.

The problem was that what he owed clients like Mygatt and Green was nothing compared to what he owed people like Quinn.

He swore to himself. What he needed was more time and information so he could figure this mess out and decide how to handle things.

"Keep her wrapped up there for now," he told Michaels. "And contact me as soon as you know more about Quinn."

"Yes, sir. I'll have to call in some extra help, though. I want to make sure we can cover this place around the clock."

"Fine. I'll call you back when I have more instructions."

Peter disconnected the call, but didn't put the phone away just yet. There was one person who might know where Quinn was, *and* if he was still alive.

THE DESTROYED

After five rings, a prerecorded generic voice kicked in. "Please leave your message after the tone."

He thought about hanging up, but instead waited for the beep to end, and said, "Orlando, it's Peter. If he's in any condition to talk, I need him to call me right away. Can you help?"

THE ONLY LIGHT entering the room came through the dime-thin space between the bottom of the door and the floor. Not daylight, though—weak incandescence from the other side.

Mila had no idea what was out there. A corridor? Another room? There was no way to know. She'd been instructed to leave her blindfold on until after they'd locked her in her cell.

Her room was equipped with a mattress on the floor and a plastic bucket in the corner, nothing else. When she walked it off, she determined it was eight feet square. There were no windows, boarded up or otherwise, and the walls were made of stone so there was no chance she could find her way through them.

It was becoming harder and harder to keep from admitting she'd failed. She wanted to believe an opportunity would present itself, and she'd be able to get away so she could finish what she'd started, but there was a growing part of her that was convinced she was done, that there was no way she would ever breathe free air again.

She knew how this was going to go. They would come in. They would question her. And, eventually, she would tell everything. She'd have no choice. Torture in the twenty-first century was a science. There were specialized methods now that *always* produce results.

Once she'd been wrung dry, they'd kill her like they'd meant to years before.

I can still get away, she thought, her defiant voice growing less convincing every hour. *I have to. I have to destroy him.*

If I don't, no one will.

CHAPTER
TWENTY ONE

"**HERE WE GO,**" Nate whispered into his comm as he crossed the street. What had happened outside Julien's place, the others showing up when they did, had not been a coincidence. There was no question in Nate's mind that there was some other reason for it, and the more he thought about it, the more he became convinced of what it had to be.

"Copy," Daeng said. He was gazing through the front window of the butcher shop as if contemplating what he might buy for dinner.

Nate knew by now their images had already been picked up by Giacona's security system. While the gun dealer had hopefully dismissed Daeng, Nate would be instantly recognized. Suppliers such as Giacona were always happy to see clients, but were not as keen on unscheduled visits.

Nate walked straight up to the door next to the butcher shop, made his presence known through the intercom, and pulled the door open as soon as the lock buzzed. As he passed over the threshold, he applied the piece of duct tape he was holding in the palm of his hand over the lock, then let the door close behind him. His other hand was already in his pocket, curled around the grip of his gun.

As he knew it would, the door at the far end of the hallway opened, and a smiling but somewhat bewildered Giacona stepped out. With him was another man, larger, no smile, and carrying a Smith & Wesson Bodyguard 380 pistol in plain sight.

"Quinn," Giacona said. "This is unexpected."

Before Nate could even answer, he heard one of the

hallway doors behind him open, and the sound of someone moving into a position that cut off any potential retreat.

Without moving his lips, he said as quietly as he could, "Set." Then he raised his voice. "I need to ask you a few questions."

Giacona shrugged. "Of course. I'm always happy to answer questions from good customers, but maybe you can come back when it's a little more convenient."

"It needs to be now."

"I'm sorry to hear that," Giacona said, his smile unwavering, "but now is not good for me. I'll have to ask you to leave."

"Let me make sure I'm clear. You're saying you don't want to help me?"

"When did I say that? I'm saying I cannot help you at this time. Perhaps you can come back in the morning? Say, nine thirty?"

"*Now* would be better."

At the street end of the hall, the door flew open. Unable to help themselves, both Giacona and the man with him looked past Nate to see who had come through their supposedly locked door. That was all Nate needed. He pulled out his gun and took two steps forward before they refocused on him.

The large man started to raise his pistol, so Nate shot him in the wrist. The Smith & Wesson clattered to the ground. The guy tried to pick it up with his uninjured hand, so Nate sent a second bullet into his foot. The man yelled and staggered back against the wall.

"Daeng?" he called without taking his eyes off Giacona.

"All good here."

While there had been no shots in the front end of the hallway, there had been plenty of grunts and groans and the sound of flesh hitting flesh.

Giacona stared at Nate for a moment, then took a quick look at the gun on the floor.

"You really going to try for that?" Nate asked. "I *am* pointing my gun right at you. But if you want to give it a go, be my guest."

Giacona licked his lips as if his whole mouth had suddenly

gone dry. "I…I don't want." To emphasize the point, he kicked the gun across the floor toward Nate.

"Good." Nate smiled. "Now why don't you wrap up your friend's wounds, then we'll have our little talk."

THEY ADJOURNED TO the workshop, Giacona helping his injured bodyguard in, while Daeng encouraged the other one along with his SIG.

"*Dottore*," the one who'd been shot pleaded as Nate motioned for him to sit against the wall.

"That depends on how helpful your friend is," Nate said in English. "Now sit."

The large man seemed to understand that much, and did as he was told.

Nate turned his attention to Giacona. "You got any coffee? Maybe some tea? Anything like that?"

Giacona looked truly scared. He opened his mouth but all that came out were a few stuttering syllables.

"Never mind," Nate said. "We can make this quick." He moved to within just a few feet of the small-time arms dealer. "True or false: You talked to someone after my other friend and I were here."

Giacona shook his head. "I…I…talk to no one."

"You want to think about that answer? Because I find it hard to believe."

"Well, no one about you. Understand? Is this not what you mean?"

"It's exactly what I mean, and thanks for getting straight to the point." Nate reached out and patted the side of Giacona's face. "See, that makes things easier, and that's something I appreciate."

"Yeah, but then there's the lying," Daeng said from where he stood guard over the other two.

Nate nodded. "Very true." He tried to lock eyes with Giacona, but the man kept looking away. "Who did you talk to about us?"

"I told you," Giacona whispered.

"You lied."

"I…I can't."

161

Nate leaned back. "Good. We're getting somewhere. At least now you admit to talking to someone."

"But I didn't ad—" Giacona stopped himself, no doubt realizing he'd gone too far.

Nate let him stew for a moment, then put a hand under Giacona's chin and lifted his face a couple inches. "Tell me who they were."

An internal struggle played out on the man's face. Finally, he said, "Americans."

"You're going to have to narrow that down a little bit."

"Government."

Nate frowned. "Government? The *US* government?"

Giacona nodded. "The request for the meeting came through a channel they have used in the past."

"Who did the request come from?"

"I only know a code name."

Nate remained silent, waiting.

"Clear Fox."

Clear Fox. Nate played the name through his memory, but it didn't match up to anything.

"What about the people you met. Who were they?"

"Four men came, but only one talked. He...he asked if I deal with anyone in the last few days. He was specifically looking for a woman, I think."

"But you told them about us."

"Yes," he said reluctantly, then in a rush, "but I had to tell them about everyone I'd worked with recently. And...and I didn't tell them your name. I didn't. I don't do that."

"You're going to tell me theirs, so you could be lying."

"They didn't put a gun to my head."

"Fair point," Nate said. "So why did you even tell them about us?"

"They are with the US. I have to answer. Maybe no gun to my head, but I didn't want to wake up the next day in prison in Cuba."

"What did you tell them about us?"

While Giacona was describing *why* he talked, some of his confidence had come back, but as soon as Nate asked for details on *what*, his nervousness returned in force. "I had to tell, understand?"

"Yeah, we've gone over that. I want to know *what*."

"I tell them…I tell them what you buy from me. I tell them about…about…"

"About what?"

Again, Giacona's tongue moved across his lips. "The tracking chip."

"The tracking chips we bought?"

Giacona looked at the ground and shook his head.

Nate froze, staring at the Italian. "What tracking chip, then?"

"I, um, put them in the equipment bags. Small, hidden in the lining. Sometimes if I hear a job has gone bad, I can have someone collect the bag before the police can find it." Looking almost guilty, he added, "No sense letting good hardware go to waste."

"So you could *track* us the entire time."

"I could, but I don't. Why would I? I don't need to."

Nate didn't believe a word of it, but that wasn't the important thing at the moment. "You gave them the frequency."

Giacona answered by saying nothing.

For a panicked moment, Nate wondered where the bag was now. Had they left it in the car? At the *hospital*? Then he remembered. In Julien's apartment.

They had led the men right to Julien's place, and then when they saw Mila arrive?

Bam.

Instead of saving her from whatever trouble she was in, they had brought the trouble directly to her. *Nate* had brought the trouble to her since he was the one who'd set up the meeting with Giacona.

Tracking chip in the bag? They could have checked for that, but why would they? *Because for us, distrust is a way of life*, Nate told himself. He'd fallen into the trap of believing in someone he'd worked with only once before. Giacona hadn't earned that trust yet, but Nate had given it to him, and now had paid the price. It was a lesson, he knew, he should never have had to learn.

"The people you met with. I want names and I want to

know how to find them."

"I don't know where they are," Giacona said.

Unfortunately for him, the look in his eyes told a different story.

"**JUST THE THREE** outside," Daeng said.

Nate's gaze stayed on the front door of the farmhouse just down the hill from where they were hiding. "And the two we saw go in the main building makes five. At least. A place this size, I think we should assume there could be up to ten."

Daeng nodded in agreement.

Giacona had not known exactly where the others were. What he *had* known was the name of the contact he had given the leader of the group that had shown up at Julien's. The contact belonged to a private organization that might have been able to arrange suitable, secluded accommodations. With only minor additional prodding, the Italian had placed a call to the contact, saying he had some equipment he was supposed to deliver to the team leader, but couldn't find the address he'd been given. Since Giacona was the one who'd put everyone in communication in the first place, the contact didn't even bat an eye when he relayed the information.

After that, it took tremendous will on Nate's part not to shoot the arms dealer in the back of the head. He settled for clubbing him in the temple with his gun, then tying him up and stuffing him in a closet with the other two. The one who'd been shot was no longer bleeding as much as before. Still, he was in serious need of a doctor, but that was not Nate's concern. In his mind, Giacona and, by extension, his men had committed an unforgiveable crime. When this was all over, Nate would make sure the rest of the freelance intelligence world knew the truth about the tracking devices and the unauthorized disclosure of information to a third party. That would terminate Giacona's career, if not his life.

The farm was south of the city, sandwiched between tree-covered hills on one side and a vineyard with row after row of maturing vines on the other. There were two buildings: a two-story, traditional-looking main house, and a taller, rectangular-shaped outbuilding that had a single door on one side, but no other visible doorways or windows.

Nate and Daeng had already done a complete circle around the property, using the vines as cover along the back, and going farther out on either side to remain unseen in the brush.

Nate nodded at the outbuilding, and said, "That's got to be where they're holding her."

If Mila was in the house, the others wouldn't have wasted manpower putting a guard near the entrance to the outbuilding. Given that a man *was* posted there, it was logical that she was inside.

"One way in, one way out," Daeng said. "If you're right, she's going to be hard to get to."

"But not impossible," Nate said.

"No. Few things are impossible."

Despite his earlier doubts, Nate was warming up to Daeng. In truth, his concerns had stemmed from the fact he hadn't known the guy, and, if he was completely honest, a tinge of unexpected jealousy that Daeng had replaced him as Quinn's go-to guy. Idiotic, he knew, but there it was. Now, that was starting to fade.

"So how do we know for sure she *is* there?" Daeng asked.

"Excellent question." Nate scanned the grounds. "If we can get close enough, we might be able to find out."

"If we both go, that'll double the risk we'll be noticed."

"True."

"So just one of us, then. Unless you're not worried about that." Daeng paused, then said, "We *could* just go in and take everyone out."

Nate had been thinking the same thing, but knew it was not the right call. As confident as he was that these were the people who had Mila, they still couldn't be one hundred percent sure. While Daeng had seen the faces of the men who'd gone into Julien's building, he had yet to see any of the same ones here so far. Perhaps Giacona and his contact had given Nate a false lead, in which case Mila wouldn't be here at all. They had to be sure before they tried anything aggressive.

"We'll save that option for later," Nate said. "For now, I'll go."

"I can do it."

"I'm sure you can, but I need to do this."

Daeng dipped his head in acceptance.

"Comm gear," Nate said, reaching into his pocket.

As he pulled out his mic and earpiece, he felt something crinkle in the inside pocket of his jacket. He reached in and pulled out Mila's envelope. In the rush to get Quinn medical attention, then to find Mila before it was too late, he'd forgotten all about it.

Whatever it contained had been important to Mila. He patted the outside of the envelope. Bunched together at the bottom were two square shapes, each a little less than half the size of a credit card. The flap was taped in place, not sealed, so he undid the top corner and peeked inside. The squares were flash drives, the bigger kind some cameras used a few years earlier. It was too dark to see how much data they held, but based on their apparent age, he doubted either was larger than a few hundred megabytes. They could have held almost anything, but ultimately it wasn't his business.

He folded the envelope and handed it to Daeng. "Hold on to this. I think it might be what Mila took from Julien's place. She'll want it back."

Daeng put it in his pocket.

"I'll check the house first. Come at it from the rear," Nate said. "You be my eyes and ears, so try not to get me killed."

The corner of Daeng's mouth rose. "No promises."

FROM HIS HIDDEN position on the hill, Daeng was able to steer Nate clear of the guards, and get him to the farmhouse. From that point it was up to Nate. All Daeng could do was watch his back.

The house was well built—perhaps *too* well. Not just any old farmhouse, Nate decided. He was sure it had been built specifically for one purpose—to be used as a safe house.

There were windows along the back, but no doors, so no easy way in. He peeked around the side, hoping for something a bit more helpful. But it was just as devoid of potential access points as the back.

"Down, down, down!" Daeng said in his ear.

Nate dropped to the ground.

"Guard coming around, walking close to the building."

Nate hugged the dirt.

A moment later, he could hear the crunch of footsteps. As the man neared the corner Nate had just peeked around, he paused.

Without moving a muscle, Nate mentally worked out the most efficient way to retrieve his gun in time to do any good.

There was the sound of a scratch, then the whiff of sulfur, followed seconds later by the strong odor of cigarette smoke.

Nate could hear the man take a couple of puffs.

Reach for the grip while you roll, Nate told himself. *Pull up and over. Fire.*

He ran the drill through his mind one more time.

A step. Not one continuing around the building, but one *toward* the building.

Come on, buddy. Turn back around. Walk away.

Unfortunately, the man didn't turn, and he didn't walk away. He came right up to the building, only a foot or two around the corner. So close, in fact, that if Nate reached above his head and slipped his hand around the edge, he could have probably grabbed the guy's ankle.

What the hell was this idiot doing? All the man had to do was glance around the corner and he'd see Nate.

Turn.

Around.

And.

Walk.

Away.

If Nate thought it any louder, the words would actually fly from his lips.

The man unzipped his pants.

No. No, no, no, no!

At first he heard the sound of a few drops hitting the building, then a steady stream. Nate had no idea how the ground that butted up against the house was grated. Would the growing puddle reach around to where he was lying?

He felt the sudden urge to jump up and run, but if he moved, the guard would hear him.

You couldn't have just used a tree?

The smell of urine intensified, which he knew had to mean it was getting closer. As carefully as possible, he lifted his head until it hovered a quarter inch above the ground.

Around the corner, the stream finally turned to a trickle. After a few more seconds, it stopped completely. The guard zipped up and walked away.

As soon as he felt it was safe, Nate sat up. The dirt where his head had been lying was indeed soaked. Nate touched the collar of his shirt, then moved his hand up the side of his head, over his ear and hair.

Dry.

"I take it he didn't see you," Daeng said.

"Almost."

"You're clear at the moment if you want to come back."

"Not yet."

Though getting out sounded like a great idea, Nate knew he still had to check the other building.

"Where are the guards?" he whispered.

"All three out front," Daeng reported. "One by the cars, one on the porch, and the last still in front of the other building."

"Let me know if anybody moves."

"What are you going to do?"

"Hopefully not something stupid."

"Copy that."

Nate headed back to the vines in the field behind the house, and used them to hide his movements as he snuck along the row. Once he was directly behind the outbuilding, he straightened up and moved quietly over to the structure.

The long backside was a flat, plastered surface with no indications there had ever been windows or doors there. Both the right and left side were equally unadorned. As he and Daeng had noted earlier, the only direct way in or out was the door out front.

He worked his way along the far end of the building up to the front corner, crouched down, and used the camera function on his phone to peek around the corner. The closest guard stood fifty feet in front of the outbuilding, his attention focused on the hills.

Nate angled the camera so he could get a better look at the building itself. The front door was about ten feet from his position.

Don't do it, a voice in his head said.

He took a step forward.

Don't!

Another step brought him fully around the corner. Keeping his pace slow, and his profile as low to the ground as possible, he crept all the way to the door, reached out, and grabbed the knob.

"Um, what are you doing?" Daeng asked.

Nate was in no position to answer, which was probably for the best since he was asking himself the same question.

He twisted the handle, half expecting it wouldn't move, but it did. When the latch was clear, he gently pushed inward until the door moved beyond the jamb.

Light streamed out from inside, not particularly bright, but, given the darkness outside, more than enough to be noticed if anyone was looking in the right direction. If he opened the door any wider, the chances of that happening skyrocketed.

He silently groaned in frustration. Unless he could get inside, he couldn't know for sure if Mila was there.

He cocked his head and listened through the narrow opening. Quiet.

"More men exiting the house," Daeng said. "You might want to get out of there."

Nate glanced at the other building, and saw movement on the porch.

Wonderful.

Having no choice, he eased the door closed, and quickly moved back around the side of the house.

"Two of them are headed your way," Daeng said.

"And the others?"

"One's still on the porch, the second's doing a sweep around the house."

"Okay."

"You *are* getting out of there, right?"

"Soon."

More guards meant more chances of being caught, but it

also signaled a potential opportunity. Nate pressed himself as close to the edge as he could get, and listened.

He picked out the two distinct patterns of steps almost immediately, one man taking longer strides than the other. Then a voice, indistinct at first.

"…bably tomorrow."

"Okay. Sure," a second voice said.

The steps continued until they reached the outbuilding, then stopped. There was the sound of metal on metal, someone opening the door and not worrying about being heard.

"Any requests and your answer is no."

"Of course."

They walked inside and the door shut behind them.

Nate replayed what they'd said. It hadn't been much, but the "any requests and your answer is no" seemed odd.

He leaned toward his mic and said quietly, "Keep an eye on it and see how many come out. Time for me to leave."

As Nate was making his way through the vineyard, Daeng said, "The door's opening again." He paused. "Two coming. One of them from before, but the other one's new."

"You're sure?"

"Positive."

Any requests and your answer is no.

Instructions to someone who's about to guard a prisoner, that's what it sounded like to Nate. And if that were the case…

Mila.

Again, not indisputable proof, but to Nate it was damn close.

MILA PACED BACK and forth in her pitch-black cell. Her captors had taken her shoes and socks, so twice she had stubbed her toe against the wall.

For a while, she had tried lying down, but that had only driven her crazy. At least the pacing was helping to quell the excess anxiety she felt building inside.

One. Two. Three. Four. Five. Turn.

One. Two. Three. Four. Five. Turn.

One. Two. Three—

Someone touched the handle on the other side of her door.

She stopped, and shifted most of her weight onto her back foot so she could sprint out of the room if the opportunity presented itself.

As the door opened, the light that spilled through temporarily blinded her, but in that initial split second she had seen the dark outlines of two men standing just outside. She eased the pressure off her leg, her potential run for freedom currently off the table.

She squinted until her eyes adjusted to the light.

Not two men, three.

She idly wondered if they were finally going to administer drugs or do whatever they had in mind to get her to talk. Part of her wished they would. Hanging around in the dark was just wasting time. Any change could provide—however small the odds—the opportunity for escape.

"Turn around," one of the men said.

She did.

"Now face me again."

She did that, too.

His gaze traveled up and down her body, stopping at her foot. "What happened?"

She looked down at her bloody toe, and shrugged. Let him figure it out.

He stared at her. "You might want to get some sleep."

He took a step back, and one of the others shut the door.

She remained where she was standing, the afterimage of the lit doorway still glowing in her retinas. Then, once she was sure they weren't coming back, she started pacing again.

CHAPTER
TWENTY TWO

APRIL 12th, 2006
ATLANTA, GEORGIA

"THAT'S IT RIGHT there," the woman said. She had introduced herself as Ms. Hafner, but by the way she'd stumbled when she said it, it was clear to Mila the woman had never used that name before.

Mila didn't care. That was the business. Some people were just better at it than others.

The package was a square box no more than two inches high. It was wrapped in brown paper and tied with twine. It reminded her of those old-time packages she'd seen in the movies. Parcels, they'd called them.

What it contained, she didn't know, nor was she even curious. That wasn't her job. Couriers seldom were told what they were carrying. It was better that way.

Having already been informed that the item being transported was small, she'd brought along her brown shoulder bag. She picked up the box and deposited it inside.

"Anything else?" she asked. There seldom was, but she always checked.

"No, that's it. You can go."

A dismissal. That didn't sit well. She may have been *just* a courier, but that didn't make her any less important than the woman. Still, she stifled the response she wanted to give, and left with a smile. Work was work. No sense in pissing off a client.

More times than not, she would travel by commercial airliner. In a way, it provided a bit of a thrill as she passed through various airport security checks carrying packages filled with the unknown. Not once had she ever been stopped and searched.

Sometimes her clients would arrange for her to fly on a private jet or even on a governmental aircraft. Those trips never required a security check. She would simply be ushered on board and directed to a seat. Those kinds of flights were a mixed bag. Sometimes they were relaxing and enjoyable, other times they were uncomfortable and boring.

On this particular assignment, she'd been instructed to go to a private airfield just outside of Atlanta, where she would be hitching a ride on a noncommercial flight to Lisbon, Portugal.

As she drove through the city, she hoped and prayed the trip would not be completely horrible. A small private jet would be nice, something with cushy seats and a stocked bar.

She was well out of the city and into an area of farms and scattered homes when she finally reached the turnoff for the airport. The drive had taken her longer than she'd expected, causing her to push the outside window of the time she'd been given to catch the plane. So when she crested the hill and saw that it was still waiting at the airport just a quarter mile away, she was both relieved and annoyed. She was going to make it, but she certainly wasn't going to be flying in style.

Though there were no markings on the side of the aircraft, Mila had no doubt the plane belonged to the US military. It was a modified commercial passenger jet. Not large like a 747, but the smaller type.

737? 727?

She wasn't sure. Identifying planes wasn't one of her specialties. What she did know was that military flights were devoid of any extra comforts. The best she could hope for at this point was not getting stuck traveling over the Atlantic with a troop of soldiers. That had happened to her once, and she'd been the recipient of a nonstop barrage of bad pickup lines.

The airport was surprisingly low-key. There wasn't even a fence around the outside, and the only building of any size was a single hangar barely large enough to house more than a handful of small private planes. There was no tower, no terminal. Just a metal roof-covered concrete slab that was home to a few picnic tables. Truly a private airfield, albeit one with a runway large enough for a full-sized passenger jet.

Mila parked the car where she'd been instructed, grabbed her shoulder bag, and headed for the plane. Before she could get even halfway there, she was met by three military-looking men in civilian clothes.

"May I help you, ma'am?" one of the men said.

"I'm Mila Voss. I believe I'm expected."

"ID?"

She pulled out her passport. She was traveling as herself on this trip, her client having told her this was a straight pickup and drop-off with no need to go covert.

The talker examined her ID, took a hard look at her face, then nodded and handed the booklet back.

"We were beginning to wonder if you were going to make it."

"Farther out here than I was led to believe," she said with a shrug.

"Hobart will show you aboard."

Hobart, the youngest-looking of the three, motioned toward the plane and said, "This way, ma'am."

They climbed the stairs and went inside. Mila had been expecting to see at least some of the seats filled. Given her late arrival, she had assumed she was last. But the plane was empty.

She looked at Hobart. "This flight's not just for me, is it?"

"No, ma'am. The others will be here in just a few minutes, and we'll be airborne shortly after that."

She felt strangely relieved by that. If the plane *had* been for her alone, she would have really begun to worry about what was in the box she was carrying.

"You're welcome to any seat in the first ten rows," Hobart said. "And if you don't mind, please use the facilities at the front of the plane during the flight."

"No problem," she said. "Thank you."

She selected a seat next to the window in the seventh row. After strapping on her seat belt, she leaned over and raised the armrests that bracketed the middle seat. Once they were in the air, she could stretch out and get some sleep.

From her bag she pulled out the book she'd been reading—*Goddess for Hire* by Sonia Singh. She'd plowed through several pages when she finally heard more people coming up the metal staircase. She looked up, curious to see who her fellow passengers were. The first two who entered were large men dressed in dark suits. Military, perhaps, or law enforcement. Behind them came a third, similarly dressed man, only he was walking backward as he held on to the end of a metal pole that stuck out the door.

When the other end of the pole appeared, Mila couldn't help but gasp. It was attached to a ring that was latched around a person's neck. Though a black bag was over the person's head, she could tell from the body it was a man. His hands were cuffed behind his back, while an additional restraint was wrapped around his chest, holding his arms to his side. His steps were short, almost a shuffle. She took this to mean his ankles and legs were also secured. Behind the prisoner came two more men in suits—one who looked to be in his late fifties, and the other younger but with the definite air of authority.

As the parade turned down the center aisle, Mila subconsciously slunk lower in her seat and pressed against the curved wall of the plane, wanting to stay as far from the prisoner as possible. But if he was as violent as the extreme measures seemed to suggest, he certainly wasn't putting up any resistance.

When the prisoner drew abreast of her seat, she heard a noise coming from under his hood. Not his voice, but stuttering, gulping breaths as if he'd never been so scared in his life. Even more surprising were the clothes the man was wearing—jeans with a casual, cream-colored shirt, not a prison jumpsuit or something similar. Then she noticed the man's fingers. They were manicured.

Who the hell was he? And where were they taking him?

Must be an extradition, she decided—a non-American prisoner being transported to Europe to answer for past crimes. She tried to remember if she'd heard about any upcoming prisoner transfers, but nothing came to mind.

THE DESTROYED

It doesn't matter, she thought. *It's not important. You don't need to care.*

That was right. She was just here to do her job and deliver the box to a woman she'd meet the next morning in a café in Lisbon.

Whoever he is, I don't care.

As the prisoner passed, the young, authoritative-looking man approached her row and stared at her, as if surprised by her presence. She tried to nod a greeting, but her head barely moved. The man leaned over to his older partner and whispered something. The other man glanced at Mila, and whispered back as they walked by.

CHAPTER
TWENTY THREE

ROME, ITALY

ORLANDO REACTIVATED HER phone the moment the plane touched down. As soon as it synced with the network, a message appeared telling her she had two voice mails. She played the first.

"Orlando, it's Peter. If he's in any condition to talk, I need him to call me right away. Can you help?"

She frowned. Peter was the one who started all this by asking Nate to find Quinn.

So you want to talk to Quinn? Tough luck, asshole.

She frowned at herself. All right, she admitted, maybe he didn't *start* it, but he definitely *re*started it, so helping him out was going to be low on her To Do list.

The next message was from Nate five hours earlier. "He's out of surgery. Still unconscious, but the doctor says he's going to be okay. Some muscle damage, but that's about the worst of it."

She closed her eyes. Muscle damage. *Thank God.*

She waited until she was off the plane and was walking toward immigration control to call Nate back.

"Got your message. Any update?"

"Last I checked he was still sleeping," Nate said.

She stopped in the middle of the walkway. "You're not at the hospital? Where the hell are you?"

"I told you. We were going to find Mila, remember?"

She dipped her head for a second. "Right, sorry," she said. "Look, I'm here."

"Here where?"

"Rome."

"Rome?"

"Did you think I wouldn't come?"

"I hadn't thought about it one way or the other. I've been a bit busy."

"Sorry," she said. "I didn't…"

"Don't worry about it."

"Can you meet me at the hospital?"

"It's more a doctor's office than a hospital, but, yeah, I can head there right now."

"I need the address."

He gave it to her.

"I still have to go through passport control, but I'll get there as soon as I can."

"NEED TO TAKE off?" Daeng asked.

Nate nodded as he shoved his cell back in his pocket. "Do you mind staying here and keeping an eye on things?"

Daeng shrugged. "Someone has to."

"I appreciate it."

"Go make sure Quinn's doing all right. I'll call you if anything happens here."

Nate nodded his thanks, then made his way back to where their car was parked.

Forty-five minutes later, he knocked on the door of Dr. Pelligrini's clinic. The woman who answered wasn't the doctor's wife.

"You are here to see your friend," she said, not a question. "My sister said you would be back."

"Sister?"

"*Signora* Pelligrini."

Nate looked at the woman anew, and though she and the nurse he'd met earlier were nowhere near identical, he did notice a few, subtle common characteristics.

"You're a nurse, too?"

"No, uh, just help."

He entered the building and she shut the door.

"Is the doctor still here?" he asked.

"*Si*, but, um, he sleep in his office. You want me to wake him?"

"Not yet." Nate took a step toward Quinn's room, then stopped. "There's another friend who should be here soon. A woman. Asian."

"If you hear knock, you can answer."

"Okay."

He entered the room and the woman followed. Quinn now lay on a narrow bed that had replaced the examination table he'd been operated on. His eyes were closed, but other than the tube running under his nose, and the bandages that covered the left side of his neck and shoulder, he looked almost normal.

"Any change?" he whispered to the woman.

"No, everything same. Good and, um...stead."

"Steady?"

"*Si*," she said, brightening. "Steady. That what doctor say. Steady."

That was good news.

"You want coffee? Tea?" She paused. "*Acqua?*"

"I'm okay. Thank you," Nate said.

"*Acqua*," Quinn whispered.

Nate whipped around.

"*Signore*," the woman said, moving quickly to the bed. "How you feel?"

His eyes slits, Quinn repeated, "*Acqua.*"

"*Si, si.*" She ran out of the room.

"Good to see you awake," Nate said, smiling.

"What...happened?"

"What do you remember?"

"Getting shot."

"We got you out of there, brought you here. Doctor fixed you up."

"How long?"

Nate looked at his watch. "Since you were shot? Almost sixteen hours."

"Worried it was...longer." Quinn took a few breaths. "What about Mi—"

The door opened and the doctor rushed in. Pushing Nate out of the way, he pulled a light out of his pocket, and leaned over Quinn. "Your head, it hurt?"

"It's…fine."

"Open your eyes."

"They are open."

"Like this." The doctor opened his eyes wide.

Quinn's slits doubled in size, but apparently it wasn't enough. The doctor spread the lids of one eye apart with his fingers, shined the light in, then did the same with the other. As he finished, his sister-in-law entered carrying a pitcher of water and an empty glass.

"*La porta*," she said.

Nate assumed she was talking to the doctor so he didn't pay attention to her.

"*La porta. La porta*," she said again.

"The door," the doctor told him.

"Oh. Oh, right," Nate said, the words finally sinking in.

He jogged to the back door, and pulled it open to find an impatient and worried-looking Orlando.

"He just woke up," he said, moving out of the way so she could enter.

When they reached Quinn's room, the doctor was still doing his examination so they paused near the door.

"Exactly where was he hit?" she whispered to Nate.

He touched the spot that corresponded with Quinn's wound.

"Ligament damage?"

He shook his head. "Not as far as I know."

At the bed, Dr. Pelligrini peeled back a corner of Quinn's bandage and looked underneath. With a satisfied nod, he taped it back down and took a step back.

"Now, rest only. Let the wound heal, you understand? And you be okay."

"Right. Rest," Quinn said.

The doctor looked at Nate. "You make sure he does. No rest, no good for heal. *Si?*"

"*Si*," Nate said.

The doctor headed for the door. "I go back to sleep. You

need me, you come get me."

As he passed his sister-in-law, he motioned for her to leave, too. Reluctantly, she followed him out of the room.

As soon as the door closed, Quinn tried to sit up.

"Whoa, whoa, whoa, whoa," Nate blurted out as he rushed over, Orlando only a half step behind. "You need to lie down."

"I'm fine," Quinn said, his voice strained.

"The hell you are," Orlando said.

Quinn jerked in surprise, then winced in pain from the effort. "What are you doing here?"

"What do you think? You get shot so I should just stay in San Francisco drinking espressos?"

He said nothing for a second, then, "You don't like...espresso."

She pointed a finger at him, jabbing the air with every word as she said, "Do not try to lighten the mood."

"Sorry." He paused. "It's good to see you."

"You bastard. You disappear for six months, and when you do finally show up, you get yourself shot. I should kill you myself."

"Getting shot wasn't exactly...part of the plan."

"That implies there *was* a plan, which I doubt." She frowned, then leaned over and kissed him.

Nate stepped toward the door. "Maybe I'll go see if I can—"

"Stay right there," Orlando said, her tone freezing him in place. She looked back and forth between him and Quinn. "Which one of you is going to tell me what happened?"

When it looked like Quinn wasn't going to answer right away, Nate said, "We were trying to, um, connect with Mila Voss."

"Connect?"

"Quinn thought there was a good chance she'd show up at Julien's apartment."

"Please, do *not* tell me she's the one who shot him."

"No," Nate said quickly. "She was with us. We were in the apartment when a strike team showed up. We got out, but they surprised us on the street. *They're* the ones who shot him."

"Mila," Quinn said. "You didn't...tell me what happened

to…her."

"After you were shot, they grabbed her and left."

Quinn groaned.

"Who, exactly, are 'they'?" Orlando asked.

Instead of answering, Nate looked at his mentor, so she turned to Quinn.

"I think they might be working for Peter."

"Peter?" There was no hiding the surprise in Orlando's voice.

"He's trying to find Mila. That's why he wanted to talk to me."

"Did you tell him you were going to look for her, too?" she asked. "Because that sure as hell seems like what you've been doing."

"Looking for her, yes, but only told him that as far as I knew, she was dead."

Her eyes narrowed as she stared down at him. "Tell me straight out, was there something between the two of you? Is that why you pretended she was dead?"

"What?"

"You need me to say it? Was she your girlfriend? Were you sleeping with her?"

Nate had the sudden wish he'd just left earlier without saying anything.

"No," Quinn said. He pushed himself up onto his elbows. "Never. Not even. She was *Julien's* girlfriend. I mean, had been…not important. I left Thailand to help her because Julien can't. But I failed, and let them get her. God only knows where she is now."

"Um, actually," Nate said, "God and me. And Daeng."

Quinn and Orlando looked at him.

"You know where she is?" Quinn said.

"Well, we think we do." Nate told them about Giacona, then about visiting the safe house, and finding the outbuilding where Mila was most likely being held.

When he finished, Quinn pushed himself all the way up into a sitting position, and started to swing his legs off the bed. Orlando stiff-armed his thigh, stopping him.

"What do you think you're doing?" she said.

"Leaving."

"Not in your condition."

"I've worked when I've been worse."

"Name once."

He said nothing.

"Nate and I can take care of this," she said.

"I'm coming with you."

"No, you're not."

"I'm not staying here."

Orlando and Quinn stared at each other in a silent standoff. Finally, she rolled her eyes and tilted her head back.

"God, you're the worst patient ever."

"Second worst. You're not so good at it, either."

She glared at him, annoyed, then turned to Nate. "Find him some clothes."

CHAPTER
TWENTY FOUR

IT COULD HAVE been the chicken dinner, or the turbulence. Most likely it was both. But whatever the reason, Mila's stomach was twisting and turning in ways it was never designed to do.

Shortly after takeoff, she'd been given a cardboard tray with her less-than-appetizing meal, but she'd been too hungry to set it aside. What a huge mistake that turned out to be. Upon finishing, she put the cardboard container on a seat in the row across the aisle, then stretched out and closed her eyes. Sleeping on planes was not something she had a problem with, so in less than five minutes, she was out.

The first bump invaded her dream, but didn't pull her back to consciousness. But the second—a drop of what felt like at least a dozen feet—woke her with a start. She sat up, and immediately pulled down the armrest on the open side of her seat.

A speaker in the ceiling crackled to life. "This might last awhile. So everybody just hang on."

It was a no-nonsense announcement that, if given on a commercial flight, would have probably resulted in the pilot being fired. No one on this plane was complaining, though.

For the next several minutes, it felt like they were bouncing along a dirt road full of potholes and bumps that threatened to shake the plane apart. It was somewhere in the middle of this that she felt her stomach clench.

She breathed deeply and evenly, her fingers gripping the ends of the armrests. The plane suddenly dipped again, and she almost lost her dinner. As soon as she had tentative control of her system, she looked around for a barf bag but there was none.

She began panting, hoping that would settle things down.

The plane jumped up and down, up and down.

Sudden movement at the front of the cabin caught her attention. One of the three men who had questioned her when she arrived at the airport had jumped up from his seat, and was weaving over to the toilet. If she was closer, she was sure she'd hear him retching, a thought that caused her own stomach to flip again.

Oh, God, she thought. It wasn't going to stay down this time.

Putting one hand over her mouth, she used the other to unfasten her seatbelt, and lurched out into the central aisle. She started to turn toward the front, but remembered the man who'd staggered into the only toilet there.

She whirled around, and headed toward the back, her mind focused solely on finding the closest open receptacle. Her free hand grabbed the top of each seat, steadying her as she moved down the aisle.

In her head *stay down, stay down* played over and over. She could feel sweat gathering on her brow and above her ears. She wanted to wipe it away but both her hands were occupied.

She was getting close now. She could see two toilets in the back, one on either side. Even better, the indicator next to each handle was green, meaning they were unoccupied.

The plane slid suddenly to the left, nearly throwing her into an empty row. When she straightened herself up again, she saw with surprise that someone had moved into the aisle in front of her. It was one of the suited men with the prisoner, the young guy who'd stared at her as he'd passed her seat. In her distress, she had totally forgotten about her fellow passengers.

"You can't be back here, miss," he said. "You need to return to the front of the plane."

"I can't," she eked out through the fingers that covered her lips. She'd never make it that far.

"There are facilities up there."

"Someone…is using them."

She could feel her stomach squeeze and everything inside boil in anticipation of its impending exit. She pushed it back down, but knew it might be the last time the effort would work.

"Please," she said, the word not much more than a squeak.

From a seat nearby, the older guy said, "Olsen, let her through."

"Sir, the orders."

"Let her through, unless you want her to puke all over you."

With a disapproving look, the young man moved out of the way. "Hurry up. Don't take long."

His instructions might have been the most ridiculous thing she'd ever heard. Hurry up? Of course she'd hurry up, but she had no control over how long she'd have to stay.

She rushed past him, threw open the door, and dropped to her knees just in time. For the next five minutes, the only thing in her world was the toilet. It wasn't until the retching finally slowed that she became aware of her surroundings, and realized that while she had shut the door, it was still unlocked. Weak from her ordeal, she reached over and turned the handle, engaging the OCCUPIED sign.

At some point, she stood again. That's when she realized the turbulence had stopped. She cleaned up as best she could, and did the same with the bathroom. She wished she'd been aware enough when she'd left her seat to grab her toothbrush and paste, but that was something she could take care of once she returned to the front.

Someone knocked on the door. "Miss, you need to go back to your seat." It was the voice of the guy who'd blocked her way—Olsen, the other one had called him.

"Just a second. Almost done," she said.

She checked her hair and face once more to be sure she hadn't missed anything, then opened the door. The man was standing a few feet outside, looking impatient.

"Sorry," she said. "Thanks for letting me by, though."

"Please return to your seat," he said.

"Sure." She paused. "I, uh, would avoid using that bathroom if you can help it."

Now that she was at least seventy percent herself again, her view of her world was no longer limited to whatever had been immediately in front of her. She could see the other guards spread out in the last three rows of seats. The prisoner was in the second-to-last row, up against the window on the same side of the plane as her seat. While the metal collar was still around his neck and the hood remained over his head, the pole had been removed. As she neared his row, he twisted in her direction.

"Please, please, help me," he said, speaking rapidly. "My name is Thomas Gorman. I haven't done anything wrong. I'm—"

The guard sitting next to him touched a handheld device against the prisoner's arm. By the way the man started jerking, she knew the device must be a Taser or something similar.

"Keep moving," the older man said to her.

Mila picked up her pace. When she reached her seat, she retrieved her small bathroom bag, and used the forward facilities to brush her teeth. She then sat again.

Though weak from throwing up, she couldn't get the prisoner's outburst out of her head. She had a hard time falling back to sleep. After thirty minutes, she finally gave up, and stared out the window at the dark.

It wasn't like the hooded man was the first prisoner to proclaim his innocence. That wasn't what had disturbed her. It had been his accent—American. Midwest or even West Coast.

Why would an American prisoner be on a flight to Europe? As far as she knew, the US was not in the habit of extraditing its own citizens. He could have been a foreigner who was just good at accents. Maybe, but it didn't sit quite right.

Thomas Gorman.

Why did that sound familiar? She knew that name, didn't she? Not a friend. A movie star? Politician? Neither of those felt right, either. There was something there, though, some little itch of familiarity.

Whatever the answer was, it wasn't coming to her.

THE DESTROYED

When the plane finally landed, she was instructed to stay in her seat while the prisoner was removed. Unsettled by what had happened earlier, she turned on the hidden camera in her bag.

What she captured was even more than she'd expected. As the guards walked the prisoner down the aisle, he started shouting again. "Please, someone, anyone, help me! My name is Thomas Gorman. These people have taken me from my home, have violated my—"

This time the electric shock came through the collar.

Something her camera also caught.

CHAPTER
TWENTY FIVE

WASHINGTON, DC

PETER WAS FINALLY alone. Olsen had just left, claiming a dinner meeting. He didn't say who he was seeing, but Peter was sure it had to be Mygatt and Green.

"Inform me the minute anything happens," Olsen had said on his way out the door.

"Of course," Peter had lied.

"When you find her this time, make sure your men *have* her. I don't want any more fuckups."

Peter had yet to decide when he should tell Olsen that Mila had already been detained. There was a growing part of him that was wondering if he should at all. What he needed to do was make a rational decision based on facts he didn't currently have.

Once Olsen was out of the flat, Peter joined Misty at her desk, and leaned over her shoulder as she brought up the security system. They could monitor the whole street via over a dozen cameras, including one directed at the nearby parking lot where Olsen always left his car.

Right on cue, Olsen stepped out of the building, walked down to the lot, and drove off in his shiny BMW 535i.

Peter leaned back. "Keep an eye on him. I'll be upstairs."

With a nod, Misty activated the software that would track Olsen's movements by way of a tiny chip she had sewn into the lining of his coat while he was in the office with Peter. There was also a second chip affixed to the undercarriage of the BMW. And if those weren't enough, three freelancers Peter trusted were doing a rotating tail so that there were actual eyes on Olsen at all times.

Peter climbed the secret staircase to the hidden apartment. Misty referred to the three-sided desk in the middle of the main room as mission control. On each side was a different computer. The one on the right was tied to the network downstairs and mirrored a machine in one of the unused offices, so if someone did a search, they wouldn't realize the computer was actually in a different room. It could access any of the other machines in the flat without the need of a password. Unfortunately, that didn't cover Olsen's private laptop since he'd taken it with him when he left. That was probably for the best, anyway. Peter would have been tempted to try to hack in, something that could have triggered an alarm alerting Olsen.

The other two computers were not linked to those below. In fact, neither was using the same Internet access as the rest of the office. Each was hardwired to a different, neighboring building.

One was used for accessing the public Internet, or the occasional hack into something a bit more private. The other had backdoor access to several divisions within the US intelligence community—not full access, but close enough.

This last was the computer Peter woke from its slumber.

When Mila Voss showed up alive in Tanzania, Peter had thoroughly gone over the file on her termination. As happened with most projects, many of the finer details were deemed unnecessary to the task at hand and were held back. It was a perfectly logical thing to do. In fact, Peter liked it that way. If he didn't need the big picture, he didn't want it. It made it easier to focus on what did need to be done. Mila's removal was one of those situations. Why she had to die was none of his business.

Not anymore.

Though Mila had worked for him a few times, he'd never had any direct contact. Hiring and briefing her had all been handled by subordinates. Peter had gone back and checked those records, and found that she had done her job, was thoroughly reliable, and had never caused any problems. Of course, he wasn't her only employer, but given how she had performed for him, he found it hard to believe the experience had been drastically different for anyone else.

Using the special-access computer, he set to work attempting to create a chronological list of jobs Mila had done. He knew there would be holes, people she might have worked for who were not official US agencies, but those gigs didn't concern him. The order to terminate had come from Mygatt through Green. They were both with the government at the time, so the project that had caused the problem had probably also come through government channels.

Peter spent two hours sifting through the digital records before Misty called and asked if he wanted her to pick him up some dinner.

"A sandwich," he said. "And put on some coffee."

"Coffee's ready whenever you are."

Just after nine p.m., he had what he considered to be as close as possible to a complete list of Mila's projects in the four months prior to her termination order. Whatever she did that had made Mygatt think her death was necessary would most likely have occurred not long before the scheduled event in Las Vegas. He thought it was pretty damn likely it had happened no more than eight weeks out.

He printed the list so he could lay it across the desk and get a clearer picture. Using markers, he highlighted those jobs on which there was an intersection between Mila and either Mygatt or Green. He then looked through these to see if something stood out, but on the surface there was nothing. Next, he concentrated on the jobs the two men were not—openly, at least—involved in. Same results.

Dammit.

He leaned back in his chair and looked up at the ceiling. What was he missing? The room grew deathly still as his mind ran through every possibility. A full ten minutes passed before he rocked forward, thinking there was another angle he could check.

Using date, time, and location information from the jobs Mila had worked, he began his new search. The list he came up with was shorter than the one he already had, but he'd expected that. It was simply a list of projects that coincided both in time and relative location to those Mila was attached to. Other than that, there were no apparent connections between the jobs.

He checked each against her corresponding project. The first was in Chicago at roughly the same time of day, but on a different side of the city so contact between the two was unlikely. The next was in DC. For a few moments, he thought that might be it, but it was soon clear, once again, there had been no overlap. The same was true of a job in Boston, and two in New York.

The sixth had been in Atlanta. Actually, he corrected himself, it had *started* in Atlanta for Mila. This time there *was* an overlap—a flight between a small airport outside the city and Lisbon, Portugal. Mila was on the flight because of its convenience for the run she was on. The other project had been using the flight to get to Europe, too, though there was no info telling Peter what they'd been up to. He didn't recognize the names of the people who were ultimately in charge of the project—neither Mygatt nor Green was mentioned—but there were four things that did stand out.

One, the flight had happened *exactly* one month before Mila was supposedly eliminated.

Two, the agent in charge of the other project was a man named Evans, the very same man who'd retired to the UK under the name Johnston and been killed just a few days before.

Three, the lead agent on the flight itself had been Lawrence Rosen, whose recent death had been caused by smashing into a Tanzania sidewalk.

And four, Rosen's partner on the flight had been Scott Olsen.

CHAPTER
TWENTY SIX

ROME, ITALY

"YOU'RE SURE YOU don't want one?" Orlando asked, holding out one of the pain pills Dr. Pelligrini had reluctantly given them on the way out of his clinic.

"No," Quinn said.

The last thing he needed was to be drugged up. There were moments when he had to pause and just ride through the pain, but, however strong it became, he handled it. Physically, he probably wasn't up to doing much, but decisions would have to be made, and he needed to be the one making them.

In all his years as a cleaner, with all the bullets that had flown in his direction, this was the first time he'd been seriously hit. He would have preferred for his lucky streak to continue, but there was nothing he could do about it now.

"How much farther?" he asked Nate.

"Twenty minutes," Nate replied from the driver's seat of their stolen sedan. "When we get there we'll have to park about a quarter mile away and walk in." His words came with an implied *do you think you can make it?*

"No problem," Quinn said. Whether that was true or not, he'd find out soon enough.

Orlando said, "We should have at least waited until morning."

"My legs are *fine*," he told her, a bit more harshly than he'd intended. He softened his tone. "Besides, morning might be too late."

With no good response, she shook her head and turned away.

Quinn glanced through the window. Outside, city had given way to country. Gentle hills and vineyards and unused fields took turns cradling the road. Scattered among them were copses of trees and the occasional old-stone home or barn.

In the early hours of the morning, they all but had the highway to themselves. A handful of trucks, another car or two, but that was it. When Nate finally turned onto a side road, the additional traffic dropped to zero.

"Will they see us coming?" Quinn asked.

Nate shook his head. "There are a couple hills between us."

"They could have lookouts."

"They could, but they didn't earlier, and Daeng's been keeping watch. He would have called if something had changed."

It felt odd to Quinn not to be the one in the know. He wondered momentarily if his own mentor, Durrie, had felt the same when Quinn had started running his own operations. Who knew what Durrie thought, though. He'd been a real ass at times. Hopefully, Quinn wasn't falling into that category.

Ten minutes on, Nate began to slow the car. To either side, grapevines moved out into the darkness. He shut off the headlights, and turned down a narrower dirt road that weaved through a break between the rows. They didn't go too far before the vines on their left were replaced by a gently sloping hill covered with trees. Within a couple few minutes, Nate veered off the path and inched into a space between several of the trees. He let the car roll to a stop, and killed the engine.

Twisting around, he looked at Quinn. "If you're not feeling up to it, I could try to drive in a little closer."

"I'm fine."

Looking skeptical, Nate glanced at Orlando, who just shrugged as if to say, "I give up."

Silently, they climbed out of the car and gathered near the front.

"We go around the edge of this hill, then up the next one.

That's where Daeng is."

Without waiting for a response, Nate took the lead.

They were halfway up the second hill when he suddenly motioned for everyone to stop.

"SOMETHING'S NOT RIGHT," Nate whispered. Daeng should have heard them by now and come to meet them. "Stay here."

He dropped to a crouch, moved quietly toward the top, and paused twenty feet shy of the crest. From there, he had a clear view of where Daeng had been stationed, only Daeng wasn't there.

Nate listened, trying to pick up any sense that there might be others around, but everything was still and quiet. Cautiously, he moved forward, his gaze splitting time between watching the woods for movement and scanning the ground for signs of a struggle that might indicate Daeng had been discovered. But there was nothing out of the ordinary.

So where the hell was he?

As he glanced toward the farmhouse, he flipped on his comm gear. "Daeng? Are you there?"

He knew there was little chance he'd get a response even if Daeng were okay. When Nate left, they had both turned off their gear to preserve batteries.

"Daeng?"

Dead silence.

Nate checked for guards, and spotted one on the porch of the farmhouse, and a pair in front of the other building.

He tried the comm one more time, then pulled out his phone as he crept back down the hill to the others. Given the circumstances, he was leery to call Daeng. If the former monk was in a delicate situation, the last thing he needed was his phone ringing.

He decided to give it a try anyway, and hit SEND.

Voice mail. Not even a message, just a beep.

"Where are you?" he said, and hung up.

DAENG HAD LEARNED from his dealings back in Thailand and Burma that when an opportunity presented itself, a person should grab it.

THE DESTROYED

About a half hour after Nate had left, two of the guards had begun a wide swing into the hills where he was hiding. Instead of panicking, he had simply circled around to the vineyard on the other side of the buildings. If the men had returned to the farmhouse right then, he would have stayed where he was, but they were taking their time. More importantly, they'd left only a single guard standing near the farmhouse to watch over everything.

This was the opportunity.

Leaving the cover of the vines, Daeng crept over to the windowless building. A glance around the front corner confirmed that the guard near the farmhouse porch hadn't moved.

Now or never.

Taking slow silent steps, he approached the door, wrapped his fingers around the knob, and tested it. Still unlocked. He turned the knob until he felt the latch slip free, quickly opened it enough so he could slip inside, and closed it again.

He found himself in what amounted to a short empty hallway that T-boned into a wider corridor going left and right. He took a step forward and leaned out just enough so he could look in both directions. No one, just a hallway with two doors to the left, and two to the right, all along the opposite wall. At the end of the corridor to the right was a metal staircase leading up to the second floor and down to a basement level.

He stopped in front of each door, listened, then tried the handles. All four were unlocked. Inside each he found what could only be called a cell. The two middle ones were about the size of the small bedroom he'd had in Hollywood when he lived with his aunt. Maybe seven feet square, perhaps eight. The two on either end were much smaller—same length, but the width was no more than four feet at best.

He moved over to the stairwell, and detected a faint, almost rhythmic sound coming up from below. If the guard was down there, no way Daeng could descend the stairs without being noticed. So instead, he lay on the floor and inched forward until his head stuck out into the empty space above the receding staircase. He tilted it down as slowly as he could.

There was little to see at first, just the start of another

corridor that looked to be a twin of the one on the ground floor. The further his head moved, the more hallway he saw. When he caught sight of the guard, he froze. The man was sitting in a chair at the far end, holding a book in his lap. Only he wasn't reading. He was sleeping.

Whatever prisoner he was watching over had to be in one of the nearby cells, probably the one at the end.

Daeng pulled back.

There was a fine line between opportunity and stupidity—one he would surely cross if he ventured downstairs.

As he stood up, he comforted himself with the knowledge that he had pretty much confirmed that there was, indeed, someone in one of the cells. It was time to head back. When Nate showed up again, he'd tell him what he'd found, and they could figure out what to do next.

He walked to the front door, slowly opened it, and looked out.

Immediately, he pulled his head back in, and used every ounce of restraint he had to ease the door shut.

The others had returned, and were huddled together in front of the main house, talking. He might have been able to sneak away, but that would have been even riskier than if he'd made a try for the basement.

He'd just have to wait a few minutes until they finished whatever they were doing. Hopefully most of them would go into the house. It would still be a risk, but—

He heard feet outside heading his way.

Panic was not part of Daeng's nature, so he calmly stepped back into the larger corridor and turned in the opposite direction from the stairs. As he reached the tiny cell on the end, he heard someone opening the main door.

Daeng opened the door, and slipped into the darkened cell. It wasn't until the door shut that he realized it had no interior handle. So while the cell doors were technically unlocked, that only applied if one was on the other side.

Which he wasn't.

Not quite what I had in mind.

He sat down on the mattress that filled most of the cell's floor, and started going through the contents of his pockets, identifying everything by feel. Euro bills and change, the passport that matched the ID he was traveling under, the envelope Nate had asked him to hold, his comm, and his phone.

He checked the reception on his cell. One bar. The walls of the building were thick, and apparently not cell-phone friendly. Still, one bar was better than none. Hopefully it would be enough to at least get a text message out.

He tried, but it failed. He tried again. And again. And again.

After pushing the mattress against the door to block any sound from seeping into the corridor, he tried calling Nate several times, but apparently one bar *wasn't* enough for either option.

He wasn't sure how long he'd been lying there when his phone vibrated. An hour? Two? He snatched it up and looked at the display.

Nate.

He punched ACCEPT, but the call failed to connect.

He tried calling Nate back, then texting him, but again, the signal wasn't strong enough.

Maybe he's close.

He picked up his comm gear and turned it on.

"Nate? Can you hear me? It's Daeng. Are you back?"

"WHAT'S GOING ON?" Quinn asked as Nate reappeared on the hill just above them.

"I don't know. Daeng's not there."

"You're sure we're in the right place?" Orlando asked.

"Positive."

"Show me the farmhouse," Quinn said.

"Okay. Down a little bit, though. Not here."

Staying at their current elevation, they moved parallel to the summit until they were a good fifty yards to the left, then snuck up the slope, dropping to their stomachs just before they reached the top.

From this angle, the farmhouse hid a portion of the outbuilding. Nate pulled night-vision binoculars out of his pack and handed them to Quinn.

The buildings were just as Nate had described them. Though they looked old, they had probably only been constructed in the last ten or fifteen years. Quinn had seen others like them, residences specifically designed to be used as mission headquarters and safe houses. The structure without the windows was particularly telling. He'd seen a similar type of building three or four times in the past, and knew without even walking through the front door that there would be holding cells and interrogation rooms inside.

He picked out the guards, then swept the binoculars around, scanning for other signs of life. The three men seemed to be it. He was about to ask Nate if there was a backup spot where Daeng might have repositioned himself, when Nate suddenly cocked his head, his eyes losing focus.

"Daeng?" he said.

He fell silent again.

"Is that him?" Quinn asked, realizing Nate was listening to the comm line.

"I'm not sure. The signal's not strong."

"Do you have another set?"

"The spares are in my backpack," Nate told him, then said, "Daeng, is that you?"

Quinn moved around Nate and zipped open the pack. He found the pouch by feel, pulled out two comm sets, tossed one to Orlando, then donned the other.

"...ate...can...me?" The words were weak and broken by digital noise, but Quinn was sure it was Daeng's voice.

"Daeng, it's Quinn."

"...uinn...how are..."

"Where are you?" Nate asked.

This time the words came back completely garbled.

"We're not going to hear him until we get closer to wherever he is," Orlando said.

Nate nodded. "You two go that way, and I'll go the other. We can meet up in the vineyard on the other side."

NATE STAYED UNDER the cover of the trees as he worked his way west along the hill. Every ten seconds or so, either he or Quinn would say, "Daeng, are you reading me?"

Most of the time Daeng answered, but his responses were still impossible to decipher. When Nate reached a point where

Daeng didn't answer at all, he knew he'd gone too far, so he cut to the north, staying low to the ground as he crossed an open field to the vineyard about a hundred fifty yards away. From there he began working his way back toward the house.

Since the grapes were planted just a stone's throw from the back of the buildings, he was able to get quite close to them while staying under cover.

"Daeng?" he whispered.

"Nate? I can…ou."

"Where are you?"

"You…ot…eve it."

"You're still breaking up. Start counting. I'll tell you when to stop."

"…ne, two,…ee, f…ix, seven, eight…"

Nate came parallel with the farmhouse.

"Nine, ten, elev…twe…irteen, fourteen, fifteen, sixteen, seventeen, eighteen."

"Stop," Nate said. He paused in the middle of a row. "I think I've got you now. Where exactly are you?"

"I'm in the outbuilding."

Nate turned toward it, as if he might be able to see Daeng. "You're *inside*?"

"Yes. In one of the cells."

"They captured you?"

"No. They don't know I'm here."

Nate paused, confused. "Back up. How did this—" He fell silent as he heard something coming down the row. Dropping his voice to the quietest of whispers, he said, "Quinn?"

"Yes." An equally quiet response.

A few seconds later, Quinn and Orlando emerged from the darkness.

"Daeng, still there?" Nate asked.

"Don't really have anywhere else to go."

"So how did you end up in one of the cells?"

"Opportunity."

"Opportunity?"

Daeng explained how he'd taken advantage of the guards moving onto the hills, described what he'd found, including the guard in the basement, and his belief that whoever they were holding was in a cell near him.

"And which cell are you in?" Quinn asked.

"First floor. End of the hall, opposite the stairs."

Nate took a moment to think, then said, "We'll position ourselves so we can keep eyes on all sides of the building. When it's clear, we'll let you know and you can get out."

"That's actually not as easy as you might think."

"Why not?"

"I seem to have locked myself in."

CHAPTER
TWENTY SEVEN

FRIDAY, MAY 12th, 2006, 5:43 PM
LAS VEGAS, NEVADA

SOME JOBS HAD pre-event meetings, some didn't. Jergins was a believer in them, so two and a half hours prior to the eight p.m. operation time, he had the team gather once more to go over everything.

In Quinn's mind, meetings like these were a complete waste. If someone on the team didn't know what they were supposed to do by now, then he or she shouldn't be in the business.

On this particular occasion, though, he had no intentions of raising any objections. He needed to be perceived as his usual, professional, totally cooperative self. If that meant sitting around and nodding as Jergins once more went over the emergency escape route for scenario 47f, so be it.

The hardest part was not pushing Jergins to talk faster and wrap things up. Quinn had a schedule to keep if his plan was going to work.

When Jergins traced the presumed route Mila would be taking to the room on a map of the hotel, Quinn stole a glance at his watch.

Five minutes. He had to be out of there in five minutes or he was screwed.

No, he corrected himself. *Mila will be screwed, permanently.*

"...and Kovacs, as soon as you're done, you'll give Quinn

the signal," Jergins was saying. He glanced at Quinn. "Then it's all yours."

Quinn nodded his understanding.

"Any questions?" Jergins looked around the room, but no one said anything. Of course, why would they? They'd been over this a dozen times too many already. "Okay, good. Setup team, you're dismissed. Get the hell out of town. In three days call the contact number for debrief. After that you'll receive your final payment."

Those involved in getting everything organized said their goodbyes, and within moments Jergins, Kovacs, and Quinn were the only ones left.

"You two are clear, right?" Jergins said.

"Of course," Kovacs replied.

"Completely," Quinn said.

"I'll be monitoring everything from a van just off the Strip, but if things go south you're on your own."

"Not going to be a problem," Kovacs said.

"You're sure you're all set?"

Kovacs sneered. "I've done this once or twice before, so what do you think?"

Assassins, as a group, tended to be a bit more prima donna than some other operatives in the espionage world. And why not? They were the takers of lives, the ones who could swing the balance of power with a single bullet. But up until then, Kovacs had kept his sense of superiority in check.

Jergins seemed to realize that Kovacs's stoic veneer was starting to crack. He leaned back and stretched. "OK. Unless you guys have anything else, I think we're done."

Kovacs stood and glanced at Quinn. "The signal will come on time."

"I'm sure it will," Quinn said, also rising.

"Oh, Quinn," Jergins said. "Could you wait just a second?"

On the inside, Quinn groaned, but he said, "No problem."

Kovacs shook Quinn's hand, and, after a slight hesitation, Jergins's. He crossed to the door and left.

"Don't worry about him. He'll be fine," Jergins said.

"I'm sure he wouldn't have been hired otherwise." Quinn wasn't worried about Kovacs.

Jergins nodded. "Been on a couple assignments with him in the past. Never been a problem."

"So," Quinn said, "what was it you wanted me to hang back for?"

"Right. You mentioned you were going to hire someone to help you, but you haven't given me the person's name yet. I need that for my report."

"Totally forgot." He hadn't. He'd just been hoping Jergins would overlook it. Fortunately, he was prepared. The morning before, he'd received an email from a guy he occasionally used who was looking for a gig. "Jered Myers," he said.

"I've heard that name before."

"He's a good guy. Quiet, does the work."

Jergins pulled a pad of paper out of his pocket and wrote the name down. When he was done, he said, "Great. Thanks. That's it."

Quinn took a step toward the door, then stopped. "Oh, a quick question for you. Do you know how many people Kovacs has working with him? I wasn't quite clear if it was two or three or…?"

"One, actually. A spotter who'll be trailing the target."

"Oh. Okay, thanks."

Quinn had assumed there'd be a spotter, but had worried that the man had other assistants.

He shook hands with Jergins and made his way out of the hotel. The first thing he did when he reached his car was to pull out his phone.

"Hello?" a male voice answered.

"Jered?"

"Could be. Who's this?"

"It's Quinn."

"Hey, Quinn. How are you?"

"Good, thanks. Got your email. Are you still free?"

"I am. Don't have anything booked for another two weeks."

"I can give you three days of work starting yesterday."

"Yesterday? Um, all right. Where do you need me?"

"I need you to stay right where you are."

"I'm sorry?"

"I want you to stay home and lie low. If anyone asks, you were in Vegas working with me."

"Cover," Myers said.

"Yeah."

A pause. "Is this going to cause me any problems later?"

"None," Quinn said, hoping he was right.

Myers took another moment, then said, "Sure, why not? I could always use a few days playing my bass."

"Thanks, Jered."

"Hey, you're the one paying me to do nothing. Thank *you*."

As Quinn pulled his car out of the parking garage, he called Julien. "Are you in position?"

"*Oui*."

"Have you ID'd the spotter?"

"Of course. Don't know his name, but I have seen him before." Julien rattled off a quick description: five foot eight, average build, brown hair cut just above the ears, wearing jeans and a Green Day T-shirt.

"And the package?"

"It's waiting for you."

"Good. I guess we're on."

"Quinn."

"Yes?"

"*Merci*, from me *and* from Mila. *Merci beaucoup*."

THE VAN WAS waiting in the self-parking garage behind the Manhattan Hotel. As they'd discussed, Julien had attached the key to the inside of the front bumper using sticky tape.

Quinn entered through the driver's door, and climbed into the back cargo area to check on the package. It was lying against the left side, a long black bag with a zipper on top. He unzipped it and found, as expected, a second zipped-up bag inside. The space between them was stuffed with several dozen broken chunks of dry ice—a necessity due to the heat of the desert, even in May.

He donned one of the gloves Julien had left on the floor, pushed a few of the chunks to the side, and unzipped the inner bag just enough so he could take a quick look inside.

The dead woman was not a perfect match for Mila. She

was at least twenty years older. Nor did she have the distinctive Eastern European facial features Mila had inherited from her immigrant parents. The woman's cheeks showed signs of busted capillaries that spoke of the love of alcohol that had probably been responsible for her death.

She was a Jane Doe, obtained from a financially strapped morgue employee in San Bernardino, California. Julien had met the man halfway at a rest area along I-15, east of Barstow. For a thousand dollars, the body and all the associated paperwork were theirs. No one would ever ask about her.

Hopefully, it wouldn't matter what she looked like. If all went according to plan, Quinn and Julien would be the only ones to have seen her.

He zipped up the inner bag, rearranged the dry ice, and zipped up the outer.

According to his watch, it was 6:32 p.m. In less than forty-five minutes, the flight carrying Mila was scheduled to land. At that point, if she followed directions, she would proceed to the Planet Hollywood Hotel, perhaps hang out in the casino for a few minutes, then, at precisely 8:00 p.m., would knock on the door of room 739.

And if she walked into that room, she would never walk out again.

Quinn's plan was to have her die before she even made it to the hotel, at least as far as anyone else was concerned.

He climbed out of the van and back into his car, made his way over to Planet Hollywood. That's where he was supposed to be stationed, so that's where he needed to make an appearance. When he arrived at his assigned room, he checked in with Jergins using the room phone, then turned on the TV so that it would sound like someone was there.

Seconds later he was out the door again. Instead of using the elevator, he took the stairs, exited the building, and made his way quickly to where a black town car with tinted windows was parked. On its rear bumper was a white number that indicated it was a car for hire.

Once behind the wheel, he opened the bag sitting on the passenger seat. From inside he retrieved a wig, hat, dark glasses, and a facial appliance that would cover from his chin all the way up to his ears, giving him a changed jawline and scruffy beard. If he'd been planning on doing any close-up work, he would have taken the time to put the appliance on just right, attaching it with the appropriate adhesive and using makeup to blend it into his face. But he was only concerned about what he looked like from a distance, so the appliance was held on merely by bands that went over his ears and around the back of his head, under the wig.

His appearance changed, he pulled onto the road, and called Julien.

"Update?"

"Her plane landed five minutes ago. Just waiting for her to come out."

"And the spotter?"

"Same place as before."

"Has he shown any interest in you?"

"No."

Per their plan, neither man hung up. From this point forward, they would stay on the phone.

When Quinn was within four minutes of the airport, Julien whispered, "I see her." There was a bit of surprise in his voice, even longing.

"Go. Now," Quinn said.

He could hear Julien moving through the airport crowd. Thirty-five seconds later, there was a faint grunt, and the Frenchman said, "Excuse me, ma'am. I didn't mean to bump into you. Are you all right?"

A pause, then a whisper. "Julien?"

"Did I hurt you?"

Recovering, Mila said in a normal voice, "Uh, no. No, I'm fine."

"I do apologize," Julien told her, then *his* voice dropped. "Black town car. Driver with black hat, sunglasses, and a beard. It's Quinn."

"Quinn?"

"Just get in the car." In a louder voice, he said, "If you will excuse me, then. Have a good day."

"Thank you," she said. "You, too."

Perhaps if Quinn had been standing there, the scene would

have looked normal, but from the audio alone, it sounded like Mila could have already blown it.

"What's she doing?" he asked.

"Heading for the door," Julien replied.

"And the spotter?"

"He sees her."

"Still not paying attention to you?"

"No."

"All right. You know what to do."

Arriving at the terminal, Quinn pulled to an empty stop near the curb, hopped out, and moved around to the other side of the car. Mila, who was standing on the sidewalk just outside the door, caught sight of him and walked over.

"Ms. Reese?" Quinn asked as she neared, using the name she was traveling under for this assignment.

"Yes."

"Any bags?"

"No, just this," Mila said, touching her carry-on.

"Very good."

He opened the back door, and she climbed inside. As he walked around the car to the driver's side, his gaze swung toward the terminal. Even if Julien hadn't given him a description of the spotter, he would have easily picked out Kovacs's man. The guy was trying hard not to stare at the town car, but only half succeeding.

That's because the car was not part of Jergins's plan. Mila had been instructed to take a taxi to the hotel to prevent drawing undue attention.

But here she was, being picked up by a town car that had obviously been arranged ahead of time. Once the spotter checked in—something that would undoubtedly happen in the next sixty seconds—Jergins would try to figure out which company the car had come from, and when Mila could have arranged it. If he made it far enough down the list, he would call a company named W. White Town Cars & Limos, and be informed that, "Yes, we do have a car picking up a Ms. Reese at the airport, arranged by a Mr. Peters."

Quinn knew the chance of Jergins calling W. White was slim, but if he did, the name Peters would throw him another curve, making the team leader wonder if Peter was the one who'd made the arrangements. This would buy even more time.

As Quinn climbed in, he caught a glimpse of Julien farther back, watching the spotter. He put the car in drive and pulled from the curb.

"Excuse me," Mila said. "I was wondering how long the drive is."

"You can relax," Quinn said. "The car's not bugged."

She immediately leaned forward so that her head was almost poking over the back of his seat. "What the hell's going on?"

"I said not bugged. I didn't say no one was watching."

She scooted back a little, but not all the way. "Quinn, what is it? What happened?"

He took a quick look at her in the rearview mirror, checked for tails, then returned his gaze to the road. Before he could speak, his phone buzzed.

He looked at the display. Jergins. "Julien?" he said. The call to the Frenchman was still active.

"*Oui?*"

"Putting you on hold."

"*D'accord.*"

Quinn glanced at Mila again. "Absolute quiet." As soon as she nodded, he switched the calls. "This is Quinn."

"It's Jergins. There's been a complication."

"What complication?"

"There was a town car waiting for her."

"So no taxi?"

"No."

"When did she arrange that?" Quinn asked.

"No idea, but I don't like it. The plan's still in effect, but be aware we might have to improvise."

"Any chance of an abort?"

"Unless the president himself calls with a pardon, I'm mission go."

"All right."

"Just sit tight," Jergins said. "I'll keep you posted."

Quinn disconnected the call and switched back to Julien. "Are you there?"

"I'm here," Julien said. Tense.

"What's going on?"

"He's got you."

Quinn's eyes immediately shot to the rearview. "Which one?"

There were almost two dozen cars behind him, nearly half of them taxis. Most of the rest were no doubt rentals full of people planning to hit it big in the casinos.

"Silver Audi A3," Julien said. "About forty meters behind you."

Quinn adjusted his gaze. Though the sun was just dipping below the horizon, he found the car, and made out the spotter behind the wheel.

"And you?" he asked.

"Behind him, another thirty."

"Don't let him see you."

"I think his attention is more on what's in front of him than behind."

"Just be careful, all right? And let me know if something changes."

Quinn fell silent, concentrating on the road.

After several seconds, Mila said, "Can you talk now?"

Might be easier if I don't, Quinn thought, but said, "They're planning to kill you."

"Who's planning to kill me?" she asked, her tone instantly leery.

"There's no package. No courier run. This was a termination from the beginning. Seconds after you enter the room at Planet Hollywood, you'd be dead."

"And how the hell do you know this?"

"Because I was the one hired to get rid of your body."

CHAPTER
TWENTY EIGHT

WASHINGTON, DC

"**DEPARTMENT OF THE** Interior, San Francisco office. How may I direct your call?" The female voice was efficiently disinterested.

"Helen Cho, please," Peter said.

"I'm sorry. Everyone has left for the evening. This is the after-hours service."

"Put her on the line."

"Sir, perhaps you should just try calling back—"

"Eight, twenty-seven, nineteen, D."

A pause, then the woman said, "One moment. I'll connect you."

Neither she nor anyone else at that phone number actually worked for the Department of the Interior or any after-hours service. While Congress had approved the budget of the organization they *did* work for, the group was hidden under so many layers, only a dozen or so people knew of its existence. DES was, in effect, the successor to the Office. Officially, their name was an acronym for Division of Environmental Solutions. Privately, those within the organization referred to themselves as the Division of Essential Solutions.

Helen Cho was the person in charge. She had once worked for Peter before moving on to bigger things within the National Security Council, then the CIA. A rising star with a bulldog attitude, she'd been a natural to take over the new, ultra-secret division.

"May I help you?" Another woman's voice, but still not the one he wanted.

"Helen Cho, please."

"Who's calling?"

"An old friend."

"Even old friends have names."

"Tell her it's Peter."

The woman said nothing, waiting for more.

"She'll know who it is."

Another moment of dead air, then, "One moment, sir."

The moment turned out to be almost a minute. Finally, the call was put through.

"I was just about to start my second glass of wine," Helen Cho said. As always, her voice was relaxed and had the hint of a smoker's scratch. As far as Peter knew, though, Helen had never smoked.

"Sorry to call out of the blue, but I need your help with something…sensitive."

"Didn't I hear they had you riding a desk? I didn't realize you were actually back in the game."

"Temporarily."

"Interesting. Hold on a moment."

The line went dead again, this time lasting only half a minute as she undoubtedly relocated to someplace easier to talk.

"Okay. So what's going on?"

"I've been roped into doing a little mop-up work. For what, exactly, isn't important."

"Who are the players?"

"William Green and Christopher Mygatt."

"*Senator* Mygatt? Last I checked, he was no longer part of the government."

"True. Maybe not today, but who knows about tomorrow?"

"Green's always been his lackey," she said, not hiding her distaste. "Why don't you tell me what you want? I'm not sure how I could help you, or even if I should."

"I guess we'll see, won't we?"

"I guess so. What's going on?"

"This mop-up—there's an aspect to it that I'm responsible for."

"So that's why you've been pulled in."

"Yes," he said. "The thing is, as I've been diving into this, I've been forced to take a look at the larger picture. What I've started to uncover is making me feel a little uncomfortable."

"Looking into things you shouldn't? Peter, I'm surprised," she said, not sounding it.

"I can only get so far. There are pieces I can't reach, not without bulldozing a path that will lead straight back to me, and keep me from doing anything that I might need to do."

"Like what?"

"All options are open."

She fell silent for several seconds, then said, "Could this damage the good senator?"

"That depends on what you tell me."

Again, the line went quiet. "All right," she finally said. "Lay it out for me. If I can't do anything, this discussion is pointless."

"Two things. First I need the details of a specific flight that occurred in April of 2006."

"I assume this isn't a commercial flight."

"No. Governmental. As best I can figure out, it was arranged by DIA." The Defense Intelligence Agency. "I need to know the purpose of the flight and who was on it and why."

"Okay. What's the second thing?"

"The DIA may have arranged the flight, but I'm positive they weren't behind it."

"And you want me to find out who?"

"Yes."

"And how does this tie into our friends?"

"You'll be the one to tell me that."

He could hear her sigh, and then she said, "I might be able to dig something up, but I can't promise anything."

"I have every confidence in your abilities. And Helen, I need it right away."

"Of course you do. Give me the details."

CHAPTER
TWENTY NINE

LAZIO REGION, ITALY
SOUTHEAST OF ROME

THE THROBBING PAIN in Quinn's neck was constant, but bearable. The biggest problem it gave him was that anytime he had to look left or right, he had to twist his entire torso, keeping the position of his head and neck steady.

"The number three guard is on the move," Orlando whispered over the comm.

After reconnecting with Daeng, they'd decided to spread out to keep a better watch over things. Quinn had remained in the vineyard, directly behind the building containing the holding cells, while Nate had moved to a spot nearer the main house, and Orlando had worked her way around until she was back on the hill in a position almost opposite Quinn's.

"Looks like he's going in," she said.

About time, Quinn thought. Now there would be only two guards patrolling the outside, more than enough for most nights at two in the morning.

"Let's give it ten minutes," Nate said.

"Copy," Orlando and Quinn said.

Once the ten minutes passed and no reinforcements had appeared, they reconvened at Quinn's position.

"Here's what I'm thinking. Orlando and I go in," Nate said, looking directly at his mentor. "You watch our back."

"The hell I will," Quinn said. "I'm going, too."

Orlando reached out and flicked Quinn's neck with her finger, right at the edge of the bandage. He jerked back.

"Why'd you do that?" he said.

"You're standing watch," she told him. "If one of *us* were hurt, you'd make a similar decision. Someone has to keep an eye on things. You're the logical choice. So don't be an asshole. I mean, a bigger one than the one you already are."

He glared at her for a second, but then gave her a terse nod. She was right, of course, but he didn't have to like it.

"Head back over to the hill," Nate said. "You'll be able to see things better there. We'll wait until you're in position."

"I *know* where I should go," Quinn snapped.

Orlando stifled a laugh.

"What?" he asked, his eyes boring into her again.

She smiled and shook her head. "You don't do injured very well, you know that, right?" She glanced at Nate. "It's kind of funny, isn't it?"

Nate nodded. "Maybe we should shoot him more often."

"Oh, there have been times I've wanted to," she told him.

Quinn looked from one to the other. "Everyone happy now? Got any more you want to hit me with?"

Nate considered the question for a moment, then said, "I'm good."

Orlando leaned forward and kissed Quinn on the cheek. "You're actually kind of cute when you're annoyed."

Quinn didn't wait around to hear any more. He headed left, paralleling the row of grapevines, then cut across the far field and moved into the copse of trees that had a front view of the farm's two buildings. He settled in and scanned the property.

"I'm in position," he whispered into his collar mic. "Still just the two guards. One by the front door of the house. The other's in the parking area, leaning against one of the cars. Looks like he's having a smoke."

"Copy," Nate said. "We're moving."

Quinn shifted his gaze back and forth from where the guards were to the detention building. It was nearly a minute and a half before he spotted Nate at the front corner.

"I've got a visual on you," he said, and checked the guards

again. "You're clear to the door. But do it slow and easy."

"I *know* how to do it," Nate whispered in a perfect imitation of Quinn's earlier response.

Quinn rolled his eyes, knowing but not wanting to admit he deserved that.

He watched as his girlfriend and his former apprentice crept up to the door, opened it, and slipped inside. As soon as they disappeared, he switched back to the guards.

Neither man had moved.

DAENG SAT QUIETLY on the floor of his cell, his mind drifting on a river of nothing. Scattered images passed by: the jungle, Wat Doi Thong, a girl in Bangkok named Om he'd been seeing, the street in Rome outside Julien's apartment. There were no meanings, no messages, just things that were.

He could see the water of the Chao Phraya flowing swiftly by, so real he could almost touch it. As the imaginary Daeng leaned toward the surface, a bright light cut across his face. It wasn't reflecting off the river, though. In fact, it wasn't in the world of his mind at all.

He blinked, then squinted. The glare was coming from the door, partially blocked by a shadow standing in the opening.

"So, um, next time, check the door before you close it," Nate whispered.

"Sage advice," Daeng said, rising to his feet.

Standing near Nate was a small Asian woman. Orlando, Daeng realized, the woman he'd heard Quinn talk about often when Dang visited him at Wat Doi Thong. She was as beautiful as the American had made her out to be, her small frame radiating with an intensity and strength that seemed out of proportion with her size.

"The girl's downstairs?" Nate asked.

"*Someone's* downstairs," Daeng said.

"One guard. Correct?"

"Yes. When I checked, there was only the one, and I haven't heard anyone else enter the building. Of course, I didn't hear you, either, and I knew you were coming, so maybe that's not such a good gauge."

Nate took in the information, but said nothing.

"Are we attempting a rescue?" Daeng asked.

"Might be our best opportunity."

"The problem is, you can't get close to the guard without him knowing. He could set off an alarm that would bring the others."

"Not going to be a problem," Nate said.

He pulled his backpack off his shoulders, unzipped the top, and removed a thin, four-inch-long cylinder.

Daeng raised an eyebrow.

"Stun grenade," Nate said. "Low power. Enough to disable one or two people if it's close enough, but the noise should be all contained to the basement." He handed the weapon to Orlando, and pulled his bag back over his shoulders. "Show me how you saw the guard without him knowing, then I'll toss this in."

QUINN'S PHONE VIBRATED. Since the only people he had any interest in talking to at the moment were on the other end of the radio in his ear, he didn't pull it out of his pocket.

Surveying the farm again, he noted that the smoker had finished his cigarette, and that the other man was rolling his head over his shoulders, stretching his neck. Neither made any indication they were aware that one of their buildings had been infiltrated.

On the comm, reception was once more a problem, and Quinn was able to hear only about seventy percent of the conversation between Nate, Daeng, and Orlando. It was enough, though, to know that things were progressing as planned.

When all talk ceased, he assumed they had moved back into the hallway, where words would be kept to an absolute minimum in case the guard in the basement could hear them.

It was amazing how slowly time passed when he could only wait for the others to do the work he should be doing himself. Convinced he would have been finished by now, he glanced at his watch and saw that not even a minute had passed.

Just relax and wait for the click, he told himself.

That would be the signal, a simple on and off click of Orlando's mic when Nate was about to set off the grenade.

THE DESTROYED

He couldn't help but look at the windowless building, as if there would be some sort of sign that it was time. Of course there was nothing, just the blank walls and single door. He switched his attention back to the guards. The one at the cars looked as bored as ever. As Quinn panned his binoculars over the patio to check the other one, he heard:

Click.

THEY WALKED SILENTLY down the hall to the stairwell. Once there, Nate looked at Daeng, who pantomimed how he'd stretched out over the opening earlier.

Nate nodded, removed his backpack, and set it on the floor. As a precaution, Orlando continued to hold the grenade until he was ready to throw it. He lowered himself to his stomach and slinked forward over the steps.

When he was out as far as he wanted to go, he dipped his head, and looked into the basement. The upside-down view was exactly as Daeng described, doors along one wall and the guard sitting in a chair at the far end with a book in his lap.

Nate extended his arm behind him and raised his palm into the air. As soon as he felt the stun grenade touch his skin, he wrapped his fingers around it, and carefully brought it forward over the gap. On the comm he could hear Orlando click her mic, but he barely registered it. All his attention was on the task ahead.

Though he knew the toss was a relatively easy one, he had to account for his inverted perspective or he'd likely throw the grenade into the ceiling. That would alter its trajectory, and could keep it from getting close enough to the guard to be effective.

A nice, simple lob was all that was needed.

He tried a practice swing, adjusted his arm motion, and tried again. Happy with the result, he brought the grenade up so he could see it, and turned the timer to five seconds. He drew his arm back and tossed the grenade into the room, then pulled himself out of the stairwell as quickly as he could.

At the two-and-a-half-second mark, they could hear the sound of metal skidding across the floor. A second later, the wooden chair below creaked as the guard must have started to wake. Then—

Boooom!

QUINN CONTINUED TO monitor the guards. Though he expected to be the only one outside the detention building to know that anything had happened, he wanted to make sure there was no reaction from the other two.

Unconsciously, he counted off the seconds after the click.

Four seconds. Five. Six. Seven. Ei—

Booom!

The sound had most definitely *not* been contained within the building.

The guards were instantly alert, both turning toward the other building. They exchanged a few words, and one started running in the direction of the sound.

"I don't know what happened," Quinn said, "but you've got company on the way."

As soon as the words were out of his mouth, he pulled back. Given his current position—the perfect place for a spotter—*he* was vulnerable, too.

As he was turning away, he heard the front door of the main house open. He took a quick look over his shoulder just in time to see at least half a dozen men rush outside.

QUINN'S VOICE. DISTANT.

Something about company.

That's when Nate realized he was lying on the floor. Which floor and where took him another second to remember. When he did, he scrambled to his feet.

Daeng was sitting against the wall, Nate's backpack somehow sitting in his lap.

Nate grabbed it from him and said, "Are you all right?"

"Uh…yeah. Fine."

A hand clamped down on Nate's back and whirled him around.

"What the hell was that?" Orlando said. "I thought you said it was low power. That was *not* low power."

Screwed by Giacona again, Nate realized, though he doubted the weapon supplier had any idea his grenades were mislabeled. But now was not the time to worry about it.

He jumped into the stairwell, and raced down to the basement. The guard, his chair, and his book were now all on the floor, and two of the cell doors were hanging open on broken hinges.

Nate ran over to the guard, and checked the man's pulse. Not exactly strong, but it wasn't threatening to stop, either. There was blood on the floor, but it appeared to be a result of the man's nose coming into abrupt contact with the ground.

Keep going! Nate told himself.

He checked the two cells with the broken doors, but they were empty, so he headed for the last cell. It had been the one closest to the guard, therefore the most likely place a prisoner was being kept. He turned the knob and tried to pull it open, but it didn't budge. At first he thought it was locked on the outside. Then he saw that the blast had warped it enough to jam it in place.

He stepped back and kicked at the door. It groaned as it moved inward. From the other side he thought he heard a voice. He kicked it again.

The middle portion of the door cleared the jamb, creating a small opening.

"Mila?" Nate called. "Are you in there?"

"Yes!" she yelled.

"Stand back."

Once more he attacked the door, this time leading with his back and ramming his whole body against it. The door broke free.

"Come on!" he yelled.

"You came to get me," she said as she rushed out.

"Come on." He grabbed her hand, pulled her to the stairway, and up to the next floor. When they reached Orlando and Daeng near the front door, Mila put on the brakes, her eyes narrowing in suspicion.

"They're with us," Nate said. "Intros later, if you don't mind."

That tempered her a bit, but not completely.

"Have we heard from Quinn?" he asked.

"Been trying to reach him," Orlando said.

"Has anyone checked the door?"

Orlando looked at him as if he were crazy. Daeng said, "You're more than welcome to, but I'm pretty sure we aren't the only ones who heard our little explosion."

"Understatement of the year," Orlando said.

"I'm *sorry*," Nate said.

Orlando shook her head. "Never mind. If we had left right away, maybe we would have made it, but by now there's got to be at least three or four of them out there."

The single exit was a choke point. The only thing the men outside would need to do was train their weapons on the doorway, and shoot anything that moved through it.

"I'll go," Nate said. "You all hide. I'll convince them I came in alone. Hopefully, one of them will recognize me as the one who was with Quinn earlier. They probably think he's dead, or at least laid up. I'll just say I was trying to finish the job of getting Mila away."

"They'll come in and look anyway," Orlando said. "They'll want to know what happened to her."

"Yeah, but they'll be splitting their forces, not coming at you all at once."

"...o it..." Quinn's voice crackled through the comm.

"Quinn?" Orlando said. "Are you all right?"

"... got...ont cov...There...an...way..."

"You're not coming through clearly. Can you repeat?"

"...ther exit..."

Nate narrowed his eyes. "Exit?

"...es..."

"Quinn?" Nate said.

Silence.

"Quinn?"

He was gone.

"If you want my opinion," Daeng said, "I think he was suggesting there might be another exit."

"Did anybody see one?" Nate asked.

They all shook their heads.

"There must be something," Orlando said. "Places like this always have an emergency exit. So I think before you go off sacrificing yourself, we should at least take a look."

Nate frowned. "Even if there is, don't you think they'll have someone waiting on the other side? Hell, maybe they're using it right now to get in."

"We have to try," Orlando said.

She was right, of course.

He looked at the door. The thing about choke points was that they worked both ways. While they searched, only one of them would have to stay behind to dissuade anyone outside from using the door.

He finally nodded. "Let's take a look."

QUINN CIRCLED BACK into the vineyards, then cut across the grass toward the rear of the farmhouse. As he moved closer, he began hearing snippets of conversation over his radio.

He didn't get everything, but it was clear Nate was planning on sacrificing himself, and hoping that would allow the others a chance to get away. Though it was something Quinn would have probably done, he didn't want them to give up yet.

"Don't do it!" he whispered into his mic.

"Quinn? Are you…right?" Orlando asked.

"They've got the front covered. There must be another way out."

"You're not coming through. We don't know what you're trying to say."

"Look for another exit! Another exit!"

"Exit?" Nate this time.

"Yes! Yes! Look for the emergency exit. There has to be one."

"Quinn?"

"The emergency exit."

"Quinn?"

He knew he was no longer getting through. But whatever they decided on, there was one thing he could do to help.

He moved around the side of the farmhouse opposite the detention building. When he reached the front, he peered out across the long porch. It was deserted. Everyone had raced over to the other building. He could see them in the open field about a hundred feet in front of it, their guns trained on the door.

He scanned them, looking for any familiar faces. Whoever

was heading up their team would be an experienced operative, and, if this was indeed Peter's operation, someone Quinn might know.

He picked out a couple men he'd seen before but didn't know their names. Tangential players on previous gigs. But, wait.

There.

The tall one near the back. His name was Michaels. A decent op who knew his stuff.

The important thing at the moment was that if he was outside, there was little chance anyone was left in the house.

Perfect.

Quinn crept across the porch and let himself in. Ten seconds later, he found the room he was looking for.

CHAPTER
THIRTY

WASHINGTON, DC

HELEN CHO CALLED back exactly thirty-seven minutes after Peter had hung up with her.

"I don't know what you were expecting, but I doubt this was it," she said.

"What did you find?"

"I shouldn't even tell you. In fact, I probably should be calling the FBI and having you detained somewhere for just asking about this."

"I told you I'm working for the government."

"For *former* senator Mygatt," she said.

"And Green. He still gets his paycheck from the same place you do."

"Green," she said, letting his name linger for a moment. "Ironic in either case. If I call the FBI, they'll check with him first, and what do you want to bet I'd get put in the cell right next to yours?"

"Helen, what did you find?"

There was a long pause. "Have you ever heard of something called Project Cancer?"

"No."

"Neither had I until fifteen minutes ago, thank you very much. Were you ever involved in any extraordinary rendition cases?"

Everybody in the intelligence world, at least those on the

front lines in high-level positions like Peter and Helen, had been involved in the transfer of citizens from one country to a secret prison in another. The post-9/11 years had been a busy time. "A few. Is Project Cancer part of that?"

"First of all, the project is a rumor. It never existed. But hypothetically, if it did, it would be a *variation* on the theme."

"What kind of variation are we talking about?"

She paused once more, then, as if reading from a book, she told him exactly what kind.

When she finished, he was speechless.

"Hypothetically, of course," she said into the silence.

"Of course."

Neither of them said anything for a moment, the full weight of what she had described filling the connection between them.

"And behind it all?" Peter finally asked.

"I did say *ironic*, didn't I?"

Mygatt and Green, he thought. "How sure?"

"Let's just say if it were an election, no one else is running."

Dear God.

"Listen carefully," she said, then gave him an email address, followed by a string of letters and numbers. "Do you have it?"

"Yes."

"Good. I'm sure I won't be hearing from you about this again."

She hung up.

Though the computers in his secret office were extremely secure, he didn't for a second consider using one of them. To check the email account Helen had given him, he needed complete anonymity.

He went back downstairs, extracted an empty black accounting case from the closet that would typically have been used for linens, and left the building. Two streets away, he caught a cab that took him on a short ride to a neighborhood he hadn't visited in over a year. He walked for several more blocks before turning down an alley.

Sixty seconds later, he was standing in front of a garage

that was part of a three-unit townhouse complex only a few blocks from Georgetown University. As far as the residents knew, the electricity meter box along the side was solely for tracking each unit's power usage. While the meters did do that, the box itself had an additional function.

Peter slipped a key into the lock on the side of the box. Others had keys to this lock, too, but his was the only one that turned in the other direction.

With a low clunk, the entire box hinged open from the wall. The back appeared to be a metal plate with another keyhole near the bottom. He stuck in the appropriate key, turned it, and opened the panel.

Mounted inside were two Dell laptop computers, two pouches containing all necessary wiring, and two thin, handheld printers. The laptops and printers had never been used before. To stay fully charged, each tapped into the electric supply running through the meter box. If anyone found them and tried to find their owners from the serial numbers, they would have discovered that the machines were listed as never having passed Dell quality control, and had been recycled.

Working quickly, he removed one computer, one pouch, and one printer, and placed them in his accounting bag. He closed the panel. If he ever needed another disposable computer, he'd be back. If not, well, who knew if anyone would ever find the remaining machine.

He walked to a park fifteen minutes away, and went directly to the bench where he knew he wouldn't be seen from the street. There were only a few others in the park, most taking their dogs on a late evening stroll.

He used a cable from the pouch to connect the computer to the printer, and fired them both up. After that it was a simple matter of joining one of the many Wi-Fi networks broadcasting from the homes surrounding the park. He picked one at random, used the preinstalled software to hack past the password protection, and went to the website where Helen had set up the email account.

It was a well-used trick. Sign up for a free account, write an email with whatever secret message needed to be conveyed, but instead of sending it, just save it as a draft. The intended receiver of the message would also have the email account information. That person would then sign on, open the draft folder, and read the message. There would be no trail of the email being sent, no warning light flashing in some NSA data collection center, no indication of anything going on at all because in the virtual world, the email never went anywhere.

Helen's draft folder contained a single message.

> What is *your* definition of domestic terrorism? Someone who sets off a car bomb on a crowded street? Someone who targets a country's leaders for death? Someone who calls for the overthrow of the government? Someone who advocates change?
>
> The slope is slippery.

Peter frowned. It was the same philosophical question the intelligence community had been grappling with for decades. If anyone had come up with a definitive answer, he hadn't heard it.

He clicked on the picture file attached to the message.

There was a delay as the appropriate program was launched.

Peter stared at it for a moment, unsure of what it meant. He recognized the face, but the name wasn't coming to him right away. Whoever it was, it had been a while since Peter had—

Wait.

He *did* know who it was, but that didn't really help him understand why Helen had sent it to him. He reread her message, and looked at the face again.

Project Cancer.

Cancer.

As the realization of what Mygatt and Green had done dawned on him, the skin on his face felt as if it had been suddenly pulled tight against his skull.

Holy shit.

If he was right, he wasn't just sitting on a powder keg. He

THE DESTROYED

was straddling a hydrogen bomb.

CHAPTER
THIRTY ONE

LAZIO REGION, ITALY

"NOTHING," NATE SAID, as he raced out of the basement cell Mila had been in.

He and Orlando had already checked the main floor and were now doing a thorough search of the area below ground.

Orlando popped out of the cell she'd been going through and shook her head.

"This place wasn't built with any other way out," Nate told her, his frustration starting to show.

"There's got to be one. There's always one."

Nate did a full three-sixty, scanning the basement once more. "Well, I'm not seeing it."

Orlando moved from one cell door to the next, scanning the room inside. As she turned away from the one closest to the stairs, she paused, her narrowing eyes focused on the door itself.

"I think it's got to be in here," she said, nodding into the cell.

Nate hurried over. "Why?"

She pointed at the inside part of the door. "You see it?"

Before he could answer, she put her finger in a small divot in the door, about a foot above the ground, and pulled out a ring handle, just large enough to get her finger into. She twisted it, and the door latch turned. In this cell, someone on the inside could actually open the door.

A quick check of the other cells revealed none had the

same ring handle.

"It's here somewhere. We just have to look harder."

Nate dropped to his knees and started feeling along the tile floor for anything usual, while Orlando made a similar examination along the wall.

"Hey!" Mila called down from the stairway. "Get up here. Something's going on."

Nate and Orlando rushed out of the room, and found Mila at the top of the stairs.

"What is it?" Nate asked.

"I…I don't know. But…" She pointed toward Daeng standing near the entrance.

They moved over to him.

"We suddenly heard a lot of noise," Daeng said.

"Maybe they're trying to get in," Orlando suggested.

"No, no. Yelling, but not at us. And something else."

"What?" Nate asked.

QUINN FOUND A dry rag and tied it around a can of tomato soup he'd grabbed from a kitchen cabinet. The matches were a bit harder to locate. He thought they'd be near the stove, but instead they were in a drawer next to the sink.

He moved over to the window, raised it as far as it would go, and used a knife to cut through the screen.

He blew out the pilot lights on the gas stove, and turned all the burner dials to high. He then did the same with the oven, leaving the door open. The second he was sure gas was spewing out, he jogged over to the window, climbed out, and shut it behind him.

For ninety seconds, he huddled in the bushes a few feet away, letting the gas fill the kitchen. As much as he would have liked to wait longer, he knew he couldn't afford to, so he moved as far away from the window as he dared, given his injury. He lit the rag, then cocked his arm back and awkwardly launched the flaming can of soup through the glass.

As he turned away, the kitchen ignited in a loud *wah-umph*.

He sprinted across the grass, making the cover of the vines seconds before two of Michaels's men rushed around the back of the house to see what happened.

Flames licked at the windows. The exterior stonewalls wouldn't burn, but everything inside would, leaving an empty husk if the fire wasn't extinguished in time.

Quinn moved off to a point where he felt safe enough to circle around to the trees on the other side so he could better see what was going on.

He'd been hoping that Michaels and all of his men would switch their attention to the fire, giving Nate, Orlando, Daeng, and Mila an opportunity to get out. Instead, only five of Michaels's men had repositioned to the main house, while Michaels and the three others remained near the detention building.

Which, of course, meant Quinn's friends were still stuck inside.

Michaels was talking to the three still with him, aiming the majority of his words at the two men on his right. When he finished, the two nodded and separated, moving out wide to either side. Quinn watched, already having a pretty good idea of what they were up to. The moment they curled back toward the building, he knew he was right. Their plan was to approach the detention-building door from both ends.

While they were doing this, Michaels and the other man moved a car into the field fifty feet in front of the building, positioned themselves behind it, and aimed their weapons at the door.

A classic solution.

The two by the door would open it, then get out of the way while their boss and the other man would shoot into the building. At some point they would rush inside, and mop up whatever was left.

Quinn couldn't let it get close to that point.

Again, the phone in his pocket rang, and again, he ignored it.

There was about a hundred and ten feet between him and the car Michaels and his man were now standing behind. He *could* probably pick them both off...if he wasn't injured. While he knew his first shot would run true, he wasn't sure how his sewed-up wound would affect the second, and he couldn't afford to make a mistake.

He had to get closer.

Which meant he had to move out into the open.

NATE PRESSED HIS ear against the front door. Whatever yelling there had been, he didn't hear it now. What he did hear was the roar of a fire.

Quinn.

His mentor must have lit up the house to give them a diversion. The problem was, they had no way of checking outside to see if the route was clear. His hand dropped to the knob.

Just a quick look, he thought.

But he couldn't bring himself to turn it.

Instead, he said, "Basement. Everyone."

THE GROUND BETWEEN the trees and the car was a patchwork of grass and dirt and weeds. His gun held firmly in his hand, Quinn stayed low as he moved in directly behind Michaels and the other man, staying out of their line of sight.

Through the windows of the car, he could see that the duo at the building had arrived at the door. Michaels waved his arm, and one of the men reached across the entrance and grabbed the handle.

Wait! Quinn willed them, knowing he wasn't close enough yet. If he tried to go faster, they would hear him.

The man started to pull the door open.

NATE WAS THE last one down the stairs. As his foot touched the basement floor, he heard something from above. A metal scratch, muffled and distant. He was about to ask the others if they'd heard it, too, when the unmistakable sound of bullets slamming into the walls of the ground-floor corridor answered the question.

"Go! Go!" he yelled, urging the others into the cell.

"Check everywhere," Orlando ordered. "There's got to be a hidden latch or panel or something we missed before."

They spread out and ran their fingers over the walls and floor. Nate chose a spot nearest the door so he could hear what was happening above. Within seconds of the initial barrage, the shooting stopped. He imagined several of the others moving into the upper hallway. He couldn't hear them, but that didn't mean they weren't there.

"I've got something," Mila said.

Everyone moved over to her.

She jiggled one of the floor tiles. It moved, not much, but enough to show it wasn't cemented into place.

"Is there a way to pull it up?" Orlando asked.

Mila ran her fingers around the edges. "I don't think—"

"Let me," Daeng said.

He was holding a twisted piece of metal that must have come off one of the doors during the explosion. He slipped the edge between the tile and the mortar, and levered it up. Underneath was another ring tab, only this one was large enough for a whole hand to grab.

"Please, everyone move back," Daeng said.

Once the area was clear, he gave the ring a yank. A three-foot-square section of the floor opened.

"Get in!" Nate ordered. He was sure the people above were heading down the stairs at that very moment.

Orlando went first, then Mila.

When Nate entered, he put his hands on the underside of the hatch, and said to Daeng, "I've got it. You put the tile back in place, then sneak around behind me."

After Daeng did as instructed, Nate shut the hatch.

MICHAELS AND HIS companion opened fire on the building.

With no choice left, Quinn ran, and was able to get within ten feet before Michaels cocked his head and began to turn. Quinn lunged forward and grabbed the man's arm, shoving his SIG into the base of Michaels's skull.

"Cease fire," Quinn ordered.

The other man noticed Quinn for the first time and started to bring his weapon around.

"Don't," Quinn said. "Throw it on the ground behind me."

The man hesitated.

"Do as he says," Michaels told him.

The man tossed the gun behind Quinn.

"Now lie on the ground," Quinn instructed. "Facedown, spread eagle."

The man did as he was told.

Quinn glanced at the men near the door of the building.

"Tell them it's all clear, and have them come back here." Quinn emphasized the command with a gentle push of the SIG's muzzle against Michaels's head as he moved so that Michael's body would shield him from their view.

"We're all clear," Michaels yelled. "Come here for a minute."

Still looking confused, the men started walking across the grass.

Without moving his head, Michaels glanced to the side. "You're Quinn. I'm glad to see we didn't kill you."

"Are you really?"

"Yes. The shot was only meant to warn you off."

"Then whoever took it needs some target practice."

The men from the building were nearing, but their pace was starting to slow as they realized something was wrong.

"Tell them to throw their guns off to the side as far as they can, then get on the ground like your buddy here."

Michaels relayed Quinn's order. While neither man looked happy, they seemed to realize Quinn had the upper hand at the moment, so they tossed their guns and lay on the ground.

"What do you want, Quinn?" Michaels asked.

"That's a dumb question."

"Look, we're just doing our job. We were hired to find the girl, so we did. I wish I could let you have her, but I can't."

"Too late."

"You already have her?"

Quinn noticed those at the farmhouse were starting to head back.

"Here's what we're going to do," Quinn said, just as his phone vibrated for the third time in the last ten minutes. He reached down and hit the button that sent the call straight to voice mail. "You're going to wait until they get—"

Michaels jerked in surprise. "Sorry. My phone. Someone's calling."

Quinn's eyes narrowed. He thought that maybe Michaels

234

was trying to pull a fast one, but then he heard the low buzz of the other phone. It rang twice more, then stopped. Five seconds passed, and Quinn's vibrated again.

What the hell?

"Don't move," he said to Michaels.

Keeping his gun pressed against Michaels's skull, he pulled his phone out. "Yes?"

"Quinn?"

Quinn smirked as he punched the speaker button. "Hello, Peter."

CHAPTER
THIRTY TWO

LOSING THE TAIL had been easy. Friday night. Vegas. Spring. The town was rapidly filling with what seemed like half the population of California. Everywhere you looked, there were cars with license plates from the Golden State clogging up the Strip.

Quinn had counted on this, and had not been disappointed. All it had taken was one well-timed acceleration through a yellow light, and they were free. Julien confirmed the tail had not seen them turn down the side road, so there was no way the spotter could know they had returned to the Manhattan.

Quinn pulled the car to a stop at the back of the casino's parking garage.

"Walk through there," he said, pointing at one of the car exits. He handed her a map he'd drawn himself. "Follow this to the safe room, and stay there until you hear from one of us."

She had yet to shake the stunned look that had overtaken her when he'd explained what was going on. Not only did she just find out she'd come within less than an hour of dying, Quinn had also explained the extreme measures she would have to undertake to remain alive.

"Be someone else…forever?" she'd said.

"Maybe, maybe not. But whoever you crossed undoubtedly has a long reach."

"I should have never—"

"Wait," he said quickly. "I don't want to know what brought this on. It's better for you *and* me if I'm out of the loop. From this point forward, Mila Voss is dead and whatever she knew died with her. Unless you do something stupid, they'll have no reason to believe you haven't been removed. Stay away from the business, contact no one you've *ever* known, find yourself a nice, uncomplicated life. That's the only way you're going to survive."

She fell into her thoughts for a few minutes as Quinn drove, then she looked up and said, "Julien and you, too."

"What about us?" Quinn asked.

"If I show up somewhere alive, they'll want to know why you said I was dead."

"Don't worry about us. My cover is tight, and they don't even know that Julien's here. But if it helps you stay hidden, then fine. You'll be endangering us, too."

That had been the last they said to each other until he stopped next to the garage.

She studied the map, but he knew she wasn't really seeing it.

"I don't mean to rush you," he said, "but if we're going to pull this off, I need to be someplace else in five minutes."

She nodded, but still didn't move. "Why are you doing this for me?"

"Don't ask me that," he said. It was not a question he wanted to even think about. Whatever answer he might have, this *had* to be a one-time thing.

Until it happens again, a voice in the back of his head countered.

He looked at his watch. "Mila, please."

"Right, right. Of course. Sorry." She pointed out the back window toward the trunk. "My bag."

"No bag."

"But—"

"No bag. Everything new. Your cell phone, too. Leave it here."

Looking shattered, she pulled out her phone and handed it to Quinn. He immediately removed the battery, pulled out the

SIM card, and snapped it in half.

"God, I can't believe this. All because of that stupid—" She stopped herself, then opened the door. "Thank you. For…my life, I guess, or whatever life I'm going to have."

He nodded, but kept his mouth shut. His words would only prolong their parting and cut into valuable time.

As soon as she shut the door, he dropped the car into drive, and sped off. For a few seconds, he could see her through his rearview mirror, standing at the side of the road, watching him drive away, but when he looked up again, she was gone.

Moving to the next item on his itinerary, he pulled out his phone.

"Nine-one-one operator. What's your emergency?" a female voice asked.

"I have passenger who collapse in seat," Quinn said, using a flawless Russian accent. "I think she not breathing."

"What is your location, sir?"

"I driving now. I pick her up at airport, suppose to take to Planet Hollywood. But go for hospital now, yes?"

"Are you close to a hospital?"

"Yes. Think only a few minutes."

"Which one?"

"I don't know what is called."

"Valley Hospital, sir?"

"Maybe. I don't know."

"Okay. No problem. Do you know your passenger's name?"

"Yes, uh, hold on." He let a few seconds pass. "Ms. Reese. Is only name I was given."

"Where exactly are you? I can have an ambulance meet you."

"No, no. Better if I drive. Faster."

"Sir, please. Where are you?"

"I drive. I—"

He cut off the connection, and hoped the message would get through.

QUINN'S PHONE RANG seconds after he exited the elevator on the eighth floor of the Planet Hollywood Hotel. He glanced at his watch. Two minutes to eight o'clock. He accepted the call.

"Yes?"

"Something's definitely wrong," Jergins said.

Quinn reached the door to his room, but paused outside, not wanting Jergins to overhear the sound of the lock opening. "What's going on?"

"The target's disappeared."

"What do you mean, 'disappeared'?"

"Kovacs's spotter was following the car she was in, but he lost her. If she was coming here, she should have arrived by now."

"It's just eight now," Quinn said. "Could be she's just running a minute or two late. Maybe she stopped to get something to eat."

"I don't like when plans don't go as scheduled."

Then I'm surprised you've lasted in the business as long as you have, Quinn thought. "So should I just sit tight, or what?"

"I need you to do a sweep."

In a less stressful situation, Quinn might have smiled. While it was the next step Jergins should have taken, there'd been no way to know for sure if the team leader would follow standard protocol.

A sweep, in this sense, meant a rapid check of local emergency services in the event someone didn't show up where they were supposed to. Accidents happened, not just in the civilian world, but in the spy world, too. It was always best to check every possibility. This particular kind of sweep, though seldom used, was the responsibility of the cleaner.

"Sure," Quinn said. "Ten minutes, maybe less."

"Less is better." Jergins told him, and hung up.

Quinn let himself into his room. On his phone, he brought up the list of law enforcement and medical facility numbers that was always prepared before the start of a job, and began making calls. It was for appearance's sake only. He already knew what he was going to tell Jergins, but it was important to create a history in case someone checked later.

Exactly nine and a half minutes later, Quinn called Jergins back.

"Anything?" Jergins asked. "She's not here yet."

"She's not going to show, either."

A pause. "What did you find?"

"At about ten to eight, a nine-one-one operator received a call from a limo driver saying he had a passenger who suddenly became unconscious. A woman he'd picked up at the airport named Reese."

"Son of a bitch."

There were two ways Quinn could go at this point. He decided on the riskier move, because, if it worked, it would be the better choice in the long run. "My first thought was that she'd found out what we had planned, and was trying to cover her tracks while she got away."

Though Jergins said nothing, Quinn was sure he'd been thinking along similar lines.

"I called the hospital where the driver would have probably taken her," Quinn went on. "I was pretty sure she wouldn't be there, but I was wrong."

"She *is* there?"

"In a way."

"What's that mean?"

"Mila's dead."

A second of thick silence. "I don't believe it."

It wasn't the response Quinn hoped for, but the one he expected. "I'm not convinced, either. I'm going over there to see for myself as soon as I hang up."

"Good. Call me the moment you're standing next to her body, *if* it's really there. Maybe Kovacs should go with you in case she's alive and in the vicinity."

"If she is, I doubt she'll be anywhere near the hospital. It'll also be easier for me to find out anything if I'm alone."

"Fine. Call as soon as you know anything."

CHAPTER
THIRTY THREE

LAZIO REGION, ITALY

GIVEN WHAT NATE could see with the light of his cell phone, the emergency escape tunnel was not in great shape.

Roots pushed through the space between the boards that lined the ceiling and walls, boards that, because of obvious water damage, looked liked they were lucky to still be intact. If the builders had really wanted this to be permanent, they should have enclosed the tunnel in walls of concrete or stone.

"Thick one up here," Orlando called from the front of the line. She pointed at a substantial-looking root sticking down a few inches.

One by one they ducked under the root.

"Door!" Orlando called out after another sixty feet.

They crowded together, one after another. The door was in the ceiling. Another hatch. Where it led, there was no way to know.

"I'll go first," Nate said.

He could see that Orlando had a different idea, but he gave her a look meant to remind her he was in charge, and she kept her thoughts to herself.

The tunnel went on for an additional five feet beyond the hatch. Orlando, Mila, and Daeng squeezed into the space so that Nate could get underneath the exit. There was a chain mounted to the bottom that ran halfway across the hatch. At the end was a metal handle.

Nate grabbed it and pulled until the rod holding the door in place moved free. He then put his hands on the bottom of the door and pushed it open enough so he could look out.

What he saw was unexpected.

"WHY THE HELL haven't you been answering your phone?" Peter asked.

"I've been a little preoccupied," Quinn said.

"I heard you'd been shot."

"Oh, you did, did you?"

"I assume you're all right."

The three men approaching from the house were getting closer. Within seconds they'd notice the two lying on the ground in front of the car.

"Fine enough. Can you hold for a moment?"

"What? I—"

Quinn touched the hold button with his thumb. "Tell your men to join their friends on the ground," he told Michaels.

Instead of relaying the order, Michaels said, "Why? You're not going to shoot me."

Though the other man couldn't see his face, Quinn smirked. "You're probably right, but are you absolutely sure? Your people shot me, after all."

"You were somewhere you weren't supposed to be."

"That's a matter of opinion. Tell your men to get on the ground."

With reluctance, Michaels repeated the instructions to his team.

The men took a moment, but all complied. Though most of Michaels's team was now lying in the grass, Quinn noticed a couple were missing. "Where are the others?"

"What others?"

Quinn jabbed the gun into the operative's head. "There were five by the house. Only three came back."

"Go ahead and pull the trigger."

Instead of taking Michaels up on the suggestion, Quinn took the call off hold. "Let me ask you, Peter. Any thoughts on who might have shot me?"

"I'm not going to bullshit you, Quinn. The team who shot

you is working for me."

"So, in effect, *you* shot me."

"If I'd known you were going to be there," Peter said with controlled anger, "I would have told them *not* to shoot. What the hell were you doing there in the first place?"

Fair question. "Looking for the girl."

"You knew she was alive before all this started, didn't you?"

Another fair question, but one Quinn wasn't ready to answer. Not yet. "I'm actually in the middle of a situation here that you're in a perfect position to handle."

"What are you talking about?"

Quinn tapped the gun against Michaels's ear. "Say hi."

Michaels remained silent.

Quinn tapped again. "Do it."

"Peter, it's Michaels."

Silence from the other end of the line. When Peter finally spoke, his voice was guarded. "What exactly is going on there?"

"At the moment, not much of anything," Quinn said. "I've got a gun to the back of your man's head here, and most of his people spread out on the ground around us."

"Dead?"

"No," Quinn scoffed. "Who do you think I am?"

"I'm beginning to wonder. So why are you pointing a gun at Michaels?"

"Because he and his men were shooting at my friends."

"I had no idea that's who was in there," Michaels said.

"In where?" Peter asked.

"They have this nifty building full of detention cells," Quinn told him. "My friends just happened to be taking a look inside."

"Quinn, what are you and your *friends* even doing there?"

"I believe I already told you the answer to that."

"Son of a bitch! This is a disaster. Why couldn't you have—"

"Drop it!" a voice called out from behind Quinn, drowning out whatever else Peter had to say.

Quinn glanced over his shoulder. The two missing men were standing a couple dozen feet away, their guns trained on him.

"I said, drop it," the one on the left said.

But they weren't the only ones back there.

"I'm afraid that's not going to happen, gentlemen," Nate said.

He, Daeng, and Orlando were another ten feet behind the men, also holding guns. A little farther back and off to the side was Mila.

After a brief hesitation, Michaels's men dropped their guns and raised their hands.

"Five paces to your right, then on the ground like everyone else," Nate said.

The men walked off the paces, and lay down.

"Everyone all right?" Quinn asked.

"We're all good," Nate told him.

"Could have sworn you were supposed to get in and out without, you know, any of these people knowing."

"Yeah, well, uh…yeah," Nate said. "We'll do better next time."

As Nate and the others walked over, Quinn lowered his gun, turned Michaels around, and motioned for him to lean against the car.

Quinn glanced at Mila. "You okay?"

She nodded.

"They treat you all right?"

Another nod.

"No rough stuff?"

"No."

"What the hell's going on?" Peter asked.

"Just gathering everyone together," Quinn told him. "More cozy that way."

"By everyone, do you mean…?"

"I mean *everyone*, Peter."

"You and I need to talk," Peter said. "Can you take me off this damn speaker?"

"Tell your friend Michaels and his team to behave, and I might be able to do that."

"No one shoots anybody," Peter's voice boomed. "No knives. No fighting. No sucker punches. No violence at all. That goes for *both* sides. Am I clear?"

"Clear by me," Quinn said.

"Of course," Michaels replied, his tone not nearly as upbeat as Quinn's.

"Happy now?" Peter asked.

QUINN WALKED TOWARD the trees at the base of the hill. Once he was out of earshot of the others, he said, "All right, we're alone."

"This could not be a bigger mess," Peter said.

"I beg to differ. So far I'm the only one who's been shot."

"I'm not just talking about what's going on there. I'm talking about *everything*! Starting way back in Las Vegas in 2006. *That* assignment should have been a no-brainer. You want to tell me why it wasn't? And why Mila Voss didn't end up buried in the desert somewhere?"

"It's complicated."

"You can say that again." There was a long pause, then Peter went on. "I've got some pretty powerful players breathing down my neck to close this as quickly and quietly as possible. The only thing they know about your involvement is what you told me initially. That you disposed of a body you thought was hers at the time."

"I said I disposed of the body I was given."

"Word games, Quinn. You led me to believe it was Mila."

Quinn made no reply, well aware of the misdirection he'd perpetrated.

"When you started popping up, I knew there was more to this than what I was told back then. I didn't want to, but I started digging. My God, what she stumbled into."

"I don't know what she stumbled into," Quinn said. "I never asked."

"You don't know? Then why did you help her get away?"

Quinn thought about saying nothing again, knowing that the truth would, rightly or wrongly, bring into question every job he'd ever worked on. But it didn't seem to matter. His future in the business was cloudy at best anyway. And if they were practicing no bullshit...

"She was a friend," he said. "I couldn't be a part of her

death."

"A friend?"

Friendships were few and far between in the business, because of the potential for exactly the kind of conflict of interest Quinn had found himself in with Mila.

When it became obvious Quinn wasn't going to add anything, Peter said, "Well, your *friend* unintentionally came across some knowledge she would have been much better off not knowing. Hell, I'm more than a little worried about what *I* now know."

Quinn didn't want to ask, but he had no choice. "What knowledge?"

After Peter told him, Quinn felt numb. "That's not possible."

"I thought the same thing, but apparently it is."

"And you're sure who's behind it?"

"I wish I wasn't."

Quinn looked up at the sky, his eyes not even registering the stars. Calling this a mess was the very definition of understatement. "They're not going to stop until they find her."

"No, they're not."

"I need to get her safe."

"Good luck with that."

"You're working with them, Peter. You could provide some misdirection for us."

Peter snorted. "I could, but it's not likely to be very effective. I'm sure they're already close to replacing me as it is. I won't be able to hide what happened there in Italy for very long. Once they find out, I'll be lucky if they don't put a bullet in *my* head."

"Then you need to make sure they don't find out."

"What I *should* be doing is sending in a backup team for the job Michaels is apparently incapable of completing."

"But you won't. You know this whole thing stinks of rot."

"Doesn't matter. Our job's not about right or wrong. Hell, there *is* no right or wrong."

"There's always right or wrong, Peter, and pretending there isn't doesn't change that."

Peter said nothing.

A dozen possible scenarios spun through Quinn's mind. Safe. Was that even possible?

"We're going to need your help," he said.

"You mean beside covering up what's happened there?" Peter asked.

"Yes."

PETER WANTS TO talk to you," Quinn said to Michaels as he returned to where everyone was waiting.

"Hello?" Michaels said once he had the phone.

Quinn waited patiently as Peter and Michaels talked. Mostly, the team leader was just listening, his expression at first angry, then confused. Every few seconds, his gaze would dart over to Quinn.

Finally, he held the phone back out. "Here."

Quinn took it and raised it to his ear. "Goodbye, Peter."

"Can you at least tell me what you're going to do?" Peter asked.

"Once I know, you'll get your instructions." Quinn hung up, and looked over at the vehicles parked in front of the burning house. "That SUV," he said to Michaels.

"What about it?"

"Who's got the keys?"

Michaels did not look happy as he reached into his pocket and extracted a set of keys. He peeled the largest one off the ring and tossed it to Quinn.

"Have a good day," Quinn said. He turned to his friends. "Let's go."

As they walked away from Michaels, several of the men on the ground scrambled for their guns and started to rise.

"Stand down!" Michaels ordered. "This project's been terminated."

CHAPTER
THIRTY FOUR

FRIDAY, MAY 12th, 2006, 8:31 PM
LAS VEGAS, NEVADA

QUINN DROVE TO Valley Hospital as fast as traffic would allow. There, he used a forged FBI badge to get beyond the waiting area and into the main part of the facility.

Finding an empty office at this time on a Friday night wasn't difficult. Once inside, he located a computer. Then, using a little of what he'd paid good money to learn, he bypassed the standard security and gained access to the hospital's system. Once he was in, he created a record for one Naomi Reese, noting that she had been dead on arrival at the ER. He listed the preliminary cause of death as heart failure, and used a line of code from his own private server to schedule the record to appear in the system the follow morning. When it did show up, it would be buried so deeply that it'd only be found if someone was looking for it specifically. There was at least a ninety-five-percent chance no one at the hospital would ever even set eyes on it.

As soon as he was done and the computer was back in its original condition, he called Jergins.

"I'm sta—"

"She's just been spotted," Jergins cut him off. "Over at the Manhattan Hotel."

The blood drained from Quinn's face. "What are you talking about?"

"Kovacs's man found her. They're converging there now."

"That's...not possible. I'm standing next to the body right now. She's dead." There was a big part of him that knew he should have kept his mouth shut. These were words that could easily come back and haunt him, but he was already committed so he couldn't back down now.

"Are you sure?"

"Yes. I'm looking at her now," Quinn said, his gaze fixed on nothing. "I'll have her out before daybreak, and dispose of her as planned."

"Then who the hell did they see?"

"I have no idea, but I guarantee you it's *not* the target."

Jergins swore under his breath. "I'll send them a message, but if they're chasing this other person, it'll probably be awhile before they get it. Hopefully they'll back off when they realize it's not her." He paused. "You've got her. I'm declaring end of mission and bugging out."

"See you next time," Quinn said.

"Hope it goes smoother for you than it has for the rest of us."

"Yeah. Me, too."

QUINN LEFT THE hospital, and drove to the Strip.

How in the world had they seen Mila? She should have been in the sub-basement safe room where no one would find her. *No one.*

He tried to reach Julien, but the call went straight to voice mail.

"Where are you?" he yelled, then hung up.

He knew for a fact that he and Mila had reached the Manhattan unobserved. From there it should have been simple. In through the garage, downstairs, hide. Even if, God forbid, she had shown her face in the casino for a reason Quinn couldn't possibly imagine, who would have seen her? The spotter should have been driving around lost while Kovacs was at Planet Hollywood.

He tried Julien again. Voice mail.

The only thing more frustrating than not being able to get through to his friend was the traffic, which had gone from bad to horrible.

He made a snap decision and pulled into the entrance for Caesar's Palace. Twenty feet in, he stopped along the side of the road and jumped out, leaving the engine still running. Horns blared at him, but he ignored them as he weaved through the cars trying to get to the hotel, and made his way to the sidewalk.

There, he turned south toward the Manhattan and ran.

CHAPTER
THIRTY FIVE

ITALY

THE QUICKEST WAY out of the country would have been to head straight back to Rome and catch the first flight available. It was also the most obvious choice, and therefore the first place someone trying to find out where they'd gone would check.

Perhaps Peter would keep a lid on things, but Quinn knew he'd be a fool to count on it. Not that Peter wasn't trustworthy. It was just that in this business, trust wasn't always a constant. Peter was obviously under considerable pressure, something he'd handled well in the past, but no matter how cool he remained as things pressed down on him, without the power and influence he used to have shielding him, his breaking point could be much easier to reach. There was just no way to tell, so it was best to be cautious.

As they neared the outskirts of Rome, Quinn leaned forward from the back where he was sitting with Orlando and Mila. "Go northeast," he said to Nate. "We're skipping Rome."

"Venice?" Nate asked.

Quinn nodded, pleased they were on the same wavelength.

"You're not going to Rome?" Mila asked as he settled back in the seat.

"No. Not safe."

"I don't care," she said. "I appreciate you setting me free, but you can let me out anywhere around here."

"No one's getting out."

"I have something I need to do!"

Quinn stared at her for a second, then looked forward without saying anything.

"I said, let me out!"

He didn't move.

"Dammit, Quinn! Let me the hell out!"

She tried to reach across him for the door. He pushed her back without looking. She then tried the same thing on Orlando's side, but Orlando's response was even rougher than Quinn's.

Mila fell back against the seat, panting heavily. "So, what? I go from one group holding me hostage to another? Is this because you're afraid that me showing up might get you killed?"

"Can I hit her?" Orlando asked.

"Not yet," Quinn said.

Mila looked around, exasperated. "Let me out!"

Again, she reached for the door next to Quinn. This time when he shoved her back, he leaned toward her, his face stopping a few inches in front of hers.

"Stop it," he said, his voice low but firm.

Her eyes narrowed. "I wish Julien were here to see this. He would never let you do this to me."

With a sudden jerk, the SUV pulled to the side of the road, and braked to a stop. Nate shoved the vehicle into park, and whipped around so he was looking straight at Mila.

"We all realize you had a pretty raw deal. But as I understand it, you wouldn't be breathing right now if it wasn't for what Quinn did. Twice, actually."

She glared at Nate.

"And let me tell you something about your friend Julien," Nate went on. "He would have *never* questioned anything Quinn did. He gave his life helping Quinn. Maybe you should think about that. Maybe what Quinn's doing right now is not so much motivated by his desire to help *you* as by his desire to repay his friend's sacrifice for him." He paused. "If there is anyone in the world I would want on my side, it's the guy sitting next to you."

He stared at her a moment longer, then put the car in drive, and pulled back onto the highway.

The rest of the car was silent. Even Mila sat unmoving, her

lips pressed together while the anger on her face faded away.

The only one who seemed unaffected was Daeng in the front passenger seat. His eyes were closed, as they'd been since not long after the group left the farmhouse, and his head was leaning against the door.

THE MEREST SUGGESTION of pink began coloring the eastern horizon as they continued on their way toward Venice. Since the incident at the side of the road, no one had said a word.

Eventually, Quinn had tried to fall asleep, but had failed miserably. Instead, he'd gone over and over the information Peter had given him about Mila's termination order in 2006. He was torn. Should he try to hide her again? If he did, this time would be different. The others would know she was still alive, and would do everything they could to find her. The only other choice would be to tackle them head-on as Mila seemed hell-bent on doing. It was something he couldn't fault her for. But how could it be done?

"I need to use a toilet," Mila said.

Quinn looked over.

"I really need to go. Please," she said.

He held her gaze for a moment, then nodded and said to Nate, "Wherever you can find a place to stop."

A few minutes later, Nate pulled into a petrol station that looked like it had just opened for the day. The attendant gave directions to the bathroom, and Mila, with Orlando tagging right behind her, headed off.

The stop finally pulled Daeng from his sleep. As Nate and Quinn stood silently near the pump, the half-Thai man climbed out of the car and stretched. When he dropped his arms, he smiled at the other two.

"I can drive if you want," he offered. "Give you a chance to sleep."

Nate shook his head. "Thanks, but it's not far now. Should be there within the hour."

"The offer's there if you change your mind."

The two women returned a few minutes later. Quinn gave Orlando a look, silently asking if there had been any problems.

THE DESTROYED

She shook her head so only he could see.

Soon, they were back on the highway heading toward Marco Polo Airport on the mainland, just north of Venice.

At first, it seemed as if the silence that had prevailed before would continue, but then Mila glanced at Quinn and said, "What…what happened to Julien?"

He thought about sugarcoating it for her, leaving out the details and just saying Julien had died in action. But Mila had worked in the business. She knew the harsh realities. The truth might have been difficult to hear, but she deserved that respect.

"He was shot."

"In the head?" she asked, her emotions hidden.

"In the chest."

Her head dipped. "Is that any better?"

"It doesn't matter."

"I'm sure he died right away," Nate said.

"How do you know that?"

"I was the one who found him."

"And couldn't you have stopped it from happening?"

"I said I found him, not that I was anywhere near him when it happened," Nate said, patiently. "I was with…"

"He was with my sister," Quinn finished.

Nate looked at Mila through the rearview mirror. "Without Julien's help, both Liz and I would be dead, too."

When she spoke, her voice was just above a whisper. "I don't know how to balance that. Julien's life for yours and…" She looked from Nate to Quinn. "Your sister's? I don't know if it's a fair trade-off."

Daeng leaned into the gap between the front seats. "There is no right answer to that, only ones that are skewed by how they affect those left behind."

"Your monkness is showing," Nate said.

"What the hell are you talking about? That's a direct quote from Mr. Archibald, my history teacher at Hollywood High."

"Smart guy," Orlando said.

Daeng grinned. "Yeah, he wasn't bad. For a teacher."

In the silence that followed, Mila seemed to be contemplating something. Finally, she nodded at Nate and said to Quinn, "Was he right? Are you trying to help me to pay back

Julien?"

"In part," he said, but it wasn't the only reason. As he'd told Peter, acting like there was no right or wrong didn't mean it was true.

"All right," she said. "Then what's the plan? How do you want to help me?"

"We can get you someplace safe," he said. "Where you can start again."

"No. Not an option. I haven't exposed myself like this just to forget about what I was doing and disappear again."

A part of him had hoped she would take his offer despite the fact it was a far-from-perfect solution, because he still had no idea how to solve her problems otherwise. "All right, then I guess we help you do what you want to do."

"How?" she asked.

He shifted in his seat so that he was facing her. "We can start with you telling us why all this is happening in the first place. Before you showed up in Tanzania. Before Vegas." While Peter had given him much of the details, Mila would come at it from a different perspective. And this way the others would know exactly what was going on, too.

Mila held his gaze for several seconds, then nodded. "Sometimes my clients would have me piggyback on someone else's travel arrangements. A month before Vegas, I was on a run in Atlanta, where that's what happened."

THE BEGINNING OF her story about her trip to Portugal was typical enough. A prescheduled flight going her way, and a client trying to save a few bucks. Quinn had had similar experiences himself.

The exception, of course, was the prisoner. While it wasn't unheard of that inmates would be moved out of the country, it *was* unusual. But these would always be foreign nationals, and more often than not they were being returned to their home country.

Where the story began to diverge from the norm was when Mila described her run for the toilet, and the prisoner's subsequent outburst. That, Quinn knew, was the moment a date with an assassin became a certainty in her future.

"When we arrived in Portugal, I was instructed to remain in my seat until after the others got off. It didn't take a lot of imagination to know that something wasn't right." She took a breath. "I had a concealed camera built into my bag. It was a security thing for me in case anything ever went wrong. Maybe I shouldn't have turned it on before the prisoner left, but I did. I caught him yelling his name again and that he was an American citizen. I also caught him getting shocked again."

"You *recorded* it?" Quinn asked, surprised.

"Yeah. That's why I was at Julien's. He'd hidden a copy of the footage there for me, in case I ever needed it."

Daeng pulled an envelope out of his pocket and held it back to her. "This?"

She grabbed it from him. "Yes. Thank you. Did you…"

"No one's looked at it," Nate said.

She nodded.

"Julien knew about this, then," Quinn said.

"I'd hinted to him about it before Vegas, but after, I told him the whole thing."

"You mean when he met up with you in Guaymas?"

She shook her head. "I mean after that. He visited me when he could. But no one else knew. It was never a problem."

Only by sheer luck, Quinn thought. If Julien had ever been followed and Mila discovered, the three of them might have already been spending eternity in unmarked graves. He gave himself a second to let his anger pass, and refocused on the problem at hand.

"The prisoner. You said he yelled out his name. Do you remember what it was?"

"I've never forgotten. Thomas Gorman."

It was the same name Peter had told him.

Orlando's brow furrowed. "*Thomas* Gorman? Are you sure?"

"Yes," Mila said. "I never saw his face, though. Only heard his voice."

"And?"

Mila shrugged. "It sounded like him."

"Because it was him," Quinn said.

"How do you kn—" Orlando stopped herself. "Peter?"

Quinn nodded.

"Do you know what this could mean?"

He nodded again.

"This Gorman person," Daeng said. "He's important?"

"Was," Orlando said. "Several years ago. He was a commentator on Prime Cable News. Had his own show."

"I remember him," Nate said. "Isn't he the one who died in that boating accident in…Virginia, or somewhere like that?"

"Hilton Head Island," Orlando corrected him. "South Carolina."

"Right."

Quinn looked at Mila. "On the same day as the flight to Portugal, right?"

"Seven hours prior to the flight," she said.

"And Hilton Head would have been less than a five-hour drive from Atlanta," Orlando added.

"More like four hours to the private airfield," Mila corrected her.

"You checked?" Quinn asked.

She nodded. "After I finished my assignment and returned to the States, I'd all but convinced myself the prisoner had just thrown out the name because he'd heard it on TV or something. But then I learned about the boating accident. I mean, how could I not? It was all over the news." She paused. "It was impossible not to make the connection. I knew I had to check. An American citizen who'd just been reported dead, being flown *out* of the country as a prisoner? Correct me if I'm wrong, but that's not something we do."

"You're right," Quinn said. "It's not."

"I looked into the accident first," she said. "The reports stated Gorman was out sailing with a friend, got a little drunk, and fell overboard. Before his friend could get turned around, Gorman drifted into the path of another vessel, and, well, death by speedboat."

"Not exactly the way I'd choose to go," Nate said.

She went on as if she hadn't heard him. "The body was mangled, the face unrecognizable, but there was no autopsy done, also no DNA, no dental check, and no prints. ID was based on Gorman's friend witnessing the event."

"But it wasn't Gorman," Quinn said.

"No. And I'm sure there was no accident, either. The friend's name was Ed Zahn. Supposedly, he was a college buddy who worked for a brokerage firm in DC. The day after the funeral he was transferred to an office in Madrid."

"Did you look into him?"

She nodded. "Both in DC *and* Madrid. Had to be really quiet about it. I wasn't sure what might happen if someone found out what I was doing." She frowned. "Except I guess they did find out."

"This Zahn guy. I'm betting he doesn't exist."

"I don't know if he does or doesn't, but no one I contacted at either office had ever heard of him."

"What I don't get is why," Nate said. "I mean, sure, Gorman was probably a pain in the ass sometimes, but—"

"Probably?" Orlando said. "Did you ever watch his show?"

"Once or twice, maybe."

"He was a nutjob like all those extremist commentators. Both sides have them. Gorman loved digging into what he considered governmental waste and reporting on it whether he had proof or not," she said. "*And* he was not a fan of the former administration."

"So he pissed them off enough that they faked his death and flew him out of the country? No way."

"I agree," Quinn said. "The administration might not have liked the things he was saying, but putting up with assholes is a rite of passage. Actively silencing him was a line they would have never crossed." He looked at Mila. "But you're not talking about the administration, are you? Not specifically. Someone *within* the government who thought it was his duty to take care of what he perceived as a problem?"

She stared at him in disbelief. "You know?"

"Who's she talking about?" Orlando asked.

"At the time, the guy was the deputy secretary of defense. Christopher Mygatt."

Orlando and Nate looked stunned.

"Is that right?" Nate asked Mila.

"Yes," she said. "I mean, I'm sure it is. That's what I've been doing—looking for proof."

"He left the administration a year after the Vegas operation," Quinn explained. "One of the senators from his home state had died of a heart attack, and Mygatt was appointed by the governor to fill the seat. The year after that, he won the position outright in a special election. Last year, Mygatt left the senate to become his political party's chairman. He's been able to manipulate things and help sway the direction the primary elections have gone. He's tight with the guy who looks like he'll get the party's presidential nom, so tight that Mygatt will be filling a very high-ranking position if his guy wins the general election. The rumor is vice president."

Mila shook her head. "I think it's something else. There was a magazine article. It broke down the possible appointees each candidate might make. It said, according to a source, Mygatt has been quietly pushing to be made director of the CIA."

"You've got to be kidding me," Orlando said.

Quinn shook his head. "It's exactly what Peter said."

Mila looked down for a moment, then glanced at Quinn. "How sure is Peter?"

"There's no question."

"So I was right." Her words were but a stunned whisper.

"This is why you came out of hiding, isn't it?" he asked.

"If…if I were able to prove to myself he was the one behind everything, then I'd have no choice but to do something about it."

"Hold on," Nate said. "You're saying someone who eliminated an American citizen, just because the guy was a pain in the ass, might be put in charge of the CIA?"

"That's exactly what I'm saying," Mila said.

"I can't imagine he was on that Portugal flight with you," Nate said, glancing at her in the mirror. "What put you on his trail in the first place?"

"Las Vegas," she said.

CHAPTER
THIRTY SIX

MILA'S LIFE SINCE becoming a courier had been an eventful one. Sure, the majority of jobs were easy, just like handling a package for FedEx, but on occasion, she'd find herself in situations that were not what anyone would consider safe.

Twice she had traveled to Baghdad, where she faced constant threats from car bombs and insurgents. Then there was the trip into Rocinha, one of Rio de Janeiro's infamous favelas, where she'd had a gun pointed at her four times. There were other trips that also left their marks on her, but none until now had ever come close to destroying her.

This time, as she huddled in the darkened room two floors beneath the casino, she felt a level of fear unlike any she'd ever experienced. Before it had always been about getting caught in situations due to her location. It had never been about her.

Now it was.

There was an assassin in this very city, here for one reason only. To kill her.

She had no idea how often assassins failed at their missions, but she guessed the percentage had to be infinitesimal. If Julien and Quinn hadn't intercepted her, her chances of living until the end of the day would have been zero, but the threat wasn't over. While her odds of survival had increased, she was unwilling to believe they had come even close to tipping in her favor.

It hadn't occurred to her until after Quinn had dropped her off that she should have asked for a weapon. Not that she could have done much with it the way her hands were shaking, but at least it would have given her a small sense of security.

When she'd entered the room, she had found a box just inside the door that contained a bottle of water, a flashlight, and a cell phone. She knew better than to make any calls. The phone's only purpose would be if Julien or Quinn needed to contact her. As for the flashlight, she'd only used it to find a place to sit. After that, she turned it off to save the battery.

The room was not large. There were built-in shelves along the two sides, and several pipes traversing the back. She had tucked herself between a couple of pipes, and drawn her knees up to her chest.

She wasn't sure how long she had been there. She thought about checking the time on the phone, but what did it matter? Her life was moment by moment now. Each second that passed was like the second before, forever repeating.

Though she could see nothing in the darkness, she closed her eyes and tried to set her mind adrift. A memory filled the void. She was young, maybe five or six. Beside her stood her father, his hand holding hers as they crossed a road. When she looked up at him, he smiled. His lips moved, and she remembered what he said.

"Always look both ways, sweetie. You don't want to get hurt, do you?"

No, Daddy, I don't.

Once they reached the other side, her father and the street faded away, and the hell of the real world pushed back in.

She tried to recall it, but the memory was full of holes this time, and when she looked up at her dad's face, it refused to come into focus.

Again it faded, and again she tried to bring it back, but this time it wouldn't come at all.

The handle on the door rattled.

She pushed back against the wall, and tried to turn on the flashlight, but it slipped from her grasp and fell on the floor.

As the door opened, she steeled herself for the inevitable.

"Thank God! I was sure for some reason you had not made it."

Julien!

She jumped to her feet and ran to him. He encircled her with his large arms, enveloping her in a hug that she'd started to think she'd never experience again. Far sooner than she wanted, he took a step back.

"Come," he said. "We have to go."

He grabbed her hand and led her out of the room.

"Where?"

"South."

"And then?"

"That is something we'll worry about later. Right now, let's just concentrate on getting you out of here."

He guided her through a different door than the one she'd used to enter the sub-basement, and into a stairwell that took them all the way up to ground level. As they exited, the sounds of bells and bongs and music and voices flooded over them.

"Stay right next to me," Julien told her. "We'll go through the casino, and out the other side, then use the pedestrian bridge to cross the street. I have a car over there."

Without waiting for her to respond, he began walking.

The air in the casino was ripe with cigarette smoke. Mila had to blink several times to keep her eyes from stinging. Rows and rows of slot machines ringed the gambling area. Beyond, radiating out from a central circular bar, were the table games. While there were plenty of open stools at the slots, most of the tables were filled with people enjoying another Friday night in Sin City.

Once more, Mila's training kicked in, and she donned the personality of someone who belonged there. Julien, too, was acting the part—laughing, exchanging a few quick observations, and generally looking like he was trying to decide which game to attempt first. But both were also scanning the crowd, looking for threats.

"Let's eat first, *oui*?" Julien said, his voice light. "Then I'd like to maybe try a little blackjack."

Mila frowned. "You always lose at blackjack." While it was part of her act, it was also the truth.

"I'm feeling very lucky today."

A laugh passed over her lips. "Like I haven't heard that before."

She expected him to come back with a witty retort, but instead his grip on her hand tightened. She glanced at him. He was looking toward the front of the casino, so she followed his gaze.

The room was actually a few stories high. At the front, a second level, reached by an escalator from the casino floor, ran partially around the edge. She could see a few stores up there, mostly places to get something to eat.

"What is it?" she asked.

He stared for a moment longer, then whipped her around and started walking quickly back in the direction they'd come. "Hurry. Hurry."

"What? What did you see?"

"The spotter," he whispered. "The one who tried to follow you from the airport."

It suddenly felt as if her whole body was pulling in on itself. "Are you sure?"

"I'm sure." He glanced over his shoulder. *"Merde!"*

Mila started to turn, but Julien yanked on her arm, pulling her forward.

"He's seen us," he said.

"No."

"Come. We'll go back downstairs. It will be safe there."

They hurried through the casino back to the hidden door. Once inside the stairwell, they dropped all pretense that nothing was wrong, and raced to the bottom level.

Mila exited the stairwell first, and paused just beyond the door, not remembering which way to go.

"To the right!" Julien yelled.

As she turned, he moved past her, and led her to the safe room.

"Get in," he said, after he opened the door.

She scooted by him, but when he didn't join her, she said, "Julien?"

"Just stay quiet. I'm going to go check."

"No. Stay here with me."

"I'll be right back."

He shut the door, not letting her say anything else. She stared after him for a second, then settled on the floor. The flashlight she'd dropped earlier was lying nearby as if it had been waiting for her return. She picked it up, thinking it wasn't exactly the best weapon in the world, but it was all she had.

LATER, JULIEN TOLD her what had happened after he left.

He'd headed straight for the stairwell, then propped open the door and stood at the bottom, listening for anyone who might be coming down. For the first couple of minutes, there was nothing, then he heard the door at the top open.

Given the hundreds, or perhaps thousands, of employees working at the hotel at that very moment, there was no way to know for sure who it might've been, but this particular set of stairs was supposed to be seldom used.

He slipped inside, and quietly shut the door behind him.

There were footsteps heading down. A single pair. If it were an employee, Julien would have expected to hear either the rapid clomps of someone in a hurry, or the leisurely yet purposeful taps of a person trying to waste a little time between tasks.

These steps were light, with no rhythm to them at all.

Step. Stop. Step-step. Stop. Step. Step. Step. Stop.

When the footsteps reached the landing for the first basement level, they paused. For a long moment, nothing happened, then the door opened. Noise from the considerably more active floor leaked into the stairwell for about five seconds before being cut off by the door closing again.

Steps once more. Heading toward the bottom now. As soon as they reached the midway landing, the person would be able to see Julien.

Careful not to make a sound, Julien let himself back out into the lower basement, then concealed himself around the side of a humming metal container that was riveted to the floor. Keeping as close to the front end as possible, he listened for the door.

Though he heard nothing, he suddenly had the sense he was no longer alone. Whoever had been in the stairwell had come into the basement without making a sound.

But where were they? Just inside the door? Already moving off? Where?

Merde!

Merde, merde, merde, merde, merde!

Reluctantly, he leaned forward to take a look.

The spotter was there, all right. Only he wasn't just inside the door, or walking away. He was standing three feet on the other side of the metal box, looking right at Julien.

Julien pulled his head back as the man's fist flew out. It glanced off the top of his ear but did no real damage.

There was no exit behind him, just a narrow space hemmed in by the metal containers. Heading in that direction would surely get him killed. He held his position until he caught the first glimpse of movement, then he rushed forward, charging like a bull.

The spotter tried to get out of the way, but Julien caught him in the ribs, lifting him off his feet and slamming him against the wall. More times than not, that would have been all it took. Julien's bulk and strength rendered most of his opponents useless.

To his dismay, the spotter was not one of those people. Even as the man's body was being smashed between the wall and Julien's shoulder, he grabbed Julien's long hair and pulled it back as hard as he could. With a groan, Julien was forced to tilt his head back just enough so that the spotter could whack Julien in the cheek.

As Julien twisted away in pain, the man pushed in the other direction and broke free.

Julien reached out, trying to grab the back of the spotter's shirt, but missed. The man ran down the narrow hallway, and Julien took off after him. The guy was smaller and quicker on his feet, so the gap between them increased.

Desperate, Julien burst forward, attempting to regain lost ground. When he reached a point only a few feet back, he grasped at the man again, this time latching on to the guy's shirt.

As the spotter tried to turn down an intersecting corridor, Julien yanked on his shirt, pulling him backward.

Chaos took over as the two men collided, their feet

tangling together. With a loud thud, they crashed to the floor.

Since Julien was on the bottom, he hit hardest, his head bouncing off the concrete. In a daze, he barely felt it when the spotter hit him in the head.

The second hit, he didn't feel at all.

CHAPTER
THIRTY SEVEN

JULIEN, WHERE THE hell are you? Mila wondered.

He'd said he would be right back, but ten minutes was not what she considered *right back*.

What should she do? Stay? See if he needed help? Make a run for it?

What?

Three more minutes, she decided. *Three more minutes and if he's not back, I'll go look for him.*

And if you don't find him?

She stared into the darkness, and whispered, "Then I run."

She began counting off the seconds in her head, each tick bringing growing certainty that something horrible had happened to him.

Sixty-eight. Sixty-nine. Seventy.

That he might even be dead.

One twenty-nine. One thirty. One thirty-one. One thirty-two.

That she would never see him again.

One forty-five. One forty—

A foot scraped against the concrete right outside the door.

"Julien?" Her lips moved, but no sound left her throat.

The knob turned slowly until it could move no more, and the door opened.

Squinting at the entrance, she instantly knew it wasn't Julien. There were two people, and neither the shape of her old boyfriend.

"Huh," one of the shadows said, surprised but not surprised.

THE DESTROYED

As they moved into the room, one of them leaned over, flicked on the light, and shut the door.

She had never seen these men before, but she was sure they were her assassins. The shorter of the two hung back closer to the door. The tall one kept coming until he was only a few feet away from Mila. As he looked down at her, he smirked.

"Mila Voss," he said. "It's a pleasure to meet you."

PAIN SHOT THROUGH Julien's head as he tried to open his eyes. He had no sense of where he was or what had happened. For all he knew he'd drunk far too much and was now paying the price. But the bed he was lying on was hard, hard as...

Concrete.

His eyes opened all the way. He looked up. He was in the narrow space between two large metal boxes.

A factory? What was I doing?

With panic, it all came rushing back. Las Vegas. The hotel basement. The spotter he'd fought.

Mila!

As he jumped to his feet, his head began to swim and everything went slightly out of focus. He jammed his hands against the metal walls, and willed his balance to return.

Mila.

He staggered out from between the boxes and found himself in the same corridor where the fight had taken place. Apparently after the other man had pounded him into unconsciousness, he'd dragged Julien out of the way.

Julien headed for the closet where he'd left Mila. Small steps at first, but growing longer and faster with each stride. He ignored the pounding in his head, and squeezed his eyes so that his vision was clearer.

He took one wrong turn, but quickly corrected himself.

Though in his gut he felt he might already be too late, his head refused to even consider it.

He *had* to get to her.

He started to run.

"I BELIEVE YOUR instructions stated that you were to go to Planet Hollywood," the tall one said. "This isn't Planet

Hollywood."

Mila kept her mouth shut.

As the man reached under his suit jacket, she could see a gun in the holster under his arm, but instead of grabbing it, he pulled out a small box from his pocket. "I can understand your reluctance, especially since you seem to have realized what was waiting for you." He opened the box. Inside was a ring. He pulled it out and slipped it on his left index finger. "I am curious, though, how did you find out? It wasn't until you arrived here, was it? Otherwise you would have never come."

He looked at her, waiting, but again she said nothing.

"I'm guessing it was your friend who was down here with you. The one who got into a fight with my colleague here? He didn't win, by the way. He's the one who warned you, isn't he?"

Julien. Oh, God. Is he...is he...

"Or was it the one in the car that picked you up at the airport? I know they weren't the same person. The one who lost the fight had been following Conner from the airport." As he gestured to the man behind him, she noticed that something was sticking out of the bottom of the ring that looked very much like a needle. "Your friend thought he was being very tricky and that Conner didn't see him. Fortunately for us, that wasn't the case."

She wanted to yell. She wanted to kick this guy in the balls. She wanted to rip his tongue out and shove it down his throat. But she stayed where she was and kept her mouth shut.

"How did your contacts know what was going to happen to you? The people who hired me are going to be very curious. So perhaps you'd like to just tell me and make everything easy."

Just get it over with, you son of a bitch, she thought.

He crouched down so that he was almost level with her. "Mila, you have tangled with a *very* powerful man. I have no idea what it is you did, and I don't care. I only know that the client wants you dead, and it's my job to carry out that sentence. I can do it quick and easy." He held up his hand and flashed the needle attached to the inside of the ring. "You'll only feel a pinch, nothing more. One second you're here, and the next...well, who knows? I can also make it painful and long." He patted the lump under his jacket where his gun was. "Is that how you want to leave this world? I wouldn't think so." He smiled. "Just tell me how your friends found out. You do that, and you'll move painlessly to the other side."

Across the room, the doorknob started to turn. Mila did everything she could to keep any reaction off her face.

"You...you were right," she blurted out, wanting to fill the room with noise. "I...I didn't know before I got here. I thought this was just a regular run."

The assassin smiled. "Of course you did."

The knob stopped.

"The man who was down here with me. I don't know him. He's not the one who told me."

The door moved inward a fraction of an inch.

"Who was it, then?"

"The man who picked me up at the airport. The driver."

"And who is he?"

She leaned forward slightly, tensing the muscles in her legs. "Someone I've worked with before. A...a friend."

"A name, Mila."

Out of the corner of her eye, she could see the door clear the frame. This was her only chance.

"Not in this life, asshole!" she yelled as she launched herself at the assassin.

She grabbed the wrist of the hand wearing the ring a split second before her shoulder slammed into his chest. He fell back onto the floor with her on top. With all her strength, she pinned the wrist down with one hand and went for his gun with the other, but he was already pulling the pistol out. She latched on to the barrel and pointed it away from her, then slipped her hand down over his as the assassin pulled the trigger.

The bullet ricocheted off the wall into the floor less than a foot away from her leg.

"Let go of me, bitch!"

He tried to push her off, but she shoved him back to the floor. She knew she wouldn't be able to keep him down much longer. Though she was strong for her size, he was stronger.

She glanced toward the front of the room. Julien stood just inside, one arm wrapped around the other man's neck, the other around the man's torso. He leaned backward, lifting the spotter into the air so the guy's feet were dangling. The man twisted and turned, trying to break free as he struggled to breathe.

The assassin pushed her again.

This time she tumbled off, but was able to keep her hand on the gun.

The assassin grinned as he whipped his other hand around, palm open. She could see the needle coming straight at her, so she slapped his arm away, and rolled to the side. The move, she immediately realized, both saved her and condemned her to death as she lost her grip on the gun.

"Long and painful, then," the assassin said as he rose to his feet.

THE MAN IN Julien's arms continued to squirm, moving just enough to get gasps of air here and there and remain conscious. Julien tried to squeeze harder, but his bulk prevented him from completely sealing his arm against the man's neck, and causing the bastard to pass out.

In the middle of the room, the other man pushed Mila to the side and tried to slap his other hand against her. Mila rolled out of the way, letting go of the gun.

There was no question what would happen next. The man was going to shoot her.

"Long and painful, then," the assassin said.

Still holding the spotter by the neck, Julien whipped the man's legs around and smacked them into the back of the gunman's head. He then tossed the guy at the assassin, and smashed into both of them, bringing them to the ground.

His first instinct was to grab the gun. What he got instead was the assassin's wrist. He slammed the man's hand against the floor over and over, trying to free the weapon.

"Julien! Watch out for the ring!" Mila called out.

The ring?

He almost reacted too late as the assassin's other hand arced toward him. At the last second he saw the needle and pushed the hand to his left, unintentionally guiding it into the spotter's shoulder.

The spotter gasped in surprise, then began to spasm before going limp.

The assassin tried to pull the gun free from Julien, but he lost his grip and it skittered across the floor away from both of them. He brought his ringed hand back, obviously trying once more to stick Julien.

Boom!

The top half of the assassin's hand blew apart, the ring gone.

He fell back, clutching his damaged hand to his chest and groaning in pain.

Julien twisted around and saw Mila standing a few feet away, holding the pistol. He pushed himself to his feet.

"Sorry," he told her. "I was delayed."

"You're here. That's all that matters."

"We need to go."

Mila didn't move.

"Someone might have heard the gunshot," he said.

"They'd have been here by now."

The assassin looked at her, trying to control the pain on his face. "We'll just keep coming after you," he said, forcing the words through clenched teeth. "You might as well give up now, because I *will* find you." As he took a deep breath, he glanced at Julien then back at her. "I'll tell you what. Our instructions were to avoid any extra bodies. You give yourself up; your friend gets a pass. How about it?"

Julien knew Quinn's plan was no longer viable. How could they fake her death now? The man who'd been sent to kill her knew the truth, and soon those who ordered the termination would know, too. The best they'd be able to do was knock the guy out, lock him up here, then get the hell out of Vegas.

"How about this?" Mila said.

MILA TOOK A step closer to the assassin. "You tell me who wants me dead, and maybe I'll let *you* live."

"How should I know? I'm just the hired help."

"You said I tangled with a very powerful man. Sounded to me like you know who it is."

He winced for a second. "Words only. Meant to get you to cooperate."

She didn't believe him for a second. There was something

in his voice earlier that made her sure he knew more. She leaned toward him. "Who is it?"

His good hand suddenly reached for the gun she was holding. She jerked back out of range, and his hand flailed as if he could grip the air and pull the pistol to him. He yelled in frustration and pain. His hand dropped to the floor near the bloody mess that had once been part of his other hand.

Almost instantly he stopped yelling, his eyes growing wide. He raised his hand back up and turned the palm so he could look at it. Sticking out of the pad near his thumb was the needle-enhanced ring.

The assassin's hand clenched involuntarily. "Oh, God."

It took Mila a second to realize what was happening. She'd thought there wasn't enough poison left on the tiny spike to kill again. But when the muscles on the assassin's neck tightened, and his jaw began to shake, she knew she was wrong.

"Do you have an antidote?" she asked quickly. She couldn't have him die on her, not yet.

He tried to smile. "Why would I…bring that?"

She knelt down beside him. "Who wanted me dead? It shouldn't matter to you anymore. Just tell me!"

He sucked in a breath that she worried might be his last, and his eyelids fluttered shut.

She dropped the gun, and grabbed his face with both hands. "Tell me!"

Silence.

"Tell me!"

She thought it was too late, that he was gone. Then his eyes opened a fraction of an inch. "The lion," he whispered.

"The lying what?" she asked.

"Lion," he repeated in a voice she could barely make out. "Lion."

There was no need to ask him again. He was done answering questions, forever.

Lying? Lie on? Lay on? Leon? Whatever it was he was trying to say didn't make sense to her.

"Someone's coming," Julien said.

He grabbed the gun off the man he'd been choking, moved to the side of the door, and motioned for Mila to join him. They pressed against the wall, pistols ready as the door eased open.

For several seconds there was no noise. Then they heard Quinn's voice say, "Mila? Julien?"

CHAPTER
THIRTY EIGHT

OUTSIDE VENICE, ITALY

QUINN KNEW THE story from there, at least as far as Vegas was concerned. The first thing they did was jam the maintenance closet door closed in a way that only they would know how to easily open again. Then he and Julien had escorted Mila to the parking garage.

The car they had procured for her escape was a nondescript Toyota Camry with California plates. Their original plan had been for her to head south with Julien through Arizona to the Mexican border at Nogales. There, using an impeccably fake Canadian passport, she would cross over on her own and continue south via bus to Guaymas, on the Sonora side of the Gulf of California. Julien would dispose of the getaway car, then work on putting a more permanent plan in place for her. Once everything was ready, he would travel to Mexico to brief her, then send her on her way to her new life.

But with the two extra dead bodies in the basement of the Manhattan, Quinn needed some help, so instead of traveling with Mila to the border, Julien stayed behind.

As soon as Mila drove away, Quinn had called Jergins and confirmed that the body he'd seen at the hospital was indeed Mila Voss, and that the person Kovacs's man had spotted was someone else entirely. Jergins was both glad Quinn would be able to handle things, and annoyed at the last-minute fire drill Kovacs's team had put them through.

"Tell him to call me," Jergins had said.

"If I catch him before he leaves, I'll let him know."

Next came the cleanup. Quinn and Julien wrapped up the bodies, collected stray bio matter, and obscured the bloodstains they couldn't remove with quick-drying paint.

They waited until three a.m. to move the bodies out. Because they were in a casino, there were more people around than they usually had to account for on other jobs, but Quinn's and Julien's movements went unnoticed and soon they were driving out of the city.

The pre-dug grave was in the middle of the desert, twenty miles from anything else, and was more than deep enough for the three bodies. After each went in, Quinn poured a thin layer of his special mix of powdered dissolving chemicals over it, adding an extra layer on the faces and hands. He'd only planned for one body, so was worried there wouldn't be enough, but he was able to stretch it out.

The project officially completed, Quinn returned to Los Angeles alone, while Julien worked out the details for Mila, details Quinn had never known. In fact, he and Julien had made a pact to never discuss Mila or Vegas again, something they had broken only once, two years later, when Julien had talked to Quinn about the apartment in Rome.

What Quinn did next was figure out how to cover up Kovacs's disappearance. He had no feelings one way or the other about the assassin. It would have been a hell of a lot better if they had been able to accomplish everything without killing him and his spotter, but that was not something they could undo.

He seeded information that made it seem as if Kovacs was doing jobs in various locations around the world that kept him on the move every three or four days. Quinn had even written up a report of the Vegas job for him, and submitted it through Kovacs's hacked email account.

The trickiest part was killing off Kovacs. Quinn had to wait a certain amount of time so that links back to Vegas would not likely be made, but if he waited too long, he risked the very real possibility of someone discovering that the last few months of the assassin's life had been faked.

He picked his time and spot with care: three and a half months later; Colombia, South America. The assignment: a drug lord assassination. While waiting for the target to appear, Kovacs and his spotter—a guy whose name turned out to be Conner Adams—were captured and subsequently tortured. According to a news report Quinn was able to get into several of the Bogotá newspapers, the chopped-up remains of two unidentified Caucasian bodies had been discovered in the jungle. From there it was a fairly simple job of connecting the dots behind the scenes so those in Quinn's world would know whose bodies they were.

It was a lot of work, and caused him more than a few anxious moments along the way, but it had succeeded. Once it was done, and Kovacs and Adams were officially dead, Quinn was able to think about Vegas less and less. Finally, there came a point when it was like none of it had ever happened.

Mila's unexpected resurrection put a stop to that delusion.

"The Lion," Quinn said. "How did you figure out it was him?"

The Lion was a label used by some people in the industry when referring to Christopher Mygatt. His mane of blond— now almost white—hair was no doubt in large part responsible for that.

"I went over those last words the assassin said again and again until it was driving me crazy. Because of the Portugal flight, it was a safe assumption that the person behind everything worked in the government. It was Julien who finally figured it out after I told him the whole story. Over the next several months, he did some checking and found the connection." She paused. "We couldn't be sure, but what did it matter? It wasn't like I'd be able to walk up to him and confront him. But then he started popping up in the news. And the rumors about his future started. And then that article."

She shook her head as if she still couldn't believe it. "If he *was* the guy who wanted me dead, the guy who'd been behind the kidnapping of an American citizen, I couldn't just stand by and let him gain power again." She drifted off for a moment, then said, "My mother came to the US as a teenager. She and my grandparents escaped from Poland. When she became an

American citizen, she was so proud. That's why I went into the work I did, my own little way of giving back to the country that welcomed my family, I guess. What Mygatt did…that's not the country my mother believed in. I knew I had no choice, *have* no choice. I have to stop him.

"The first thing I had to do was make sure I wasn't blaming the wrong guy. It took me a while, but I was able to identify one of the men who'd been watching the prisoner on the flight. I was hoping he would confirm the Lion's identity, or at least point me in the direction of someone who could. I was supposed to meet him in Dar es Salaam. He showed up at the hotel, but he didn't make it to the rendezvous point. I got nervous, so I bugged out, then…"

"We've seen the footage," Quinn said.

"Footage?"

"Hotel security camera. Lawrence Rosen crashing into the sidewalk, you running up to him. That's how they found out you were still alive."

She closed her eyes. "Camera. Right. I knew it was there, but I didn't think I'd be noticed." She opened her eyes again. "After that, I was desperate. The only names I had were Rosen and another guy named Olsen. I found out Olsen is pretty entrenched in DC, so getting to him would be a last-resort option only. I needed another name, someone I could talk to." She told them about Stockholm, and finding out about an agent named Evans who'd had a part in both the prisoner flight and her attempted termination. "I saw it on his face, and knew that the Lion and Mygatt were the same, but he tried to kill me before I could make him talk. I had to shoot back." Her jaw clenched in anger, and she looked at Quinn. "You found out for sure, though. Now I know."

Quinn looked out the window, lost in thought.

He understood that those fighting terrorism would, at times, need to employ extreme measures. Sometimes he agreed with the method, sometimes he didn't. But abducting a US citizen and sending him to a secret foreign prison to die?

What Mygatt had done was unimaginable. He had violated Gorman's fundamental rights as a US citizen, in a way worthy of a place like North Korea. Furthermore, he had covered it up so thoroughly no one suspected the truth. There was no doubt in Quinn's mind that the senator would use all his resources to find Mila and eliminate her. Permanently. And if he succeeded in becoming director of the CIA, those resources would be unstoppable.

He had told Peter he needed to get her someplace safe, but the only way Mila would ever be safe was if they accomplished what she'd set out to do.

By the time they reached Marco Polo Airport, Quinn had come up with a very loose framework for a plan. At his suggestion, they purchased tickets for Geneva and made their way to the gate.

Once there, Quinn pulled Orlando to the side and sketched out his idea. Once he finished, she stared at him, her face stone. If he didn't know her so well, it would look like she thought he was crazy. But that wasn't it at all. Her mind was spinning, playing out all the possible scenarios, considering details he hadn't even thought of yet.

A full thirty seconds passed before she moved again. When she did, all she said was, "I need to get to work." She then pulled her computer out of her bag, and found an empty seat near their gate.

Nate was next.

"Whoa," he said, once Quinn had finished. "That's a bit...risky, don't you think?"

"Beyond risky," Quinn said. "If you don't feel comfortable with it, you can walk away. No judgment."

"Not an issue. I'm not going anywhere. I was just pointing it out."

"It might be our last job."

"Well, something has to be. But, just to go on the record, I'd prefer that it's not." Nate seemed to lose focus for a moment, then pulled out his phone. "I should...I should call Liz."

Quinn was momentarily caught off guard by the mention of his sister's name. "Don't tell her."

"Seriously? You think I'm that stupid?"

"No. Sorry."

"I just want to see how she's doing." Nate paused.

"Maybe have a little phone sex."

"What?"

"Kidding! All right? Kidding." He started to walk away, then looked back. "Half-kidding, anyway."

When Quinn pulled Daeng aside, instead of telling him the plan, he said, "When we get to Geneva, we'll put you on a flight back to Bangkok. You've been a huge help, and I can't tell you how much I've appreciated it."

"Is that a good idea?" Daeng asked. "It seems to me you're not through here." He looked over at Nate on the phone, then at Orlando huddled over her computer.

"It's going to get dangerous," Quinn said. "I can't ask you to risk your life. People back in Thailand are counting on you."

"You mean risk my life *again*."

"Yeah."

"Out of the four of you, only two are at full strength. You're far from it, and the girl is, well, under a lot of stress. So you're telling me you can't use a third, healthy person?"

"I can't ask for your help again."

"Perhaps this isn't just your decision. Nate?"

Nate looked up, his phone still held to his ear.

"May I ask a quick question?" Daeng said.

"Hold on," Nate said into the cell, then put his hand over it. "What's up?"

"Have I proven useful?"

"Definitely."

"And could you use my help moving forward, or would you rather I return home now?"

"That's up to you, but we could absolutely use your help."

"I agree," Orlando called out, her gaze not leaving her computer screen.

"I guess I'll be staying," Daeng told Quinn. "Now, what is it you have in mind?"

THE LAST PERSON Quinn pulled aside was Mila.

"Don't even attempt to talk me out of it," she said.

"I'm not," he said.

She looked surprised. "Oh…okay. Just so we're clear."

"We are."

"I'll take off when we get to Geneva."

He gave it a beat, then said, "There *is* another way." He laid it all out for her.

When he was through, she stared at him, slack-jawed. "Is that even possible?"

"I guess we'll find out."

For the first time since they had reconnected, Mila smiled. "It's a lot better than what I had in mind. Thank you."

"Quinn?" Orlando called out, waving at him to join her.

"Excuse me," he said to Mila. He sat in the chair next to Orlando. "What is it?"

"I was thinking we could use a little more ammunition."

"Definitely," he said. "What did you find?"

She hesitated. "Something that might change the plan a bit."

"For the better?"

"You tell me." She turned her laptop so he could see the screen. On it was a low-resolution image that had obviously been pulled from a video. The person in the shot had the look of a homeless man—hair and beard long and matted, face thin and dirty.

Quinn shot Orlando a questioning glance.

"The footage this was pulled from is about six months old."

"Okay," he said. "But who is it?"

"If I'm not mistaken, that's Thomas Gorman."

CHAPTER
THIRTY NINE

WASHINGTON, DC

IT WAS JUST after eight a.m. when Olsen walked into the townhouse.

The moment he entered their shared office, Peter jumped up. "I'm glad you're here. I was just about to call you."

Olsen laid his briefcase on his desk. "Did something happen?"

"They have her."

Olsen froze. "You're sure?"

"Yes. One of my teams tracked her down in Switzerland about four hours ago."

"Four hours?"

"I didn't know myself until just before you arrived. Apparently there was a bit of a dustup, and they weren't able to contact me right away. The good news is, in the middle of it all, they were able to sneak her on a plane. She's on her way here now."

"Wait, what? Here? No. We don't want her here."

"I already okayed the order to do that in the event she was caught."

"I never gave you permission for that!"

"Your instructions, Mr. Olsen, were to make *sure* we had her this time, that there were to be no 'fuckups.'"

"That has nothing to do with bringing—"

"That has *everything* to do with bringing her here. I want to see her right in front of me. I want to take a sample of her DNA and her prints, and I want to prove beyond a doubt that the woman we have in custody *is* Mila Voss. I thought you wanted the same thing."

"We can't have her here," Olsen insisted.

"It won't be for long. I've routed the plane to a private strip about thirty miles northeast of here in Virginia. No one is even going to know she's in the country. We'll put her on a second plane that'll be standing by, and process her. You just tell me where you want her flown after we've got what we need, and that's where she'll go."

Olsen mulled over the plan, then said, "All right, all right. We can make that work. It's actually not a bad idea."

"Thanks," Peter said, not hiding his annoyance.

"I'll have to run it by the senator and Mr. Green, but unless you hear from me otherwise, it's a go."

"If it is, I assume you'll want to be there, too."

"Absolutely."

The neutral look on Peter's face remained unchanged, but inside he cracked a smile.

CHAPTER
FORTY

VIRGINIA
THIRTY-FOUR MILES NORTHEAST OF
WASHINGTON, DC

THE PRIVATE JET descended toward the airport. As instructed, the flight crew had remained behind the locked cockpit door. There were no other crew members on board.

"Last chance if anyone wants out," Quinn said.

There were no takers.

He, Nate, and Orlando were dressed in forest camouflage outfits, with dark brown ski masks resting on their heads. Daeng was wearing a dark suit and holding a pair of tinted glasses. Mila was the only one still wearing the clothes she'd been in earlier.

Quinn touched her arm and said, "It's time."

"Okay," she replied, nodding.

"It's going to be fine."

"I know."

"Shall I?" Nate asked. He was in the seat next to her.

"Thanks," she said. She gave him the pair of handcuffs she'd been holding, and then raised her hands in front of her. Once the cuffs were secured, she took a deep breath.

"Daeng will be with you the whole time," Nate said.

Another nod.

From the angle of their descent, Quinn knew they were almost there. "Shades," he said.

They moved quickly through the cabin, closing all the

window shades so no one could see in after they land.

After they were all seated, Quinn thought through the revised plan one more time. They had taken every precaution possible, but there were still at least a million ways it could go wrong. The number one being if Peter decided his interests were better served elsewhere and screwed them over. They'd know the answer to that soon enough.

The plane bounced as its rear wheels hit the runway, then stayed down. Once the front gear settled on the ground, the engines wailed as they worked hard to kill the momentum that had carried them across the Atlantic Ocean. Once their speed slowed enough so that the plane could safely turn off the runway, everyone but Mila jumped out of their seats.

As soon as Orlando turned off the interior lights, Quinn raised one of the shades a few inches and peeked out.

There were two medium-sized hangars, and a long, one-story building that fit with the description of the terminal Peter had given him. On the tarmac near the terminal was a plane not much different than the one they were in, and in front of it was a single car.

So far, so good.

"All right," he said. "Looks like we're a go."

PETER POINTED AT the distant white dot moving toward them in the afternoon sky. "There she is."

As soon as Olsen spotted it, he nodded. "I want this transfer to go as quickly as possible."

"That's the plan. Once she's transferred to the other plane, we'll proceed with identification. That should take no more than fifteen minutes. After that, she'll be back in the air." Peter had hired Steven Howard and Rickey Larson at Quinn's request to serve as "protection" for Olsen and the former Office chief, and to handle the identification process.

Peter's explanation seemed to satisfy Olsen. He touched his hands-free earpiece, waited a moment, then said, "It's Olsen, sir...Yes, almost here...How's the visual there?...Good, good... Call me if there's anything you want to ask her."

Tucked half a mile away in the woods was a trailer, but not the kind someone would take camping to Yosemite or the

Rockies. It was a high-tech surveillance station, complete with monitors; recording equipment; microwave, satellite, and radio receivers; several comfortable chairs; and a stocked refrigerator.

The trailer had been moved into position three hours prior to the scheduled landing time, ready for its guests to arrive.

This had been the hardest part of Peter's end of Quinn's plan. Hardest, that was, next to agreeing to help in the first place. If *anything* went wrong, they were all doomed, but knowing what Mygatt and the others had done, there was no way Peter could just stand around and do nothing. The secret world was not always the most moral of places, but there were lines that should never be crossed. Mygatt and Green and Olsen hadn't just stepped over one of the lines, they had rocketed miles onto the other side.

After convincing Olsen that bringing Mila to Virginia was the right thing, Peter had waited thirty minutes, then offered up another idea.

"If you'd like, I could have cameras set up, and the senator and Mr. Green could watch the identification remotely."

As Peter knew would be the case, Olsen loved the idea.

In a hesitant voice, he added, "We could do a satellite feed or even route it through the Internet. It all depends on how worried you might be about someone hacking the signal."

Again, Olsen's reaction was predictable. "That is something that *cannot* happen."

"Chances are, everything will be fine, but if you're asking for an absolute guarantee, I can't give you that."

Olsen frowned. "We'll just record it, then. They can watch it later."

"Sure, that makes sense." Peter paused the appropriate amount of time, then said, "There is another option, if you're interested."

"What would that be?"

"I can get access to a remote surveillance trailer that we can set up close to the airport, and use a microwave link to relay the feeds. No one will be able to tap in. It's the most secure way if they'd like to watch live."

Olsen said he'd ask, and when he came back ten minutes later and said both Mygatt and Green would like to utilize the trailer option, Peter wasn't surprised. When presented with an opportunity to micromanage an important event, he had found that people in power seldom said no.

The plane landed with a squeal of rubber. The roar of the engines took over, and finally the aircraft settled down to a pedestrian pace as it headed over to where Peter and Olsen were waiting.

The jet made a large circle just before it reached the terminal. When it stopped, it was beside the second plane, facing in the opposite direction. This would make it easier to move the prisoner from one craft to the other.

As the engines wound down, the door opened. Standing at the top was a tanned man in a suit and tinted glasses. Peter had never seen him before, but that was probably good. It meant Olsen was unlikely to know him.

The man lowered the built-in staircase and disappeared back into the plane for a moment. When he reemerged, Mila Voss was with him.

A low, satisfied grunt reverberated from Olsen's throat. "It's definitely her."

"Just to be safe, I think we should still do the checks."

"Fine," Olsen said, though it was a halfhearted assent.

Only the suited man and Mila exited the plane. Peter had explained to Olsen that the idea was to keep things low-key on the off chance someone might be watching. Mila even had a coat draped over her hands, covering the cuffs around her wrists.

As she and the suited man crossed the tarmac, Peter folded his arms, right over left. Mila walked with her head drooped, as if defeated, while the man with her kept a steady hand on her back. When they were within five feet of Peter and Olsen, the man told her to stop.

To Peter, he said, "I was instructed to see her all the way onto the plane."

"Correct," Peter said. "Proceed."

"Let's go," the man said, guiding Mila toward the stairs.

Just before they reached the first step, Peter called out, "Hold on."

The man turned back around. "Yes, sir?"

Peter walked over, his back now to the other craft. As he'd hoped, Olsen did the same.

"I just want to take a look," Peter said.

He put a hand under Mila's chin and lifted up her face. Her eyes seemed unfocused, as if she hardly knew he was there.

"What are you doing?" Olsen asked.

Ignoring him, Peter asked the man, "Is she drugged?"

"No, sir. She's been like that since she boarded the plane."

"What about when you captured her?"

"That was a different part of the team, sir. I was waiting at the airfield so I can't say."

Peter moved Mila's face side to side as if checking for cuts and bruises.

After a few seconds, the tanned man said, "She *was* asleep right before we landed."

That was the cue.

"All right," Peter said. He took a step back. "Go ahead. Take her on."

QUINN WATCHED THROUGH a narrow slit at the bottom of one of the window shades as Daeng walked Mila toward the other plane. They stopped in front of Peter and the other man, shared a few words, then continued toward the stairs.

This was another point where Peter could blow things for them, but Daeng stopped and turned, Peter and the man with him walked over, their backs now to the newly arrived aircraft, just as discussed.

"Now," Quinn said.

In silent succession, Nate, Orlando, and Quinn exited the plane, slipped under the fuselage, and made for the trees fifty yards on the other side. As soon as they were safely under cover, Quinn took a look back. Though his view was limited, it looked like the others had boarded the second plane.

"This way," Orlando whispered. She was looking at the map on her phone that showed their current location in relation to the trailer.

They made their way through the woods, careful to make as little noise as possible.

"I don't know, Quinn," Peter had said after Quinn laid out

everything for him before boarding the plane in Venice.

"You have a choice to make. It's not a small one, I know, but let's be honest. Is there really any answer but yes?"

"You've got to give me a little time to think."

"You have until we get to Geneva."

Peter's response would come in one of two ways: either Quinn and the others would be taken into custody in Geneva upon disembarking the flight from Venice, or they wouldn't. That would mean the plane and the equipment Quinn had requested would be waiting for them.

Option two turned out to be the winner.

Somewhere in the woods ahead they would find three guards. They knew this because of the way Peter had been holding his arms when Daeng approached him—folded, right over left.

When Quinn, Orlando, and Nate were within one hundred and fifty feet of the trailer, they pulled down their ski masks, circled to the left, and quickly came to the dirt road where two cars were parked.

One of the three guards was sitting behind the wheel of the car in back, but the other two were nowhere in sight.

Quinn pointed at Nate, who nodded, then headed along the edge of the trees toward the car. When he came level with the vehicle, he dropped down so as not to be seen, and moved around the rear over to the driver's side.

Quinn could no longer see him at this point, but what he could see was the man inside. For a few seconds, everything was as it had been, then the man looked over, surprised, as his door was jerked open. Before he could do anything, he slumped forward as the shot of Beta-Somnol Nate had jabbed into him took effect.

The crown of Nate's head appeared for a second as he arranged the man back into a sitting position so it would look like nothing was wrong. He then shut the door and returned to the others.

It took them two precious minutes to find the next guard. He was wandering the woods, beyond where the cars were parked. Once more, Nate did the honors, shoving the needle into the man before the guy even knew he was there.

Quinn knew the third guard would be positioned close to the trailer, most likely on the side with the door, so they came at the surveillance vehicle from the back. When they reached it, Nate went one way, Quinn and Orlando the other.

As he and Orlando turned the corner, they came face to face with the third man. The guard pulled back in surprise, his hand automatically going for his gun, but before he could free it, Quinn had an arm wrapped around him, and a hand over the man's mouth. Orlando quickly injected enough of the drug into the man's arm to keep him out until morning.

With her help, Quinn laid him on the ground. He grimaced as he straightened back up.

"You okay?" she whispered.

"Fine," he lied.

They reconnected with Nate around front, and gave him the sign that told him the third man was taken care of.

Quinn checked his watch. Nearly five minutes had passed since they'd left the plane. They needed to speed this up. Without wasting another second, Quinn wrenched the door open and the three of them rushed inside.

Most of the opposite side of the trailer was taken up by a wall of monitors. On the largest screen was a shot showing the inside of the second plane. Mila was having her fingerprints taken. Two men—Mygatt and Green—were sitting in chairs in front of the wall where they had been watching the action. But now, they were looking toward the door in confusion.

"Hands where I can see them!" Quinn yelled.

"What the hell?" Mygatt said.

"Hands where I can *see* them!"

Green got the message first, and put his hands on the counter in front of the monitors. Mygatt didn't budge.

"You've just made a huge mistake," the former senator said. "There are half a dozen men out there right now undoubtedly surrounding this trailer. You need to put down your—"

"You know, I'd love to play who's got the bigger set of balls but we don't have time," Quinn said. "Hands where I can see them." He slapped the barrel of his gun against Mygatt's head.

The politician screamed out in pain, and complied with the order.

"What do you want?" Green asked.

"We've got what we want."

"There *are* men outside. They will kill you unless you put down your guns."

"We've already met them. They won't be a problem."

Green started to look nervous for the first time. "Who the hell are you?"

Quinn held a hand out to Nate. His former apprentice gave him an empty black cloth bag and a pair of handcuffs. While Quinn put the cuffs on Mygatt, Nate did the same with Green.

Then they both opened the bags.

"Mr. Mygatt, Mr. Green, I believe you are both familiar with the term extraordinary rendition. Consider this yours."

As he and Nate pulled the bags over the men's heads, Orlando administered the needles.

PETER AND OLSEN were in the private room at the back of the second plane. Mila was sitting in the chair in front of them while her suited escort stood quietly against the wall near the door.

As Peter knew would happen, when they were in the middle of taking Mila's photos and the necessary samples to verify her ID, Olsen had started asking her questions. Playing her part, Mila refused to respond. This only made the agent more determined, which was why he didn't seem to hear the car driving up outside.

Several seconds later, feet pounded through the plane, then someone knocked rapidly against the door. When Daeng opened it, the man named Howard was standing there.

"Yes?" Peter said.

"Sir, a car just drove up with a group of armed men," Howard said.

"Who are they?"

"I don't know, sir, but they're not our people."

Peter glanced at the man who'd escorted Mila into the plane. "Go with him. Figure out who these people are. If they're a problem, subdue them."

"Yes, sir," the man said, heading for the door.

"And tell the pilot to get ready to leave."

The man went with Howard.

When Peter turned back around, he saw that Olsen had his phone to his hear. Olsen frowned, pulled it down, and hit another button. "They're not answering."

"Who?" Peter asked.

"The senator and Mr. Green."

"They're safe at the trailer. The team will protect them."

Olsen shoved his phone into his pocket. "I need to go check on them."

"You're not getting off right now."

"They might be in trouble!"

"Perhaps, but you're not going to be much help if you're dead."

Right on cue, the sound of the plane's idling engines began to increase. At almost the same moment, shouts came from the cabin. This was followed by what sounded like muted gunfire. Then something slammed into the outside wall of the room.

"Please tell me you're armed!" Olsen said.

Peter nodded, and pulled a pistol from his shoulder holster. "I'm going to go see if I can help."

"No! Stay in here."

"If I stay here, we're dead for sure. Out there, I might be able to do something to stop this."

Not waiting for a response, he ran out the door, making sure to shut it behind him.

QUINN WAS WAITING five feet away when Peter exited the room at the back of the plane. He motioned for his former client to run past him. Once Peter was clear, Nate threw himself against the wall again, this time letting out a loud groan.

Quinn aimed the gun that was loaded with blanks at one of the empty seats, and pulled the trigger twice. As soon as the echoes of the shots died down, he motioned for everyone to stop making any sounds.

He gave it ten seconds, then walked to the door and threw it open. What he'd expected to find was either Olsen cowering in the corner, or perhaps using Mila as a shield. Instead, Olsen was on the floor and Mila was straddling his chest, one leg pressed down on each of his arm.

"Hope you don't mind," she said, looking back at Quinn.

He shook his head, and removed a syringe from the case on his belt. "Would you like to do the honors?"

"Please."

Quinn released her from her cuffs, and handed her the syringe.

"Goodnight, Mr. Olsen," she said as she stuck the needle in the man's arm.

CHAPTER
FORTY ONE

MYGATT, GREEN, AND Olsen were propped next to each other against the wall of the back room, black bags over their heads, their hands and legs restrained. The amount of Beta-Somnol they'd been given had been carefully measured so that they'd only be out for approximately thirty minutes.

Right on schedule, Nate exited the room and said, "Two of them are waking up."

"Good," Quinn said.

He rose from his seat, walked into the room, and closed the door behind him. There was only one chair inside now. He pulled it as far from the three men as possible, and sat down.

It was another five minutes before the first one was fully alert.

"Hello?" Olsen said, his voice at first tentative, but quickly growing in strength. "Hello? Is anybody there? Hey, anyone!"

Quinn remained silent.

"Hello? Somebody! Anybody!" As Olsen tipped to the side, his shoulder knocked against Mygatt. "Who's that? Hey, who are you?"

Mygatt groaned.

"Shit," Olsen said.

A few seconds later, Green moaned and said, "What the hell? Take this thing off my head!"

"Mr. Green?" Olsen said.

A pause. "Olsen? What are you doing? Get this off my head!"

"Sir, I can't. I'm tied up and my head's covered, too."

"Have you tried to get free?"

"I've only been awake a minute or so, sir."

"Dammit," Green said, his tone even more urgent than before. "Is the senator here, too?"

"I don't know."

"Senator Mygatt?" Green called out. When there was no reply, he said, "Olsen, what the hell happened at the plane?"

"We were attacked. I'm pretty sure they killed the other men. Peter, too. He went to see what he could do, but I heard gunshots right after. Then a man came into the room who seemed to know Voss. They shot me up with something. That's all I remember."

"Same thing happened to us. Hit us in the trailer. Goddammit! Any clue where we might be?"

"Sir?" Olsen said. "Don't you hear it?"

"Hear what?"

"The drone? We're on the plane, sir. Or *a* plane, anyway."

Quinn decided this was as good a time as any to give them something else to think about. He shifted in his chair, intentionally causing it to creak.

The two men's heads jerked toward the sound.

"Who's there?" Green asked. "Senator Mygatt? Is that you?"

Quinn said nothing.

"Who's there? I can hear you! I know you're there!"

For several more minutes, Green and Olsen took turns trying to get Quinn to talk. Finally, as Mygatt was waking, Quinn stood up, and noisily left the room.

PETER WATCHED THE plane until it disappeared into the night. Not that he would have, but there were points during the last twenty minutes when he could have turned the tables, and stayed in the good graces of Mygatt and Green. Now, there was absolutely no turning back.

He headed to his car. He'd been able to set up most everything before he drove to the airfield with Olsen, but there were still a few things that were incomplete and one very important phone call he had to make.

Despite Helen Cho's stated desire not to discuss the

Gorman matter any further, Peter had called her three hours earlier as he was helping to put Quinn's plan in motion. Now, as he drove back toward DC, he punched in her number again.

"What?" she said as she came on the line.

"Do you have it?"

"I swear to God, Peter, I should just—"

"Do you have it?"

She was silent for several seconds. "Yes."

"Is it enough?"

"More than enough. But…"

"But what?" he asked. "Helen, you know who Mygatt really is. You know what he and Green have done. What's going to happen to you and your little group there if Mygatt becomes the director of the CIA?"

"I get it. You don't have to lecture me."

"Noted."

Knowing that Mygatt and Green were guilty was one thing; making people believe it would be an entirely different matter. Helen now had in her possession the hard proof.

He gave her a timeline of what she had to do next.

"If this ever comes back on me, I'm coming after you. You know that, right?" she said.

"I'd expect nothing less."

"As long as we're clear."

"There's one more thing."

He could hear her take a deep breath. "What is it?"

He told her the final part of Quinn's plan.

"You have got to be kidding. No way!"

"All I need you to do is open the door. Do that, and you won't have to deal with either man ever again."

"And if I don't?"

"It's going to come out anyway, and, naturally, there will be some collateral damage."

"Are you threatening me?"

"I'm informing you. So what's it going to be?"

This time she was quiet for nearly half a minute before she said, "You asshole."

OVER THE NEXT couple hours, Quinn took turns with Nate

and Orlando silently sitting in the room for ten or fifteen minutes at a spell, then leaving again. At first, their three guests were belligerent and demanding, then they became more imploring, offering to make some kind of deal. Finally, the perceived reality of their situation set in, and fear took full control.

At this point, Quinn and the others left the men alone, letting them live with their imagination of what might happen next.

"Will Peter be able to pull it off?" Orlando asked as they waited in the main cabin.

Before Quinn could answer, Mila said, "I don't trust him. He tried to kill me."

"Who? Peter?" Quinn said. "That may be, but he was only doing the job he'd been hired for, and it seems to me he's trying to make up for it now." He glanced at Orlando. "So, yes, I think he'll be able to pull it off."

"I hope you're right," she said.

IT TOOK LONGER than Peter had hoped for all the parts to come together. By the time he was ready to make his second-to-last call, he'd been back in the townhouse for several hours.

He picked up the phone and dialed the number.

"Prime Cable News," a pleasant female voice said.

"Dick Tillman, please. He's expecting my call."

She transferred him to a secretary who put him through to Tillman.

"I hope to hell you're not fucking with me," the network executive said.

"I'm not. I assume you contacted our mutual acquaintance?"

His voice lost some of its aggressiveness. "Yeah. He vouched for you."

Peter had needed to pull several strings to get the retired general to talk to Tillman, but he knew it would do the trick. "And your camera teams?"

"The one here is no problem, but we don't have anyone in Romania. On the word of your friend, I've sent a team there from Paris. They should arrive in Bucharest within the next three hours."

"Good," Peter said, then relayed a set of coordinates. "The Bucharest team will have ninety minutes after they land to get to that location. Tell them to do nothing to draw attention to themselves. They should get in a position that allows them a view of the gate. They'll know what that means when they get there. Then they just wait."

"What are they waiting for?"

"They'll figure it out."

"What about the other team?"

Peter gave him another set of coordinates. "Their timeline will mirror that of your team in Romania."

"And I suppose you can't tell me what they need to watch for, either?"

"No, I can't. But I can tell you, Mr. Tillman, you don't want to miss this."

FOUR AND A half hours after they'd taken off from the airfield in Virginia, Quinn's phone rang.

"Yes?"

"I've just received the final confirmation. Everything's in place," Peter said. "Is two hours enough?"

"Hold on." Quinn grabbed the walkie-talkie that connected him with the flight crew. "We're ready to take her down. How long until we can be on the ground?"

"Forty-five minutes. Fifty, tops," the pilot reported.

"Whatever you can do to make it sooner will be helpful." He added the estimate to the time it would take them to drive to their final destination. "Two hours should be doable, but it'll be tight."

"You want a delay?" Peter asked.

"No. Any later will be less effective. We'll make it work."

"All right. Good luck."

"Thanks, Peter. You really came through." Quinn hung up and looked at the others. "Time for that chat."

They all pulled on ski masks, and relocated to the back room. Nate and Daeng each held a video camera, so the rest stayed behind them to make sure that the only ones in the shot would be Mygatt, Green, and Olsen.

"What's going on?" Mygatt asked.

"Where are we?" Green threw in. "Someone, please talk to us!"

"We felt the plane turn," Olsen said. "Are we landing?"

"Yes," Quinn said. It was the first word any of them had spoken to the prisoners since takeoff.

"What do you want? Who are you?" Mygatt said.

"Who I am isn't important. What do I want? Well, *Senator* Mygatt, what I want is an explanation."

"Explanation? About what?"

"Thomas Gorman."

Mygatt delayed a second too long before saying, "Who?"

"We're not going to do that, senator. Let me make this clear. As soon as we land, there are two groups of people we can give you to. One who will make sure you get home, and one who will tear you apart." He gave it a beat, then said, "So, tell us what happened to Thomas Gorman."

What started as dribbles of denial and deflection soon became a flood of reality as the story came out. Even then, Mygatt tried to paint himself as a hero, protecting his country, but his attempted ruse sounded empty.

"Moving in," Quinn whispered, as soon as the senator was finished.

Both Nate and Daeng zoomed their lenses in so that only the black bag covering Mygatt's head was visible. Quinn then walked over to the man's side.

"How much of this story is true?"

"All of it," Mygatt said. "Everything. And I'd do it again."

As he said the last sentence, Quinn pulled the bag off, revealing the former senator's face.

"Again," Quinn said. "The story you just told, is it true?"

Mygatt's eyes widened as he noticed the cameras.

"Senator?"

"Yes," Mygatt whispered.

"Yes, what?"

"Yes, it's all true."

"So you faked the death of an American citizen, and flew him out of the country to a secret prison in Romania?"

Mygatt looked at him, surprised. "Romania? How did…It's

not like that! He was a menace. I did what everyone else wanted to do. It needed to be done. *For* the US."

"And these men were with you?" As Quinn asked this, Orlando moved around and pulled the bags off Green's and Olsen's heads. "They were part of this?"

Nate and Daeng waited until she was out of the way, then panned their cameras over to the two newly revealed faces.

"These men are patriots," Mygatt said.

"Were they part of this?" Quinn asked.

"They were also doing what needed to be done."

Quinn stood up and nodded at Nate and Daeng. They switched off the cameras and lowered them.

"Thank you, Senator Mygatt, Mr. Green, and Mr. Olsen. That'll be all."

The bags went back over their heads.

"Hey!" Olsen called out.

"I did what you asked!" Mygatt shouted.

"You did," Quinn said. He ushered the others out of the room and shut the door.

THE PILOT PROVED to be more than capable, getting them on the ground in thirty-eight minutes instead of forty-five.

As Peter had promised, a sedan and a white panel van were waiting for them. Logos on both sides of the van proclaimed that it belonged to KFR Catering, but the decals, along with the actual color of the van, could be removed in just a couple of minutes, changing the van to an unmarked dark blue.

As the prisoners were hustled out of the plane and into the van, Orlando sent Peter copies of Mila's secret video footage of Thomas Gorman, and the three men's confessions, which he would then distribute to the appropriate channels. These same channels would also receive the additional information Peter's inside source had been able to unearth.

"You guys are released," Quinn said to Howard and Larson.

"Easiest gig I've had all year," Howard said as they shook. "You guys be careful."

The two men walked over to the waiting sedan, and left.

Though the plane had been in the air for several hours,

they had actually landed just a few hundred miles to the northeast from where they had taken off. That, of course, was information they did not share with their captives.

To ensure that Mygatt and company didn't figure that out, Quinn slipped one of the CDs that had come with the van into the vehicle's old stereo, and turned up the volume in the back. Each disk was labeled with the name of a different country, and contained recorded radio broadcasts from that particular nation. The one Quinn selected was from Kazakhstan.

As soon as everyone else was in, Quinn glanced at Nate. "Let's go."

DEWAYNE BEETNER WAS not in a good mood. Why the hell he and his cameraman, Zach Yates, were in some Romanian backwater town, hiding out in a car outside what looked like a deserted factory, he didn't know. But the assignment had come from high-up PCN management, so here they were, before the sun was even up, waiting for…something.

"Gotta take a leak," Yates said.

Beetner grunted his indifference as Yates climbed out of the car. It wouldn't be long before he had to do the same thing.

This wasn't the first time Beetner and Yates had been sent on an assignment without adequate information. Occasionally tips would come in that their bosses back in New York would deem worthy of checking out. More times than not, they turned out to be nothing more than PR stunts that were a complete waste of time.

Beetner was beginning to wonder if this was even going to reach that level. He had the distinct feeling that absolutely *nothing* was going to happen.

His gaze drifted up to the stars above the town. Out here, away from the big city, they glowed with an intensity he seldom had a chance to see anymore. When he'd been younger, he would have been able to pick out most of the constellations, but he'd lost that knack long ago.

At least it wasn't raining, he thought. That would have truly sucked.

Light flickered at the bottom of his vision. He tilted his head back down. A high, solid wall ran the length of the block, broken only by the closed gate they were told to keep an eye on. On the wall next to the gate, a rusty-looking lamp had just come on.

Beetner reached across the car and opened the passenger door. "Zach!" he whispered loudly. "Get back here!"

Yates ran back and climbed in.

"What is it?" the cameraman asked.

"That light. It wasn't on before."

"Okay. Is this it?"

"Hell if I know, but be ready just in case."

Yates grabbed his camera from the backseat and aimed it toward the gate.

For a full five minutes nothing happened. Beetner had all but written it off as another meaningless moment in a night full of them, when, without any warning, a small door that was built into the gate opened.

"Get this. Get this," Beetner said, still doubting whatever was going to happen would be newsworthy.

For another several seconds, nothing more occurred.

Then a foot hesitantly stepped over the threshold.

The man it belonged to emerged a moment later. His thin frame made him look small, but in height, he was probably the same as Beetner, around five foot ten. His face was gaunt and incredibly pale.

He took several tentative steps away from the gate, and looked back. Though the door remained open, no one else emerged. He then looked both ways down the road as if he were unsure where to go.

"Is he why we're here?" Yates asked.

"I...I don't know." Beetner thought for a moment. "Come on. We might as well talk to him."

As the two men climbed out of the car, the thin man turned to look at them. For a moment he did nothing, then his eyes widened in fear. He twisted back in the other direction and started walking away at a pace Beetner guessed was as fast as he could go.

"Hold on!" Beetner yelled, hoping the man understood English. "We don't want to hurt you. We just want to ask you a question."

The man glanced back but kept moving.

Beetner might have given up right then, but there was something about the guy that was familiar. He started jogging, and could hear Yates grunting along behind him.

"Sir, please. We're not going to hurt you or anything."

This time there was no response at all.

As he passed the gate, Beetner glanced over at the open doorway. He'd assumed from the way the other man had looked back that there were others with him, but the reporter saw no one on the other side, just a starlit courtyard and a decrepit building beyond.

"Sir," he called out. "I'm not sure if you can understand me, but we just want to talk. We're from PCN. The news network?"

At the mention of PCN, the thin man's steps faltered.

Beetner thought he heard the man say something, but he wasn't sure. "Sorry. I didn't catch that," he said.

"Trick," the man grunted as he kept walking.

He'd spoken English.

"No, sir. No trick."

"Trick," the man repeated. "Not real. Leave me. Leave me."

Not only had he spoken English, but his accent was American.

"We're not going to hurt you," Beetner said. He jogged the final few feet between them and put a hand on the man's shoulder to stop him. "We just want to—"

The man jerked away, twisting as he did so that he ended up facing the PCN reporter. "Leave me! Leave me!" He stumbled backward a few steps, then whipped around and continued walking away.

Beetner stared after the man, unable to move his feet.

"Oh, shit," Yates said from behind him.

"You saw that, right? I'm not crazy."

"I saw," Yates said, his tone of disbelief matching his colleague's.

Beetner remained rooted where he was for another second. Finally, he broke free and began chasing after the biggest story he would ever have.

CHAPTER
FORTY TWO

QUINN CHECKED HIS watch.

They would be cutting it close, but even at eleven p.m., it had been too much to hope that they wouldn't run into any traffic as they drove into New York City. Their timing had to be perfect, otherwise they risked getting detained and questioned themselves. Something that was out of the question.

"Seven minutes out," Nate said.

Quinn nodded, and glanced at Daeng. "Let's get them ready."

Mygatt, Green, and Olsen sat on the floor of the van, tied and hooded as before. Speakers in back blasted the prerecorded radio station directly at them. Quinn lowered the volume then said, "How's everyone doing?"

"We did what you asked," Mygatt said. "Now let us go like you promised."

"I think I promised to give you to people who wouldn't necessarily kill you."

"What does that mean?"

Quinn didn't respond.

"You will *never* get away with this," Green said. "Kidnapping a US dignitary and high-ranking officials and taking us out of the country is going to get you the death penalty, my friend. And I'm not talking from a court. I will personally see to it that you are *all* tracked down and killed in the most painful possible ways."

"And you feel you'll be in the position to do that because…?"

"Let us the fuck out of here!" Green yelled.

"Well, you're in luck. That's exactly what we're going to do," Quinn said. "Now, boys, we're going to remove your restraints for a moment, so when it's your turn, don't try anything stupid. If you do, we're going to have to shoot you, and I'm sure you'd rather avoid that. Correct?"

The men uttered their agreement, though Quinn suspected Olsen and Green were thinking this might be the chance to make their move.

They started with Olsen first, having him lie flat on the floor of the van, then cutting loose his hands and ankles. Twice the man's muscles twitched as if he were preparing to strike out, and twice Quinn rapped the back of Olsen's head with the barrel of his gun. They stripped him down to his underwear, replaced his clothes with a pair of bright orange coveralls, and restrained his hands and ankles again.

They repeated the procedure with Green and Mygatt, neither man attempting any kind of escape.

"Why did we need to change?" Mygatt said.

Instead of answering, Quinn turned the radio back up and returned to the front, leaving Daeng to watch over them.

"We're close," Nate said.

Quinn saw that they were only a few blocks from the exact position they needed to be. He called Peter.

"Almost there."

Peter took a second before he said, "No calling it off, huh?"

"Not an option."

"Yeah, I know. Okay, I need three minutes."

Quinn put a hand over the phone and leaned toward Nate. "Slow down."

IT HAD BEEN a less-than-interesting news day. The presidential primaries were over, each party's candidates all but decided. Most of the day had been spent discussing the preparations for the upcoming convention, going over the merits of each candidate, and arguing over who was going to have the best chance in the fall. In other words, the same stuff they'd been hashing over for the last week.

THE DESTROYED

Something was brewing, though. Norm Geller sensed it the moment Patty Vinton, the late-shift news director, had hung up the phone and rushed out of the control room. Geller was the TD, the technical director. His job was to operate the switcher board that cut between studio shots, pretaped segments, and live location feeds, then funneled the final product up to the satellite and onto the air. He'd been doing the job for nearly a decade, so his instincts were pretty honed about these things.

Though he didn't say anything to anyone, his money was on a political scandal. There had been far too few of them up to this point, and with the conventions not far away, wild accusations were bound to start surfacing. An affair, an illegal campaign contribution, a supporter who was not exactly on the up and up—could be any of those things.

When Patty came back into the room, he wasn't surprised when she said, "We're about to get a live feed. And Frank's in Bay Seven cutting a piece we'll want to slot in right after."

"No problem," Geller replied.

"What's going on?" one of the producers in the back asked.

Patty ignored him and said to Wendy, their graphic person, "We're going to need a lower third."

"Sure. What's it need to say?"

"The reporter is Dewayne Beetner. Location—'Outside Bucharest, Romania.'"

That caught Geller off guard. "Romania?"

As Patty nodded, the phone rang. She picked it up, listened for a moment, then said, "We go in thirty seconds."

IT DIDN'T MATTER that it was just after eleven p.m. Times Square was packed with tourists.

As always, the neon and video screens that lined the buildings lit up the area like it was day. Excited, beaming faces moved from one bright spot to another, taking in the wonder of a city most of them had probably never been to before. The only locals were those working—in the stores, at the carts along the street, in taxis.

Several television networks had giant video boards silently carrying their feeds. One such board was owned by Prime Cable

News, also known as PCN.

Nate pulled the van to a stop at the curb, seventy-five feet from the building with the PCN monitor.

"Gentlemen, we're going to be sorry to see you go," Quinn said.

He nodded at Daeng, who cut the ties around the men's ankles.

Orlando started to open the door.

"Wait," Mila said.

They all knew they only had seconds before a cop approached and told them to keep moving, but Quinn motioned for Orlando to hold on.

Mila knelt down in front of the man who'd caused her to lose the life she used to have. "I want you to remember something, *Mr.* Mygatt. I want you to remember that Mila Voss is responsible for everything that has happened to you and will continue to happen to you. And if I could do more, I would."

"Don't worry. I won't forget you," Mygatt said.

"Good. Because you're going to wish you could."

She stood up and nodded at Orlando.

"It's on the screen," Nate called back. "My God, it's really there."

The door swung open.

Quinn and Daeng grabbed Olsen and Green first, shoving them outside, then together they pulled Mygatt to his feet.

"You're through, Mr. Mygatt," Quinn said. "I'm sure you don't believe that now, but in a few seconds you'll know I'm right."

They threw him out of the van.

Before Quinn closed the door, he looked back at the three men in their bright orange jumpsuits as they tried to pull the bags off their heads. He could also see the PCN camera crew rushing toward them from half a block away. And the large screen that could be seen from almost anywhere in the square was broadcasting a live camera feed from "Outside Bucharest, Romania" that was focused on an aged and horribly thin Thomas Gorman.

"Go," Quinn ordered as he shut the door. "We're done."

CHAPTER
FORTY THREE

SELDOM WAS THERE a bigger story in an election year than the election itself. The Thomas Gorman scandal was going to be one of those exceptions.

His resurrection was littered with the bizarre. The facility he had been released from turned out to be an abandoned factory. PCN reporter Dewayne Beetner and his cameraman Zach Yates had searched the place themselves, finding absolutely no signs that it had been used at any point in the last decade. Wherever the prison was that Gorman said he had been held in, it wasn't located in that building.

Strange occurrence number two happened at almost the same instant, half a world away in New York City. If a PCN crew hadn't been assigned to do generic on-the-street interviews near the PCN monitor in Times Square, it was possible this second event would have been covered up. But the crew couldn't help notice the three men in orange jumpsuits with black hoods on their heads being pushed out of a van. They had rushed over, and had been in time to see the men pull their hoods off moments before two SUVs screeched to a halt nearby. From inside, several men in dark suits jumped out and grabbed the three in orange. They quickly ushered them into their vehicles and drove away. But the faces of the men in jumpsuits had already been recorded, and within minutes producers at PCN identified them as former senator Mygatt, a high-ranking CIA operative named William Green, and another member of the intelligence community named Scott Olsen.

Even more interesting was that these were the same men

implicated in a set of anonymously leaked documents, which included recorded phone conversations between the senator and Green that clearly showed they were responsible for Gorman's faked death and incarceration.

Not surprisingly, before the sun had even risen the next day, both the current and former administrations publicly denounced the men, anxious to separate themselves from Mygatt and his associates' grossly illegal actions.

QUINN AND THE others drove straight from New York to a safe house outside Philadelphia.

The next day a package arrived from Peter. In it were the contents of yet another new life for Mila.

When Quinn showed it to her, she looked less than enthusiastic.

"There might still be those loyal to Mygatt or Green who would want to take out their revenge on you," he explained.

"I know," she said. "I just hadn't thought this far ahead."

"You did the right thing, Mila."

She held up the package. "And for that, this is my punishment."

"Not a punishment. An opportunity. A chance to do something you wanted to do, perhaps."

"Yeah, I guess."

"Julien would have been proud of you."

A smile touched her lips. "He would have, wouldn't he?"

A few hours later, a car came to take Mila to her new life. Where and what that was going to be, Quinn and the others didn't know. It was better that way.

They all gathered at the front door to see her off.

"Thank you," she said. "All of you, for coming after me. I would have failed on my own."

"You would have found a way," Nate said.

"I don't know about that."

"We do," Orlando told her.

Mila gave each of them a hug, saving the longest and last for Quinn.

"I'm sorry you were shot."

"Part of the job."

"Hopefully you won't have to find me again."

"If you need us to, we will."

THE DAY WAS sunny with only a few scattered clouds moving along the southern edge of the bright blue sky. The sound of the boat's motor hummed as its propeller churned through the river.

As soon as the familiar dock came into view, Quinn could feel the release of the tension he'd been holding on to. In an odd way, it felt like he was coming home.

The scaffolding was still erected around the temple, and while he could see some work had been done, they were not nearly as far along as he'd thought they'd be.

No matter. It would get done eventually.

The engine died as the boat pulled against the dock.

"So this is it?" Orlando said.

"Sorry you came?" Quinn asked.

She smiled. "Not at all."

"Please tell me they have Wi-Fi here," Garrett said.

Quinn patted Orlando's son on the shoulder. "Sorry, buddy. No Wi-Fi."

"PlayStation?"

"No."

"Wii? Xbox? They at least have cable, right?"

Quinn shook his head.

"Well…what am I going to do?"

"Don't worry. You'll find something."

As they climbed out of the boat, three monks appeared at the end of the dock, smiling broadly. Both Quinn and Orlando gave them a deep *wai*.

"Welcome back, *Khun* Jonathan."

"*Khob khun, krap*," Quinn said.

He took Orlando's hand, put his other on Garrett's back, and walked across the dock to the temple grounds.

"THANKS, QUINN," THE client said. "We'll see you the day after tomorrow."

"Right. See you then." Nate hung up.

The job he'd just taken was a simple one. In fact, as was

often the case, the client wasn't even sure he would need the cleaner's services, but was hiring Nate as insurance just in case. Once the gig was done, Nate thought he might take a week to go visit Liz in Paris.

He looked across the room. "Puerto Rico. Ever been there?"

Daeng, sitting on the couch in the living room of Quinn's Hollywood Hills home, shook his head. Instead of heading straight back to Bangkok, he'd come to L.A. to visit some old friends from his high school days. Nate had offered him the guest room at the house.

"Interested in going? They've budgeted me for an extra man."

A shrug. "Why not? Sounds like fun."

"Fun? Hopefully it's boring, but I guess we'll see." He paused for a second. "There *are* a few rules we should probably go over first."

"You're the boss."

ACKNOWLEDGMENTS

As always, there are many who I will forget to mention, so apologies ahead of time for my lack of memory and unintentional slights. Yes, I make mistakes. All. The. Time.

Huge thank-yous to editor extraordinaire Elyse Dinh-McCrillis and excellent friend/author/book-cover designer Robert Browne. Thanks to Danielle Perez for guiding me through the origins of Quinn, helping him (and me) mature as a character (and author). Suzette Pirozzi for the Italian translations. Any mistakes would be mine. And to Jovan Paskota for his last second, much appreciated assist.

To my friends old and new who keep me sane—and slightly insane—thank you. And Ronan, Fiona, and Keira—you, as always, are the reasons I smile every day.

Made in the USA
Charleston, SC
11 September 2012